BLOOD FOR GHOSTS

BLOOD FOR GHOSTS

stories

JOHN HUGON PERRYMAN

Stephen F. Austin State University Press
Nacogdoches, TX.

For more information:
Stephen F. Austin State University Press
P.O. Box 13007 SFA Station
Nacogdoches, Texas 75962
sfapress@sfasu.edu
www.sfasu.edu/sfapress

Book design: Tinesha Mix
Cover design: Tinesha Mix
Cover photo: Susan Bauman
Author photo: Sally Perryman
Distributed by Texas A&M Consortium
www.tamupress.com

LIBRARY OF CONGRESS CATALOGING-IN-PUBLICATION
DATA
Perryman, John Hugon
Blood for Ghosts / John Hugon Perryman

ISBN: 978-1-62288-124-6

FOR MY PARENTS,
AND FOR MY BROTHERS AND THEIR FAMILIES

CONTENTS

ACKNOWLEDGMENTS:

This work would not be possible without the support and friendship of many. After more than a few years of trying to see all or portions of this collection into some sort of print, one accumulates many debts, some of which cannot now be fully repaid. This does not diminish the need to try to settle accounts. The following is an attempt to thank as many people as is possible in a limited amount of space.

First and foremost, I must thank my parents. This work is written in honor of my mother and in memory of my father. I will never know a kinder, humbler, more decent man. Also, to my brothers and their families: thanks for your love and support. Y'all mean the world to me. Along the way, I have benefitted from the advice of the entire family; their suggestions greatly improved this work. Any mistakes or shortcomings contained herein are my fault alone. I am grateful to Perrymans and Hemphills everywhere.

A thanks is due to three generations of the Foote family. Thanks are also in order to the following, whose friendship for over thirty years (and in some cases over forty), is deeply appreciated: the Buffins, Castros, Denigers, Dunstons, Hunters, Rovinskys, Rubins, Warrens, Winfields. Thanks also to the Stiffel/Paddocks, Ware/Wilsons, and Iozzo/Brodskys. I deeply appreciate Michelle Lenihan's support and friendship.

I am in profound debt to the many excellent teachers from whom it has been my good fortune to learn. At Greenhill: Emily McLaughlin, Becky Choate, Doug Thomson, Karen Hagood, Sue Roman, Dick Williams, Christine Eastus, Barbara Graves, Barb Currier, Marilyn Stewart, Wells McMurry, Dick Hall, Thomas Holodak, Mark Samide, and Bob Witman. At UTD: Tim Redman, Dennis Kratz, Charles Bambach, and Jeffrey Perl. Special thanks to Fred Turner, whose friendship and encouragement made this work possible.

In addition, a whole host of friends from Greenhill, St. Barnabas, and St. Mark's deserve mention, though space will not allow a comprehensive list. I am grateful to Scot Casey, the Gibbons, Hubbard, Cotton, Stenberg and Ferrell families, the entire Upper School Office, Jerry Lacey, Dwight Phillips, and Jay McAuley.

A tip of the hat must go to the classicist Hugh Lloyd-Jones, whose book title I gratefully borrow. I owe a similar debt to Hawthorne for "The Wives of the Dead."

I have enjoyed working with Kimberly Verhines and Tinesha Mix, both of SFA Press. I appreciate their assistance, time, and patience.

Finally, a thanks is due to a certain few from a valley far to the north: did we not once gather in East, Dennett, and Thompson? Did we not once compete on the friendly Cole Fields of strife?

- "The Taking of Names" first appeared in *The South Carolina Review*. Spring, 2000.
- "Holy Ghost Man" first appeared in *descant*. Volume 40, 2001.

BLOOD FOR GHOSTS

And up out of Erebus they came,
flocking toward me now, the ghosts of the dead and gone.
Odyssey, Bk. XI

The past is never dead. It's not even past.
Faulkner, *Requiem for a Nun*.

NECROPOLIS

In the middle of the night, usually when she was vacuuming the large office on the southwest corner of the thirty-second floor, she would look down and see the ghosts ambling homeward up Central Expressway. Away from the bright lights of downtown two miles behind. Vague, desperate shades, lit only by the flickering street lamps. They would have vanished by the time she vacuumed and emptied the trash of the office next door. Having made their way up the entrance ramp, along the frontage road, and through the gateway into Freedman's Cemetery, they'd step down into their earthy beds as if descending through a cellar door. Remedios would smile after finishing with the hallway's final office, glad that they could settle back down to slumber. Ease their aching bones. At least someone somewhere was getting some good rest, she thought. It had been like this for several years. Since they'd begun the expansion on the expressway, and the construction crews and engineers had dug up bodies from the old graveyard that folks had forgotten about. The burial ground that hadn't been marked by maps or signs. The cemetery that, according to official city records, did not exist. The place that only a dozen or so old folks remembered ever having seen and that so few talked about that even their kin would nod their heads impatiently and glance down at their watches as they heard tell of the old graveyard.

So when the heavy machinery appeared on the scene and started turning up bone-rich strata, people began to get nervous. Instructions were discreetly delivered to the construction workers to cover up this unpleasant discovery, for a fear had quickly arisen that the revelation of each new skull might require an additional permit from the city to proceed. Traffic studies had made it clear that progress must not be delayed. So a decision was made to move the remains out at night in large dump trucks, to a landfill near Waxahachie. But the bones kept spilling out onto the expressway, cast up from a deep that seemed to find them unfit for burial. Clavicles would reach up and trip surveyors. Skulls would peep out and nudge cables and wheels. At night especially, bones were everywhere, mushrooming in the moonlight. One of the contractors ended up swearing the earth itself was pushing them out and got frightened and tried to withdraw his bid, but the city wouldn't let him, so he got to where he never visited the site but only sent his chief foreman to work on the dig. The company finally hired a P.R. firm to spin the rumor as an urban legend in case word leaked out. Press releases had been written and were ready for immediate dispatch to media outlets. The strategy was to undercut the story by likening it to various tabloid hoaxes. But the strategy failed. Word didn't leak out. It exploded. But by then the folks downtown already knew.

For weeks, phone calls flooded 911, City Hall, and the construction company headquarters. Usually, the callers were timid or embarrassed, but some were hysterical, saying they'd just seen a bunch of ghosts traipsing down the expressway. Not along it. *Down it.* Eventually, the calls slowed to a trickle—an amount acceptable to City Hall because in the end, after the initial shock wears off, people really don't want to be confronted with such things.

Nonetheless, enough suspicions had been raised that emergency City Council meetings were held and a determined few started trying to preserve the burial site. Soon it was decided that a task force needed to be formed to investigate the matter. One especially industrious council member found an old person to speak about the graveyard, and before an assembled crowd of maybe two hundred, including dozens of members of the press, the ninety-three-year-old told how his folks were buried there and how his granddad had been a slave who'd picked cotton in Brazoria and wound up running a little juke-joint next to the graveyard and just down from the legendary Black Elephant saloon. The crowd teared up, but when he went on about how he'd also been elected King of Paris but was exiled to Malta when his bunions flared up, his sponsor gently escorted him from the podium and wheeled him out of the council chamber. Nonetheless, word of the lost graveyard eventually reached the press, and soon a rumor could be overheard in the corridors of power that Susan Sarandon would be Grand Marshal of a parade to benefit the cause, for no matter the spokesperson or officiant, the dead demand proper burial.

Remedios herself knew these dead, and she'd even given some of them names. The pretty one who always wore the bright dress she called "La Roja." Another reminded her of her uncle in Guadalajara; he wore a stovetop hat and limped down the highway with a cane. She called him "Tio Theo" because he always seemed to do things in twos: tip his hat to friends, swat away birds, blow his nose into a handkerchief. She knew them all and imagined stories of their lives to help her pass the time. She even talked to them and laughed with them from the thirty-second floor, at least until her supervisor would cast her a stern look of disapproval. But Remedios couldn't help it. And she couldn't finish her vacuuming and move onto the next floor until she'd seen the last of them enter through the distant gates. She knew the tired walk of their wandering souls. Though most returned to the cemetery singing and joyful, a few returned as if they'd just come from a funeral or a failed evening of shooting craps. Others returned rubbing their blistered and aching hands as if they'd spent the day swinging a sledge-hammer. One or two returned anxious, nervously looking behind them all the while, as if they'd spent the day in the arms of a cousin's wife. But they all had something in common: they all wanted peace and rest. Remedios hoped she herself would have as much when she died, for she had always worried that she would have to wander the earth as a shade, too. At least for a time.

And so for her the scene was hardly strange or unbelievable. To Remedios, what was unbelievable was that she could be vacuuming the offices of the most prestigious law firm in town—one that did business on every continent except Antarctica. To her, what was strange was that she could be living in Dallas when she'd been born seventy-six years ago to a pair of teenagers who lived in a remote mountain village in southwestern Mexico where the wealthiest man in town owned three pigs, where people still spoke Nahuatl (the vanished language of Aztec royalty), and where no one had ever heard of a book, much less seen one. To her, the fact that she now lived in Dallas was much more unbelievable than that these ghosts would want peace and rest. Who couldn't believe that? So she'd never thought it worth mentioning to anyone what she regularly saw, and in fact she usually forgot about it until the next night's work, when the pageant would again bring her the comfort and peace that familiar and pleasant scenes always bring one during the toil of a long day: would again bring her the beautiful La Roja and the determined Tio Theo. With these thoughts in mind, she once more gazed down upon the two pink, granite columns that rose gracefully into an arch above the gateway to the park. This time she thought she saw the dark bronze sculptures, embedded within each column, wink at her in the flicker of street lamp.

She smiled, reached for the St. Christopher pendant around her neck, brought it to her lips, and then watched silently as the throng of shades passed through into a dark beyond, the very place that City Councilman Jamaal Akbar Madison was viewing at that same moment as an empty space. These were the same columns and figures that he'd lobbied to raise funds for and which, after they'd been finished, he scorned as poorly conceived and constructed. Too tired and emaciated. Like victims of a concentration camp. Not regal enough. These were the columns that he, too, found himself staring at, having returned to the cemetery in the middle of the night, a place where he'd been not eight hours earlier, during the cemetery's Grand Opening—or "Grand Reopening"— as he insisted on calling the occasion. It was then that he'd become fixated on what he was convinced was an anachronistic detail in the tribal costume of one of the figures. He suspected a conspiracy to undermine the cause. All the sensational media talk about hauntings he thought to be a waste of time, a distraction calculated to shift attention from the construction delays. He himself had never seen the ghosts, only the graves, and he hadn't seen much of them as he'd been trying to parlay his cemetery activism into campaign capital. But he'd lost the mayoral race. Again. Even though he'd delivered on the dead. And though a year had passed since the race, his thoughts during the Grand Reopening were still consumed by this failed campaign.

So throughout the ceremony, Madison found himself gazing down at his watch while the mayor gave her opening remarks. This moment should be his, he believed. No white person should be given the honor of delivering the opening remarks at an event like this. Especially no thirty-something white woman. Not that he had anything against women or white folks. Most of them, anyhow. But it just wasn't right. He shook his head in disbelief as she flipped back her hair, making a production of how the wind blew the long blond strands across her face, while the Reverend Bishop Isaiah Harkrider made his way up to the podium. "Thank God a brother's gonna speak," he thought, "even if it's a Tom."

Harkrider's pace was slow, befitting an eighty-three-year-old who had marched on Selma, grown the seventeen member Holy Ghost Temple of the Revelation into a four thousand member congregation, co-chaired a multi-ethnic committee ordered by the federal government to monitor the desegregation of Dallas public schools, and helped found a Pastors Coalition—now made up of over seventy churches in the greater metropolitan area. His movement was slow but spellbinding in its hard-won dignity, and the crowd could not help but reflect back upon his life as he ascended the scaffold. Each step up to the lectern brought to mind the years of struggle and suffering: the weeks he'd spent in jail during the height of the Civil Rights movement, the hunger strike he'd led during Vietnam after the death of his only son, the financial trouble he'd delivered his church from in the late eighties, and the recent and sudden loss of his wife to diabetes. The silence of the expectant crowd was pregnant as the gray champion of its causes summitted the platform and made his way to the lectern. The setting could not have been more appropriate, he thought, as he retrieved and unfolded his handwritten remarks from a pocket of his jacket: the dais and the lectern were both situated within the shaded threshold of the gateway, providing an impressive frame for him to speak within. He stood in the darkened way, smiled out upon the gathering, and began.

"Exactly one hundred years ago this week, brothers and sisters, the great WEB DuBois"—his voice lingered over the name, aware of the power of this invocation, one with which none present could take issue—"made a telling insight into this great nation of ours. Dr. DuBois said that the problem of the twentieth century would be the problem of race. Brothers and sisters, we can look back over the past hundred years—over the lies of Jim Crow, the courage of Mrs. Parks, the struggles of Birmingham, and the triumphs of Dr. King—and see how prophetic his words proved to be."

The crowd murmured in unified approval.

"And it is with his words in mind, brothers and sisters, that I say to you, that the problem of the twenty-first century," he paused to bait the eager crowd, "the problem of the twenty-first century, will be the problem of history."

He waited to let his words sink in, drawing himself up to his full, impressive height during the break, then continued.

"That's right—*our* problem is history. Who tells it, how it's told, and most importantly, what's told. Because in the twenty-first century, brothers and sisters, we can no longer afford to let others tell our story. In the twenty-first century," he thundered, "we tell our *own* story!"

Stepping back from the lectern, he gestured with an arm and ushered the crowd's reverent gaze into the solemn yard behind him. It was a sparsely grassed yard, distinguished only by a dozen or so crooked post oaks. It could have been the yard behind a thousand Texas farmhouses. After several moments, during which time the assembly shouted with approval, he returned to the lectern and grabbed its edges as a captain might a ship's wheel in storm. Sweat now poured from his brow, and he shook like flame. "Have I gotta witness, brothers and sisters? Have I gotta witness?" he shouted out upon the gathering, looking—almost defiantly—from side to side before him. His words stirred them, like a wind across waters. The crowd responded in percussive outbursts and shook with frenzy. Arms shot skyward. Fists clenched and shook. Eyes closed and heads nodded.

"Brothers and sisters, this cemetery is our history. This cemetery is our story. This cemetery is our past, our present, and our future! This is our promised land, our Canaan, our cemetery!" And as he cried out this last word, his hands flew upward like doves released into flight, and the crowd roared and swayed with approval.

But the mayor had seen none of this, staring, as she had been, at a liver spot on her own hand and trying to rub it out. And in fact, she wouldn't have even looked up then had her attention not been grabbed by the very word she had heard her husband repeat countless times that morning over breakfast.

"'Cemetery'? It's not a 'cemetery,' Trish. It's a g—damn 'graveyard,'" he had insisted. "I mean, I'm for the dead and all—I don't have anything against them—but a 'cemetery'? A 'cemetery''s…it's a special place. And a special word. There aren't a lot of them—cemeteries. 'Arlington National Cemetery,' for instance. Not any burial ground is a 'cemetery'. You can't just call a place a 'cemetery' and make it a 'cemetery'."

She remained silent, hoping his little outburst would pass.

"It just doesn't work like that. 'Cemetery.' Hell, that's kinda like…that's like Harkrider calling himself a 'bishop' and all."

"Honey, settle down."

"Well, what if I start calling myself a 'bishop'?"

She shook her head dismissively at his remark. She'd heard it all before.

"No. I'm serious. Why not?" He hated when she acted this way.

"Why stop there," she muttered without any enthusiasm but enough sarcasm to get him going.

"Maybe I won't. Hell, maybe I'll even proclaim myself Pope. How 'bout that? The world's first Texan Pope? We already gotta few presidents. We need a Pope. Pope Jimmy the First. No—Pope Jimmy the Generous. I'll throw out candy at Cowboy games, and I'll canonize Willie and Waylon both. How 'bout that?"

"Knock yourself out, honey. If you want to play at being Pope, then you just go right on ahead and say you're Pope." She snapped the newspaper out in front of her and returned to her reading.

"Oh, don't get that way with me. You know what I mean. I just don't know if it qualifies as a 'cemetery'."

He made a face at her, and as if sensing it, she set down the paper, pulled her glasses down to the tip of her nose, and clasped her hands atop the table.

"So what exactly qualifies as a 'cemetery,' Pope Jimmy? I didn't know there was some criteria for such…such exalted status."

"You know exactly what I mean."

"I do?"

"Yes." He shook his head at her and snarled his upper lip. She sipped her coffee and chose her next words carefully.

"You think an African American can't be buried in a 'cemetery'? That that's where generals and poets and presidents and… and Popes are buried and no one else?"

"Oh, don't use the race card on me. Save that for City Hall."

He was pissed. If there was one thing he couldn't stand it was how she'd taken to referring to "blacks" as "African Americans" ever since she'd taken office. This newfound habit was as bad as her recently acquired reverence for the papacy.

"It's not a black/white thing, Miss Mayor. It's just, I mean, I don't think it's a 'cemetery'. Maybe it's not a 'graveyard' either. I don't know. Hell, what should you call the place where you… you put to rest dead slaves…bury them. Where do they go and all? Is there a word for it?"

"How about 'heaven'?"

"Don't get all self-righteous with me."

"What?"

"I know there are slaves in heaven, I think. That's not what I'm talking about anyhow, and you know it." But before he could reformulate his thoughts, she cut him off.

"First of all, they were 'freedmen'. Second of all, 'graveyards' are for slasher flicks and Marilyn Manson. If I let this thing be called a 'graveyard', there's no chance in hell I could run again. So 'cemetery' it is."

This was almost more than he could bear. If she wasn't trying to be politically correct she was trying to be hip. He was beginning to think it was a mid-life crisis. In a moment of vindictiveness, he thought he'd arrange an intervention for her the way she had for him a few years back, but he knew no one would go in on it. None of her friends or sisters would show up. They were too afraid of her. He was, too. And it was this quality of hers that had more than one pundit convinced that the governor's mansion was well within her reach.

Still, her attempts to be hip with the kids and spout off about the latest bands and movies were driving him crazy. And it was only getting worse. A few months ago one of their daughter's friends had said in passing that her new haircut made her look like Kirsten Dunst. And then a few weeks after that, while they were at Border's to buy a birthday gift for his mom, he'd caught her flipping through a tabloid that had a cover shot of Kirsten Dunst on it. Then he'd caught her watching The Tonight Show when Katie Couric was the host and interviewed Kirsten Dunst. They'd gotten into a big argument about the decaying state of the American media, and he thought she'd ended up being embarrassed and ashamed of the whole thing. Apparently not. And this latest episode was making him sick to his stomach.

He chose his next words carefully.

"I see. So it's all about re-election. All about image."

He could tell by the look on her face that he'd struck a nerve. Her response was quick and her tone of voice ice cold. He had always envied her ability to respond in such fashion, even when he was on the receiving end.

"No—it's all about what's right. 'Cause it's gotta be something. It can't be nothing. And as I'm mayor and you're not, if I say it's a g—damned 'cemetery', then it's a g—damned 'cemetery'."

This came out in a bitchier tone than she had intended, and she immediately went into damage control. Though she had intended to humiliate him, she hadn't wanted to emasculate him and scorch the earth en route. She softened her voice and used the royal 'we' that always seemed to appease him.

"Besides, if we let it be called a 'graveyard' then we'd have more nuts phoning in saying they saw more ghosts while they were driving down the highway. We'd never hear the end of it."

He nodded his head in agreement. He didn't want his wife to emerge victorious from this, but she was right on this one point. As the vice president of the city's second largest construction company—his father's company—one that had won the bid for the expressway's expansion five years earlier, he knew first hand that the office had been inundated with calls during the first few months of the dig. His dad had assured him that they were random bodies. That there couldn't be a graveyard at that location, and he'd done more digging in Dallas than just about anyone. Then he reminded his son that it was imperative that they move forward with the construction and end the halt to progress. Yet he wondered now if everything his dad had told him could be wrong.

He hadn't thought there were so many crazies out there. But the first two weeks alone he'd received one-hundred-and-twenty-three calls from people saying they'd seen ghosts moving through the construction site at night. Climbing on equipment. Napping on flatbeds. Dicing in wheel wells. It didn't seem right to him that a bunch of dead folks could put a halt to progress, but that was what had happened.

The Police Department and City Hall had also been swamped. The calls had slowed since it had been announced that the site would be protected and preserved, and he figured if calling it a 'cemetery' was a charm that could make the ghosts or the freaks go away, then it was an argument he would gladly concede. He looked back up and saw his wife smiling at him. It was the smile he hated, and she knew it. The smile that signaled her ascendance and victory.

And it was that same smile that she thought she saw on Harkrider's face as they made eye contact, and she was shaken free from the memory of breakfast with her husband and returned abruptly to the dedication of "Freedman's Cemetery." She had no idea how long she'd been distracted, but as if pleased with her return, the minister continued.

"Prayers, brothers and sisters, prayers are not enough," his rich, gravelly bass intoned. "Because you gotta put legs on those prayers. That's right, you gotta put legs on those prayers," he repeated looking around, pleased at the crowd. He smiled and nodded his head, and then summoned them to his side: "Can this body say 'amen'?"

The crowd nodded its head amid a sea of "amens," and he drew strength from their affirmation.

"Gotta put legs on those prayers, brothers and sisters. That's right, you gotta pray for our story. That it all might be told. 'Cause the colored folks' graves have been covered up and forgotten. The colored folks lives have been forgotten and hidden. Lost in the courthouse. Lost in the schoolhouse. Even lost in the school yard….but not in the graveyard. Not in this graveyard! Not in our cemetery! And not on our watch!" he screamed, pounding the lectern for emphasis.

Shouts of affirmation burst like fireworks above the crowd.

"For these lives must not be forgotten. Will not be forgotten. Will not be lost in the archives. Thrown out with the trash. Will not be forgotten." He was now shouting at the gathered crowd of perhaps two hundred. Only then did he become fully aware of their presence, taking out his handkerchief to daub at the beads of sweat that had gathered across his face. Only then did he see the mayor nervously wringing her hands, unused to being in the presence of so many vocal and confident blacks. And only then did he become aware that Wells Moreland—star reporter of News Team One—was motioning his hand vigorously at him to make sure that when he spoke he addressed the camera to the front left of the podium. He made eye contact with Moreland, and gave a quick nod, leaning an elbow down upon the lectern so that his natural bent would be toward the camera.

"These graves—our graves—have been forgotten. Not by us, mind you. But by the city. That's right, these graves have been forgotten…but not the white folks' graves."

This elicited some more nods and shouts from the crowd. The mayor looked down at the ground and then toward her watch, which was slightly covered by the sleeve of her blazer. Way too hot, she thought, silently cursing herself for taking the wool blend Versace out of her closet that morning.

"And I hear folks say, 'Well, you gotta pay cemeteries to look after the graves. Gotta have a caretaker.' And I think to myself—'Gotta pay cemeteries to look after graves?' I thought that's what cemeteries did. I thought that's what cemeteries did…but not in 2003. And not in Dallas, Texas!" he thundered.

"Amen," the crowd exclaimed, swelling excitedly toward the podium. Wells Moreland motioned toward his cameraman to pan the crowd for reactions, and Harkrider skillfully waited for the camera to resume its focus upon the lectern, and when it did, he exploded—"and not if you're colored folks!"

This was almost more than the mayor could bear. She felt the crowd pressing in on her, was suddenly burning up in her blazer. She flipped her hair back, brushing her bangs to the side to resist the wind.

"No, no, but it's something else I got to say. It's something else I got to say," Harkrider insisted, chopping his hand sideways through the air as if dismissing possible objections. "I don't care if my grandfather, the son of a slave, died in 1925. His grave's gonna be dignified. His resting place's gonna be clean. His name's gonna be known. His life—HIS LIFE—it's gonna be visible to the whole world. His name will be spoken and his story will be told and his voice will be heard so that the whole world knows that he did not live in vain!"

The crowd nodded its thousand heads, rolled like a great sea, shouts crashing in affirmation across the plaza in front of the burial ground's entrance. The crowd was ready to charge, the mayor thought, looking back down at her watch. Her palms were wet. She'd sweated through the armpits of her blazer. She looked back up and again found Harkrider gazing right at her.

"Yes, his story will be told," he nodded, smiling at her, before returning his focus to the sea before him. "Yes, his story will be told. So that son of a mayor or son of a slave or son of a CEO or son of a president, he will not have lived in vain! He will not have lived in vain. His story will be told!" He was shaking now—stamping and shaking and she suddenly lost awareness of how much she was sweating and grew afraid that he might fall over and die and then she forgot even this as she gazed up at his enormous figure and then she too felt herself begin to surge forward with the crowd and sway with its power and shake like flame.

"HIS STORY WILL BE TOLD! THEIR STORY WILL BE TOLD! YOUR STORY WILL BE TOLD! HIS STORY WILL BE TOLD! OUR STORY WILL BE TOLD! THIS STORY WILL BE TOLD! IT ALL WILL BE TOLD! IT ALL WILL BE TOLD! IT ALL WILL BE TOLD! SO HELP ME GOD TO BE TOLD, ALL TOLD, AMEN!"

The crowd broke into applause as loud as the crash of waves

on a beach.

This must be what it felt like to drown, Steve-O thought, forgetting that his camera was still on, then panning back out over the crowd as it rolled and nodded and cried and swayed. He knew Wells would want plenty of crowd shots. He looked back down at his watch and wondered how much of it they'd have to cut for the evening news. "They're not gonna believe this back at the station," he thought. "But the camera don't lie," he smiled to himself, "the camera don't lie." Which is what he still was thinking as he swung it around and zoomed in on the mayor who was trying her best not to tear up when she magically sensed the camera on her—"Damned if she don't have a sixth sense," he thought—and composed herself and began nodding with confidence and even clapping some as a sort of show of support for Harkrider.

But deep inside the mayor was not pleased. "The little punk," she thought to herself. "Like he's more comfortable here than I am. I ought to rip him a new one the next time I get him alone. This better not make the fucking news. I swear to G— I'll have his little-bitch-ass fired," she thought, still smiling and clapping but now squinting and peering at the camera out of the corner of her eye to see if it was still trained on her, and then giving a few flips of her hair when she sensed it had moved on. After a few seconds she looked back over at it and saw the camera focused again on Harkrider. A few more seconds passed when Steve-O again looked her way, and then back to Harkrider, clearly terrified at the look she'd shot him.

His fear of the mayor was replaced by another fear when Wells Moreland tapped him on the shoulder and motioned his hand across his throat in a cutting gesture. He wanted to continue, but he knew he couldn't waste the video. And he knew there was no way they'd make the six o'clock newscast. Fortunately, they'd filmed the story's lead-in before the ceremony had begun. He looked down at his watch. But even if it were the last story, they only had twenty-three minutes to edit it down and send it in.

Then the crowd surged forward again, and he and Wells Moreland, who'd taken out his Binaca to freshen up, were knocked sideways. When Steve-O recovered, he looked up and found himself staring at the mayor some twenty feet away. She was wiping tears away from her eyes. Tears. He couldn't believe it.

"There is a God," he thought to himself as he again swung the camera around and turned it on and looked through the eyepiece. But a flash of bright color—a red jacket or dress—flew by in front of the camera and jostled him. He looked up, knowing exactly what he'd find even before spotting the assailant. He knew the type; some prankster wanting to get on the nightly news. There was one in every crowd. He shook his head and bit his lip in disgust.

Finally, he refocused the camera on the mayor. There was an instant of eye contact—when the feisty career of the brusque, attractive, and undeniably brilliant young mayor dissolved in the fading light of day and he saw before him only a vulnerable thirty-five-year-old woman—but then the crowd surged again and the shot was lost and when he looked back up she was glowering at him with a hate he had never seen before. Wells Moreland stepped in the way and turned the camera off, not realizing the shot he'd interrupted.

"Prepare to wrap it," he said. "We gotta end it soon and head out to Mesquite." Those were the last words Steve-O wanted to hear, because the last time they'd been out at the rodeo had been the worst day of his life. In fact, the Mesquite Rodeo had a long history of humiliating cameramen, a history he'd played no small part in. But this most recent episode of his had been one of the worst. While he had been trying to get some footage of a cowboy riding Dakota, the prize bull shrugged its massive neck and flung a shot put sized mass of snot onto the camera lens and into his face. He'd come down with a cold. Friends at the station began messing with him, telling him he had anthrax and that he should take penicillin. He laughed it off but ended up going to the doctor anyhow. As if to make matters worse, none of the cowboys had been able to ride the bull, and they had no footage to use for the news that night. And here his boss was telling him to wrap up this shoot where he'd gotten footage of the ice queen mayor crying so they could head back out to Mesquite. He could wait. This ceremony may be a freak show, Steve-O thought, but freak shows were good copy, and he didn't want it to end. And apparently neither did Harkrider, for the minister then started to rail about beginnings.

"That's right—some folks fear we'll find the beginning's bones," he scream-sang. "They're afraid of it. Cry themselves to sleep over it," he lamented, shaking his head before continuing with renewed conviction. "But I pray for it. Wake up in the middle of the night and shout for joy for it. That's right, brothers and sisters, I pray we'll find the beginning's bones. 'Cause I want to naaaaame them bones. Wanna naaaaame them bones!"

The crowd was dancing now.

"Name them bones….and do you know why, brothers and sisters?" he asked rhetorically, a playful smile crossing his lips. "I say do you know why?" The crowd shouted its answer, and he laughed in affirmation.

"That's right. 'Cause them bones gonna walk around. Gonna walk around. Gonna sing and dance and shout and—praise God, hallelujah—gonna tell their story! Praise God, them bones. Praise God we've found our beginning's bones!"

The crowd swelled and rolled and spat Jamaal Akbar Madison out toward the front of the podium, where he would have been embarrassed were it not for the brash behavior of a young woman in a bright red dress who was convulsing and dancing at the words of Harkrider, attracting attention in the process. He was embarrassed for her, ashamed even. She was standing next to that annoying Wells Moreland, who was himself confused at the sight. It was an absurd juxtaposition. Madison sized up the two: the waifish, barefoot woman and the portly Moreland, perhaps the vainest man in town. Italian suit. Toupee. Trump tan. He immediately thought of Whitney Houston's meeting with Ariel Sharon; it was a pairing that ludicrous. And as absurd as he believed Moreland's existence to be, this dancing, flailing teenager was giving the silver-haired broadcaster a run for his money. Madison knew the type: some melodramatic celebrant. Dressed in an African fabric. Probably a college student studying post-colonialism, he mused to himself. Trying to play the part. Replacing a lost tradition with a fake one. He shook his head and descended back into the crowd, making his way toward the far side of the plaza side. And only when he thought he had resettled into the anonymity of the swirling mass, did a voice called out to him.

"Timmy Madison, what are you doing here?"

Madison knew the speaker without even turning around. Without even having heard the voice in over two years. He knew the ironic and challenging tone. He'd spotted her right before the ceremony had begun, and he tried to avoid her. He couldn't now, but he could pretend not to want to speak too loudly as if out of respect for others who were trying to listen to Harkrider. He knew he had to respond, though, and in a confident, unflustered manner. He turned and confronted his five-foot-two-inch antagonist.

"What do you mean?" he asked casually, without greeting her by name.

She crossed her arms, leaned all her weight on one hip, and looked up at him. She wasn't buying his cool act. Hadn't bought it when he'd first mentioned he was considering changing his name, either. He knew why, recalling his moment of weakness a few years back when toward the end of a date he confessed to her that the woman who had married his grandfather had been full- blooded Irish—straight off the boat from Dun Laoghaire—and that a great grandparent had been of mixed race from the Caribbean. She loved to tease him about this. "O'toole," she'd say, grabbing a doughy handful from his ample waistline, "what sort of middle name is that?" But most of all she loved to kid him about his initials: "How appropriate," she'd say playfully. This confidence confused him: after all, she had been raised in Utah (of all places), and had even considered changing her name to a Swahili one after entering graduate school (which she hadn't finished), and she was actually even lighter skinned than he (and got reddish freckles in the summer). But you'd never have known any of this from her bold body language. And so he felt obligated to try to defend his presence at this august occasion.

"I came to honor my people," he continued, returning his attention to the podium and attempting to bring to her attention the fact that a speech was being made not a hundred feet away. She could have cared less, and this was the very quality of hers that intimidated him so much.

"Your people?" she asked skeptically, nodding her head as if to be sure she'd heard him right. She was unconvinced. Amused, even. He was terrified other people had heard her and picked up on her tone of voice. Suspected he was a phony. Why did she have to talk so loud all of the time, he thought. Finally, he managed a response, trying to sound as convincing as possible.

"Yes, *my* people."

"Your people, hmm? Okay. I just wanted to be sure."

He continued to look straight ahead and pretend that he was paying attention to Harkrider, hoping she would disappear. She didn't.

"Good turn out," he finally said, giving a vague nod to the hundreds gathered at the gateway but actually trying desperately to change the subject.

"So, did you see my poems?" she asked, cutting off his final word as if he had nothing of value to say.

He'd been afraid she'd ask that. He feared she'd seen him before the ceremony began, reading the poems inscribed into the two obelisks that stood beyond the gateway and in the cemetery itself. He felt certain that she must have heard the poem he had entered in the contest had been rejected. Though the gates to the cemetery had been closed before the ceremony, he'd been able to read both of her poems through the wrought iron fence. Engraved in large letters across the base of two enormous obelisks, the short poems were easy to make out across the narrow footpath on the other side of the fence. He thought they were awful and couldn't believe that they'd been immortalized in stone. He actually thought it was a bigger scandal than the fact the mayor was presiding over the events of the day.

He straightened his bow tie—a habit he always succumbed to before he told a lie—and replied, "Yes. They were…interesting." Though he had not converted to Islam, he had begun the process of legally changing his name from Timothy O'toole to Jamaal Akbar and adopted the uniform of the Nation because he sensed most people found it vaguely menacing. He was hoping it had this effect on her and that his unimpressed tone of voice would burn her up.

But she was too enamored of her poems' canonization and the prospects of her own immortality to detect or be concerned with his attempts at irony. "I love the way the sculptor worked them into the stone. They brought him over from Italy just to do the inscription. They told me he loved the poems, especially the one about the Middle Passage. It's Tuscan marble, and they say the poems will be there forever. My grandkids can come out here and see it all. Yours too. It's so exciting."

He suddenly felt nauseous, but he recovered—and admirably, he thought: "Yes, hopefully future generations will be coming here to remember and honor these dead ancestors." But she'd forgotten about the hundreds lying beyond the gateway in unmarked graves.

"There's a picture of the western obelisk, that one there," she said pointing, "on the cover of my new book. Had you heard I was getting another one published?" He thought about making some sarcastic comment about a chapbook not being a real book, but she didn't give him any time for a reply. "It's a beautiful shot. The sun's setting in the distance and the surface of the marble looks like the ripples of the ocean. The colors are incredible. And it's spring, so the flowers are in bloom, too. The photographer is really an artist. I want to work with him again. On my next book."

He had tuned her out and was now trying his best to focus in on Harkrider and not to acknowledge her presence, but it wasn't working. She continued, undeterred.

"Anyhow, I have a signing this Sunday. At the new Timbuktu Tea and Books on Hampton. You should come by. It's four to seven. I think you'd have a good time. Bring a date, if you like."

Though she'd said "like," he knew she meant "can." This really pissed him off, and as he was trying desperately to think up some sharp response, he found in his left hand—without being aware of how it got there—a yellow piece of paper with green and black trim that contained on it all the relevant information about the signing. He realized that this must have been the same piece of paper that he'd noticed under all of the cars' wiper blades as he'd been trying to find a parking space for the ceremony.

"Thanks," he said, adjusting his tie, "I'll try to make it."

"Oh, we'll have fun," she teased, in a tone of voice that shook his attention away from Harkrider. She was smiling at him—mocking him, he thought.

"I'll be reading selections and then signing copies."

"Fantastic," he said coldly.

"Then I'll see you there, Timmy?"

He thought he might have nodded.

"I'll have one already signed for you, ready to pick up."

He grunted a response and returned his attention to the podium.

"See you then," she whispered, pressing his hand, and giving him a peck on the cheek. And then she mercifully disappeared, to slip the rest of her announcements into the few remaining empty hands present at the ceremony.

Out of the corner of his eye, he watched her leave. He'd been humiliated. And worst of all, she knew it, too. In truth, he thought her poems weren't terrible. They just weren't good. Certainly not good enough to warrant being immortalized in stone. But neither had his poem been. He'd submitted it in the same contest, but apparently her poems had won. Her poems, and those of two others, would be remembered in stone. This galled him. But the truth was he had known "The City of the Dead" was bad the whole time he'd been writing it. He was hoping some vaguely worded lines would sound suggestive. They didn't. And he wondered if that wasn't really what was pissing himself off.

For as long as he'd known her, going back to before they had dated to the time when they'd just been friends, he'd thought her work had been incredibly mediocre. He never told her that. Especially not when he began to sense that he might be able to close the deal with her. So he'd tolerated the poetry readings. The coffee shop gatherings. The grad student get-togethers. Until he'd finally had enough. He just stopped returning her calls. It seemed like the best way to end it. He would have done anything to escape her poetry.

Her worst work reminded him of bad Maya Angelou, whose poems he had always despised. He was convinced that, after "On the Pulse of Morning" had been read at Clinton's inauguration, every woman he met thought she was a poet. Oprah's Book Club wasn't helping matters either, he felt. Everyone can't be a writer; he was sure it didn't work that way. It couldn't. All his professors had told him so. This he believed more than anything else. You just couldn't say you were a poet and be a poet. But some people—like his old girlfriend—thought you could. And now she had a couple of stone obelisks to show for it. They'd argued about this type of stuff during the entire six months they'd dated. Their bookshelves could not have been more different. For years he'd read Sowell, Mansfield, and Keyes, but one day he suddenly stopped. Yet when she tried to get him interested in West, he would have none of it. She decided she had no time for his stubbornness and suspected a mid-life crisis. The final straw had been when he said he couldn't stand Oprah. She lost it after he'd said that. Started questioning his "blackness." Said he was a "traitor to the race." As if Oprah was the litmus test for one's authenticity. "If it makes you feel any better," he insisted, "I hate Martha Stewart, too." But she wasn't listening to him. They hadn't talked since the breakup. Until now.

He'd actually stopped reading poetry for months after the breakup, which was tough for him to do because he loved reading. Walcott was one of his favorites. So was Giovanni. He'd just bought her latest. It was probably his favorite. That or "Howl"—he'd never forget the first time he'd read that. He thought Hughes was way over-rated—though he'd never have said it in public—and he had a secret crush on Dickinson. And this passion was his great-est source of shame. He liked the work of this dead, frail woman the most. This wealthy, white recluse. Somehow, she reached out to him across time, place, and race. He felt they were soul mates. And he thought that this shouldn't be so. In his heart of hearts he wondered if this wasn't one reason why he despised the mayor so much. And his old girlfriend.

For only this troubled him more than white people's power: black people's power. Or rather, the power of some black people. Those who had told him when he was a kid that he couldn't like Star Trek and Thelonius Monk. Jim Taylor and Jim Brown. Now that was power to be feared. And as much as he loved his Uncle Timothy, he feared him even more. Before he had headed off to college, his uncle had cornered him at a family get together and warned him—stared him right in the eye and said something to him that he'd never forget: "The only thing that's messed with black folks more than dope is Harvard—you know what I'm say-ing? Hmm? Just remember who you are."

He'd nodded his head. The truth was his uncle's warning had terrified him as much as any nightmare about cross burnings. For this warning had the veneer of respectability. No, not the veneer. His uncle *was* respectable and intelligent and decent—the most im-pressive person he knew. But there were times when he wondered if everything his uncle said was right. And this was why the warn-ing had been so confusing. And still was. All through college, he'd struggled with it. He knew that it was one thing to boycott some businesses and to lead rallies against companies that had interests in South Africa, but where did it end? Should you hate Star Trek? Seinfeld? Should you renounce Hollywood or just parts of it? Or should you take it back further, condemning the Enlightenment and so many of its developments and innovations? What about the Constitution? The English language? He thought his uncle's advice could get absurd if you carried it out all the way. His greatest fear was that once you start down that path, you have to take down the whole house. Everything. Or else you're a liar. Why not just renovate a room or two? Add on a new wing?

He turned his head from Harkrider to where the mayor was standing, not fifteen yards away, but her attention was transfixed on something else. He turned to see what she was staring at but saw only the annoying Wells Moreland and his cameraman. He couldn't figure it out.

But Steve-O, who sensed the mayor's stare, could. By some quirk of fate, he had been reunited on a regular basis with his middle school girlfriend. Shortly after eighth grade, their paths had parted for good—or so he'd thought. He'd go to Tech and study communications, working his way through smaller markets as a cameraman before winding up in Dallas, and she'd go to Texas on Plan II, pledge some sorority (he didn't remember which), and eventually end up at S.M.U. law school, during which time she'd clerk for her father, a judge, before marrying early, having two kids, and then beginning a private practice at thirty, and—incredibly— becoming mayor at thirty-four. Yes, their paths had parted dramati- cally, but he'd always have the goods on her. And they both knew it. They weren't damning goods. Just weird ones. And he could tell ev- ery time he drew an assignment to cover an event she was at that it tore her up inside. He'd actually forgotten about it until they'd been awkwardly reunited at a campaign event a year and a half ago. He'd pieced it together as the source of her scorn after she'd pretended she didn't remember him after he'd reintroduced himself to her for the second time that night. She insisted she didn't remember him. But he knew she did.

And she did. She remembered every second of that fateful encounter they'd had years before. So did he. At Dubecks' Skate- world on Greenville. At Bobby Carlyle's twelfth birthday party ("Whatever happened to Bobby?" Steve-O wondered). A couples' skate. The lights had been dimmed. Peaches and Herb was on the P.A. It had begun innocently enough. She'd asked him to skate, which wasn't unusual at that age since the girls are usually bigger and more assertive. In fact, she was a good four inches taller than he was. They'd made a couple of loops around the rink holding hands and were nearing the party room that looked out onto the skaters when the unbelievable happened. Something that would live on in the lore of Walker Middle School for months. He'd first felt the rumbling in her hand, which suddenly tightened its grip on his. In an instant she had yanked him closer, bent down, and given him a peck on the cheek. He hardly knew what had happened. And to make matters worse, she met his horrified gaze with an equally horrified and astonished look and screamed out, "Who did that?" This was more than he could take or process at the time. He was overwhelmed, and though her question didn't seem to make any sense, he did begin to wonder who had done it. He was confused. The skate ended unceremoniously, and he didn't see her for the rest of the party. But his friends had seen what had happened. And the word spread.

At least that's the way he recalled the story now, years later, though the more he thought about it the more he wasn't sure if the strange comment had followed the kiss or if the whole incident wasn't something he'd heard had happened to a guest on a late night talk show. Something like it must have happened, he reasoned, for it's what he'd been telling folks for years. Especially during the past year, since the mayor had taken office.

And as Harkrider resumed his speech, Steve-O lost himself in the thought of a seventh grade couples' skate. Suddenly, Wells Moreland, who had just returned his Binaca to the pocket of his News Team One blazer, yanked on his arm and drew him near.

"Let's go. The sonofabitch is running over."

He'd turned to his boss, with the camera still trained in on the mayor.

"Let's go," Moreland whispered. "Don't waste any more video. He could go on for days. I've been waving my hand at him for the past five minutes trying to get his attention, but he doesn't care. We gotta head to Mesquite. Now," he said, tapping his watch.

Steve-O turned the camera off. "I thought he said he'd try to limit it to fifteen minutes so it could make StreetLife?"

"He did. So what," Moreland answered, breathing into his palm and then, apparently unsatisfied, retrieving the Binaca for another shot.

"And the mayor…didn't she ask him to keep it short, too?"

"She did."

"Well," he said, biting his lip, hoping Moreland would follow his train of thought. He didn't.

"Let's go. He's way over. He saw me trying to get his attention but went on. He doesn't care. Besides, we got enough footage to tell the story."

"But they really wanted us to get it all. Even if it's just for the archives. So they can use it later," he said, trying tactfully to remind Moreland of what they'd been told back at the station.

"Listen, you heard Harkrider himself. He promised he'd keep it to fifteen minutes. Well, he didn't. I'm sorry, but I don't feel bad at all about leaving. We're already gonna have to edit it down. It's his own fault. He got greedy. And we got places to be. It'll take us fifteen minutes to get to Mesquite. And they want that piece on Cowboy Poker to air tonight."

Steve-O stared blankly into space, then began slowly to pack things up.

Then, as if to make his case more convincing, Wells Moreland continued in the annoying, paternalistic voice Steve-O hated. "Esteban Luis Ojeda, my man, don't feel so bad. It's not personal. It's business. His time's no more valuable than any other story's. Or any commercial's, for that matter. They're all equal. And they're all interchangeable. You've been in the business long enough to know that. Parts is parts. Even when the part belongs to the great Bishop Isaiah Harkrider."

There was nothing he hated more than when Moreland called him by his full name. It was Moreland's patronizing attempt to exert control over him, all in the guise of casual familiarity. He'd been doing it a lot more since all the cameramen at the station had nixed his idea for them to go on assignment sporting a ridiculous pin that had written on it: "News Team One: History's First and Final Draft," refusing again when he amended it to simply "First and Final: News Team One." Still, Steve-O nodded his head at his boss and thought back over the conversation they'd had an hour ago with the mayor and the minister. It didn't seem right to leave.

"How many cameras you got?" Harkrider had asked.

"Just one."

"One?" the mayor asked, a bit shocked.

"One," he'd nodded.

The mayor shook her head with contempt, as if all the media was incompetent and guilty of some greater crime. She felt herself about to explode, but she checked herself. Even though she knew that her husband had been right, that entertainment and news were turning into each other—"Isn't that what Katie and Jay's little switcharoo was all about?" he'd snarled at her—she wasn't convinced that you only had to have one camera at events like these. This was historic. She'd even worn her blazer. Had gotten it dry-cleaned the week before. She was pissed.

But Harkrider was more forgiving and patient. His patience was legendary, and the mayor herself had experienced it first hand before (though she'd never confessed this to him), when she'd been a sophomore in high school and he'd shown up on campus the first day kids were bussed in. He'd held the front door open and greeted kids all morning long. Stayed even after the principal had returned to his office, and the parking lot cop had gone off to lunch. Stayed put. Welcoming anybody who crossed his path. Welcoming them all. Each and every one. With a smile that was as much a blessing as it was a greeting. A smile that could reconcile all.

And he was smiling again when he said to Moreland, in his deep gravelly voice, "All right. One'll do, just be sure to get it all."

"Don't worry. We will," Moreland said, looking down at his watch. "But keep it to fifteen minutes. We've got to head out to Mesquite after all."

"I'll do my best. But when the spirit moves me…"

Harkrider didn't have time to finish his thought for the mayor had grabbed his arm and was already guiding him toward the podium, when he nearly collided with a young woman in a red dress. He made as if to help her up, apologizing, but the mayor dragged him on. She had no patience for such displays and only looked at the girl with disdain. She knew the type. She'd seen her earlier that afternoon, wandering barefoot through the cemetery itself, picking flowers. Tacky, she'd thought. And probably homeless. Later, right before the ceremony began, she was sure she'd heard her singing a song to herself in Spanish while moving through the crowd. That and the raggedy red dress were enough to make the mayor take a mental note to write D.C. about tightening immigration laws to send back such undesirables to wherever it was they came from.

She couldn't stand how community events—events that were designed to bring everyone together—were being undermined by such thoughtlessness. Kids, and even young adults, hadn't learned respect for such civic events. Had no discipline. They didn't know how to act. Or dress. Probably had never been taught. They didn't understand how to behave in public. That there were some things you just didn't do.

The mayor understood all this, and she also knew there was a tight schedule to be maintained, and by God she was going to abide by it. And she'd force them all to do the same, even if it meant grabbing this enormous hulk of a man by the elbow and leading him up toward the podium. It was for his own good, she thought.

And so an hour later, when Harkrider saw the News Team One cameraman packing up his gear and heading out quietly toward the parking lot, he knew that he'd gone off schedule. He didn't even need to look down at his watch. And it didn't really matter to him, either, for he'd always felt that the building of God's kingdom on earth didn't conform to human schedules. Didn't cut itself off short so that it could be wedged into prime time. Wouldn't be bulled out of the way by a story on cowboy poker. It had its own time.

"So brothers and sisters," he said, smiling out on the audience, "I'll conclude my remarks today by reminding you all that we are now standing at a threshold."

Standing in the gateway, he gestured outward with both arms, reaching them toward the columns that framed the cemetery's entrance. He paused…stared out on the gathering. On the silence. Somewhere in the distance, a van started.

"There's much work to do yet in our New Jerusalem. For all

that our tomorrow can be, is contained in our past. So let us not cross lightly into the promised land of our past. This gateway is a holy place, an intersection, crossed three times by past, present, and future. Every step you take—each and every day—is a step through that gateway. Not a step *away* from the struggle of the past. But a step with the struggle of the past. *Into* the struggle of the past. *At* the center of that struggle. Each and every step. Let us not forget how easily the past can be covered up and forgotten. That generations before us were not able to embark upon this journey. To consider all that now lies before us. Nor let us enter through these gates in vain. For when you are dipped into the pool of the past you must emerge a new man. A new woman. You must be born anew. For this is a special moment. Unlike others. And with this new birth must come new responsibilities."

"Amen"s leapt upward from the crowd like fish from a sea.

"I say to you right now, that if you look closely on this matter, you will see that the past is always with us. The past walks among us. Breathes in the air we breathe out and gives it back to us again. It doesn't lie stretched out behind us like a timeline. It isn't a skin to be sloughed off. The past is with us just as surely as the future is in us and the fullness of time is upon us. So do not fall asleep. And do not be made drowsy on the wine of contentment. Be watchful. For history is now. The future is now. And this now is with us and is so for all time. What was and what will be now *is* at this very moment."

The sea rolled and splashed with approval.

"So as you step through this gateway and the sun greets you anew on the other side, know this: that all of time has moved toward this moment. All of time is indeed contained in this moment. Stars have burst open and galaxies exploded to give birth to this moment. Empires have fallen and kings risen for this moment. Leviathans have dived and rockets surged skyward for this moment. Sparrows have dropped to earth and prayers ascended—all for this moment. Your moment: and that moment, brothers and sisters, that moment is NOW!"

And with that word, the gates to the cemetery were thrown open and the crowd surged past the podium and into the land beyond. As he looked out over the gathered mass, a crowd that he now imagined to be shaking like a thousand flames, he could only smile to himself. Not even the terrible odor could dampen this moment. No, he thought, not even the stench from the highway construction—that most unpleasant byproduct of progress— could undermine the building of this new city. It was a stench you couldn't forget. A stench that was made worse by the oppressive heat of the late afternoon.

A stench Jamaal Akbar Madison read as coming from the cemetery itself and not the construction. For some reason, he thought he'd caught a whiff of the thousand corpses from the yard beyond the gates. Unburied and rotting. He had even had night- mares about the stench rising from the mass grave. He didn't think any ceremony led by a two-bit preacher man was gonna make the stench go away. He resented old timers who thought they could just turn their collar around and win a following. Who thought that gave them some precious clout. That it counted for more than intelligence and education. And yet he wondered if his feelings for Harkrider weren't rooted in jealousy, or something like it: an awareness of the fact that he, with his Harvard diploma, could never command a crowd the way this unlettered, old man could. And though the stench was overwhelming, it didn't distract him from these thoughts, or from the final words of Harkrider—words whose sentimentality was making him nauseous. Hollow, self- important words. Confused words about the past and oppression. Words ripped right out of the pages of pop psychology and Ann Landers. Stuff Little League coaches told their teams before games: all that "stay in the now," crap. No, the stench didn't distract him from these pitiful words.

But the young woman in the red dress did, when she gently brushed by him on her way toward the gates. By his count, he'd seen her at least three times that afternoon, and that was more than enough. He was now officially pissed off. She was dressed inappropriately, and her behavior was bizarre. It was like she didn't realize the solemnity of the place or the significance of the event that was unfolding around her. Even if it was an event for which he felt scorn. He scanned the crowd for some uniformed officers. If there'd been a cop nearby, he would have asked him to have the annoying woman removed from the ceremony or at least reprimanded and detained in the parking lot, for he didn't realize that the young woman was La Roja. And that La Roja was the ghost of his great-grandmother—the one he had never known—who'd been born in the Dominican one-hundred-and-forty years ago, buried in Freedman's Cemetery seventy six years ago, and disturbed from her rest last spring.

It wasn't this realization that brought him back to the cemetery in the middle of the night. He never had this realization. What had brought him back was something else. At first, he thought it had been the stench that woke him up in his bed, soaked with perspiration. But the more he thought about it, the less this seemed likely. Dreams don't stink. No matter how bad they are. He figured it must have been something else that made him return. Exactly what, he couldn't say. But whatever it was, it was powerful, and it had led him to the empty space before the gates.

The same space that Remedios, who at precisely the same moment had stopped her vacuuming, saw was still teeming with figures—with La Roja and Tio Theo and dozens of others. Gazing down upon the scene, she knew she might not see them again after tonight, the last night of their wandering, for the cemetery had been dedicated and the ground finally made hallowed. Their burial now seemed complete. She placed her hand against the windowpane. It was cold. Moisture gathered at her fingertips.

The night was cool. The noise of the city faded, and a light breeze shook sound from the treetops. For several minutes, Jamaal Akbar Madison sat across from the obelisk, staring at the poem. Seeing it. Tracing the letters with his eyes, but blind to the words. And then the wind rose and returned his thoughts to the matter at hand, and he found himself looking up from the jagged outline of obelisks and historical markers to their clean echo in the buildings that lined Central Expressway. In an upper floor of a distant building, he thought he could see a greenish light. Then the movement of a shape at a window. Suddenly, he grew afraid. Self-conscious.

He stood up and tugged at where his bow tie had been, then began walking quickly toward the gate. He needed to leave. Feared that he'd been found out. He couldn't bear the thought that someone had watched him stroll through the grounds. Seen him seated before the obelisk. Witnessed his silent confession. His deep confusion. Madison stared into the dark and empty space before him, and in the flash of a moment, a possibility was revealed: that he was the most alone man—banished and betrayed and welcomed by none. And as he crossed through the gates, his anxiety turned to anger. He cursed the night. Wanted to burn it all to the ground. Buildings, gates, graveyard. Everything. And he thought the place to begin might be with the shape in the distant window.

A shape that now turned off the lights to the corner office. Her work now finished, Remedios made the sign of the cross and shifted her attention from the cemetery to thoughts of the bus that would leave in an hour. The ride home was so much better than the ride to work. There was no traffic. She loved the early morning. Its clean air and empty roads and silence. She could see so much from her window. For above it all—above the cemetery and the highway, the media and the mayor and even Madison himself—above it all was Remedios: cleaning and humming and embracing the strange beauty of the world before her, wondering what the verdict would be on her paper work. Though she wasn't yet an American, she hoped to be one soon. High above the bright, new city, above the quick and the dead, the living and the already living, she was there. She was there, and she could see them all. She could see them all at once. And she was smiling.

The Taking of Names

The Lebanon Fishshack wasn't really a fishshack but a place where you could do some shopping while filling your tank up with gas, maybe even sitting at one of the tables in back behind the Quaker State display and talking with Wesley and some of the fellas while eating a Country Boy Breakfast—two eggs any way you like, Texas Toast, three slabs of bacon, and a cup of coffee—as the sun begins rising over the far shore of Texoma, just barely visible beyond the trees through the back window. 'Course you could buy your bait there too. Borrow a couple of bucks of gas for your boat, long as Wesley had it on him. But everyone in Lebanon knew it wasn't really a fishshack. Not just a fishshack, anyhow. Folks there have never been too particular. That's how it's always been in Lebanon, and how it still is. And that's what they'd named the place a long time ago, but no one knew who'd done it or when, though someone thought it might have been Wesley's dad since he used to run the place.

What was even more peculiar than all this was that it turned out the Lebanon Fishshack wasn't even in Lebanon but about two hundred yards outside of town. As far as I can tell no one had ever known this 'til some judge in Oklahoma City told Bobby to throw out a disorderly conduct citation he'd given a man because the shack was out of his jurisdiction. Some hotshot from Dallas with a speed boat hitched up to his Suburban. They're always coming up to Texoma getting drunk and thinking they own the place. Not that any of this mattered to anybody but Bobby. He was mighty pissed. Moped around for a week. But he got his satisfaction soon enough. Later that summer he came across the same guy fishing without a license. Claimed he'd left it on shore in the glovebox, but Bobby was riled up when he recognized who it was and said you gotta have the license with you at all times though he'd let me off the hook a dozen times for the same offense. The whole thing got me and Ruthie to thinking one day about if we even lived in Lebanon, but we figured it didn't matter 'cause wherever it was we'd been there for thirty years and it was too late to get worked up about it. We did know what county we lived in, though. That's on our voting cards. And I know for sure the county line cuts the lake in half and that our house ain't straddling the lake.

None of this would have mattered a lick if Wesley's sister, Wanda, hadn't caught wind of it. She said the place should change its name. Said how could any self-respecting man say something was in Lebanon if he knew it wasn't in Lebanon. Said it was false advertising or something and that she might just call the Better Business Bureau unless something was done about it. Bobby suspected her husband put her up to it since he ran the other store in town, but Bobby was always suspecting somebody of something. "Yankee sonofabitch," he'd grumble to himself when he'd see them out on the lake in their new pontoon even though he knew Big Al was from Maryland. It didn't matter none to Bobby, 'cause he was sure she'd married Big Al just to spite the family.

The truth is Big Al wasn't a bad guy, too good for Wanda, in fact. He just didn't know how to run a place, and she was jealous of Wesley's success and how he'd already had to expand his place twice. In fact, the rumor was that she couldn't even bear to enter the store 'cause it hurt to see how good the Fishshack was doing. She'd even drive the long way to the lake just to avoid going by the place. If you knew her you'd know that's not hard to believe. That's how Wanda is. As for me, I just don't know how she came up with the big idea that'd make her think she could change the name of something she never used. It just doesn't make sense. Anyone in their right mind would have to admit that. I didn't lose any sleep over it, though. At least not at first.

Anyhow, every Sunday after church that entire summer she'd call up Wesley ranting and raving and saying she was fixin' to sic Ralph Neighbors on us, but we all figured if the customers knew it wasn't in Lebanon there was nothing nobody could do about it. Just in case, Wesley even put up a sign in the front window that said: "All customers hereby be notified, the Lebanon Fishshack is NOT in Lebanon." Still, we weren't sure if this would do the job. Word got 'round about Wanda and folks didn't know what to make of all this, didn't know if they were violating some ordinance by shopping there, and so late that summer business slowed to a trickle.

One day Wanda finally did storm into the place while a few of us diehards were eating breakfast and started raising cane and Bobby made like he was gonna cuff her but I said, "No Bobby, this ain't your jurisdiction," and he sat back down slowly and clenched his mug tight and muttered real low, but not too low, "Bitch." That perked her ears up good. We figured since we had a lawman on our side, that we were alright. Not that we could have actually used the law, but that's not the point. Just the thought that it's there should be enough. That's what Bobby used to say, but he's been a cop for twenty-five years. He figured you gotta respect the badge even when it doesn't really mean nothing. All hell'll break loose if you don't. That's what we were banking on, anyways. But that Wanda's an ornery little cuss, and apparently no one had ever told her that business about respecting the badge, about what it's supposed to mean and all. Fortunately for us, she's a frisky one and don't know much about respecting anything, period.

And that's what led me and Bobby to hatch our plan to save the Fishshack. It was no secret Wanda liked to flirt, sometimes even with Little Al's high school friends. Little Al himself knew she did it. The whole town knew it. Everybody but Big Al. And being as Wanda'd left us no alternative, we were gonna have to use her weakness against her. Still, we would have backed off if that inspector hadn't shown up that day and started asking Wesley questions and talking like he was gonna shut the place down. We figured these were idle threats and all, but we couldn't say for sure. He just said their office had been flooded with calls from some crazy woman saying we were breaking the law in Lebanon and that law-abiding citizens were fed up with it. At first he paid her no mind, thought she was some kook, but the phone calls kept coming. "What?—are there no real men working for the state, men who'll stand up to liars and crooks?" And then later it got worse: "Are you afraid to uphold the law, or just too damn lazy? Hmm? Answer me, boy! Well, I see, excuse me if I've inconvenienced you, if this little idea called the law cramps your style you yellow-bellied coward" and on and on and on. We'd heard it all before. The truth of the matter was my heart kinda went out to that inspector when he started telling us this. He nearly broke down in the Fishshack right there in front of me and Wesley. We fixed him up with an RC Cola and some Corn Nuts and he managed to pull himself together, thank the Lord. Poor boy. It was plain to see he was no match for Wanda. Way out of his league. A guy can only take so many insults to his manhood. We'd seen Big Al suffer enough from these kinds of attacks.

This was when me and Roy and Bobby wrote out our letter from the Entrepreneur Society of America, mailed it to Roy's cousin in D.C. and told him to mail it to Big Al inviting him to a grocers' conference in Dallas. We'd worked out every detail, down to the minute. There were lectures, question and answer times, a hospitality room. The place even had an indoor swimming pool.

The works. But then Roy started to think and got worried. He said Big Al wasn't really an entrepreneur or not much of one anyhow and probably wouldn't get this sort of an invitation and Bobby said it wasn't the point that we knew that, so long as Big Al didn't know it. This shut Roy up, but he still looked as troubled as Ruthie the time before our first Christmas together when she'd found out she was overdrawn. She came home from the store pale as a ghost, then burst into tears. That's a look you don't ever want to see, especially on a mug like Roy's.

Anyhow, we got Big Al his room at the Ramada off of Harry Hines in Dallas, and he took the bait. With things being the way they were, we figured he'd jump at any chance to get away from Wanda. We worked it out for a Friday night when we knew Little Al had a basketball tournament up near Stillwater so that he'd be out of the picture. And that's when we sent over Bobby's nephew, Handsome James, to ask Wanda if he could borrow some gas for fishing early Saturday morning. Not long back Bobby'd overheard James bragging after church 'bout how she'd patted his rear once in her store and stared at him on a couple of occasions in the D.Q., licking her lips all hungry-like and how even once at a slumber party for Little Al he woke up with her hunkered down next to him making sexy eyes. Needless to say, Bobby was impressed. He knew any boy as cocksure as James would be up for the plan. So we rigged up a microphone with wire and tape and all, and James thought it was pretty cool, like some cop show. We all waited 'round the block in Bobby's Cutlass while Handsome James rang the doorbell. Not more than five minutes after he'd entered we figured we'd recorded enough to shut Wanda up. Maybe even enough to make Jerry Springer. It was that sorry of a scene.

We kicked back in the Cutlass, chuckling to ourselves while the tape was rewinding, but we didn't chuckle long. When Bobby checked to make sure he'd recorded it all, the tape got chewed up. He tried to untangle it by hand and play it, but there was nothing—just dead silence. I swear I'll never forget it. We couldn't run back to my place for a tape because who knew how long James

could hold out. I didn't know what to do and was out of ideas.
But Bobby wasn't. He's a cool customer. He popped the tape out,
flipped it into the air, caught it, and stared at it: "Our only hope,"
he said, shaking the tape for emphasis, "is to make believe there's
something here." And that's what our grand plan to restore peace
and order to Lebanon had come down to, which means it had
come down to pretty much nothing. Fortunately, Bobby's got a
damn good poker face, and when I have to I can lie with the best
of them. The truth of the matter is I hail from a long line of bold-
face liars, a fact I'm secretly kind of proud of. So Wanda was gonna
have to call our bluff. That's all there was to it. It was our only shot.
We figured we'd better get over there before she scarred James
for life, so we stumbled out of the car cussing and made the short
walk over to her house. It was warm for a November night, perfect
for fishing. I swear I'll never forget that walk over, thinking about
how the lake would be calm with few boats on it, the wind not too
strong but just right.

We figured we didn't have to knock since we'd heard her
groping and panting and trying to wrestle poor James to the floor.
Sure enough, when we got into the den there was James doing his
best to wrench her mouth free from his neck. To this day Bobby
laughs about how scared James looked. At first, from where I was
standing, I couldn't really tell. Then I got a good look after Wanda
stopped biting about his ear, and I saw he looked like a deer in your
headlights. He didn't know what was happening to him. His hair
was standing on end, bags under his wide eyes. His face was pale
and had lipstick all over the place. I didn't think the poor boy would
recover from this disturbing encounter. He's a fine nephew, taking
one for the team like that. Not every boy would have done that
'cause Wanda's pretty scary though she's got the little hard body of
a sixteen-year- old cheerleader, which is what she was thirty years
ago. It was likely James's dad put him up to it, and judging from the
looks of it, James was regretting that decision.

Right there in front of us Wanda kicked her shoes off across
the room without losing her grip on his shoulders and then let out

some husky moans. Anyhow, we watched for a good minute while Wanda bucked about and tossed her hair back like in the late-night movies, grabbing and gasping every which way. Frightened James had seen us enter the living room and was making hand gestures for help. Finally he just broke down and cried out, "Damn it, Uncle Bobby, help me! Please, please help me!" Wanda stopped dead in her tracks and spun around and started putting on her shirt and pulling her hair back. But it was too late.

Bobby stepped up to the couch and spoke, real slow. He'd been waitin' for this day for months. It was even better than he'd hoped for. "Well, well ,well—what do we got here? It's a fine predicament you got yourself into, Wanda. Preying on this poor, helpless boy. Whaddya you got to say for yourself? Hmm, hmm?" Wanda was too busy buttoning up her shirt to answer. Bobby went right on, "That's what I thought. Well, here's what I got to say. I reckon if you can call yourself a 'wife' then we can call that place a 'fishshack' and we can say it's in Lebanon. Or Fort Worth. Or even New York City for that matter. Any of that'd ring more true than you calling yourself a wife. So from now on you stay away from the New York City Fishshack, you hear?" he said, tapping the tape recorder while James wiggled free and tugged loose the wires and mike taped to his chest, holding them out at Wanda like a preacher'd hold a cross at a vampire.

Wanda had finished with her shirt and put on some more lipstick and was now looking angrier than the devil himself. She held her tongue as her face turned red, but as we were walking back to the car and Bobby was comforting Frightened James, who was about in tears and shaking all over, she came running onto the porch and burst out, "Ain't none of this over, boys. It's all far from over. I'm taking names, I swear I will. As many as I have to. I'll find out what's behind all this. Did you hear me boys? I swear to God it ain't over! Nothing is! Not unless Wanda says it is!"

Truth is we didn't really care if it was over or just begun. We just wanted to fish. Before we headed back over to the Fishshack, me and Bobby dropped off James. Poor boy'd done got spooked.

Seeing a middle-aged woman all hot and bothered like that'll rattle the horniest teenage boy. Even one that thinks he's a stud like James. His dad answered the doorbell and let him in and set him down and got him some water. We didn't want to stick around because James was still shook up and looked sick and we didn't want to embarrass him by maybe seeing him lose his dinner. A young quarterback don't need to deal with that. Bad for his confidence.

Back at the Fishshack, we watched with pride as Wesley took the sign out of the front window and tore it up for the trash. He smiled real big and said, "Boys, the Lebanon Fishshack is back in business." Then he disappeared into the kitchen and made a big pot of coffee and a bunch of us sat down at our old table with a twelve pack. Because Big Al wasn't such a bad guy, we all vowed never to discuss the events of that night. We did have to laugh when we got to thinking about what he was doing down in Dallas, though. Poor boy. He'd probably come back like there'd been a conference, spouting off about the interesting people he'd met or the things he'd seen. That was alright, we figured, because we knew deep down inside that he'd suspect Wanda'd been up to something. And as for Wanda, we were sure she would be able to cover her own tracks. She's cunning as they get. We figured we'd shut her up, though. Everyone was shaking their head and cutting up when Bobby told the look on her face when she spun around and saw us standing in her living room, me holding out her shoes to her and Bobby her bra.

Everyone was slapping their knees and bellylaughing. Everyone, that is, except Roy. I was the first to notice how quiet he was being, and I asked him what could be the matter. He was looking real troubled and pouring packet after packet of Sweet 'n' Low in his mug and watching it disappear into his black coffee before he realized I'd said something to him. Then he said, real nervous and to no one in particular, but we figured to Wesley more than the rest of us, he said, "If we ain't in Lebanon, well, where are we then?" Nobody said a word. I looked at Bobby and he was stumped and looking at me and so I looked down at my coffee, and then at the empty packets in front of Roy. Finally, Wesley spoke up, with the same big-ass grin on his face he'd had when he tore up the sign. "Roy, I can't say for sure where the hell it is, but wherever we are I'd say we're doing good, and likely to do more. That's all anyone can ask for." And it was true. We were all of us agreed on it. No one could say for sure where it was, but it didn't matter, 'cause we were laughing and carrying on all through the night, right there in the place we'd been using for years and had always called the Lebanon Fishshack.

Holy Ghost Man

"No. No, sir. That no storm, sir."

I remember being somewhat taken aback by his response. In truth, his tone was not insolent or challenging, but sincere—even humble. I thought, too, that there was a little bit of fear in his voice, and this was what struck me as most peculiar. Not offensive, but peculiar. At this time in the South, it was practically unheard of for a black man to answer a white man thus. Certain protocol was maintained. Fear of Klan activity was very real, and though I despise that abominable fraternity, and indeed had been moved to set up my practice in the countryside in part to defy such prejudices, I was stunned by his response and tactfully wanted to provide him an opportunity to explain or retract his remark. I slowly walked up alongside of where he stood on the edge of the porch, gazing off into the distance, and repeated my statement.

"I say, looks like a storm's gathering."

I glanced at his profile, then at the distant cloud, then back at him, waiting for a response. He was oblivious to my presence, but after a long silence I thought I discerned him to have mouthed three words, three words that altered the course of my life. He did not speak them so much as form them on his lips. It was as if he were exhaling a secret name, one forbidden to say aloud. And that had been my introduction, fifteen years ago, to Holy Ghost Man.

Of course, at the time I had not known it was a man I had been inquiring about. I'd merely remarked to the father of my patient that a storm was preparing itself in the distance. I had just delivered his teenage daughter's baby, a delivery greatly complicated by her premature labor. I was sympathetic with the situation and sensed he secretly hoped that I would suggest the necessity of a certain procedure. I was attuned to such a feeling, for I had once been convinced that such a procedure would have spared my wife. As it turned out, she was lost during the birth. And I was left with a misshapen son, one I was not prepared to raise, an innocent child who suffered my incompetence and wrath. His death raised in me lurking suspicions that I could have done more. The suspicions were shared by neighbors. And so not a year after burying my wife, I decided it best to leave town in order to preserve my integrity. I moved to Atlanta and then Texas and set up practice to deliver babies to the likes of this family on whose porch I then found myself.

But glancing up at the grandfather once during the birth, I knew I had not escaped the past. He had dark thoughts in his mind. Thoughts I knew well, for I had once been tempted to act on them. The situation was beyond my control, I reasoned. As it was, the birth was difficult and required my full attention. I quickly convinced myself that whatever course of action he eventually chose was his to make, and his alone. To this day I wonder if I chose wisely.

And so I'd retreated to the front porch of the tattered shack after the birth to allow the family some privacy. The new grandfather joined me shortly thereafter. Though clearly anxious, he was thankful and touched by my humanity in visiting his house. It was evident he had probably never engaged in a meaningful conversation with a white man before, and in truth my contact with blacks had been limited. He wanted me to know he appreciated my visit. In 1912, it wasn't often that a white doctor made house calls to blacks in this part of the country.

He had handed me a cup of coffee, and we sat in awkward silence for some time in the warm October sun, when I pointed to some clouds gathering in the distance. He had stood up and squinted and walked to the edge of the porch. Though I remained behind him, I could see his shoulders and arms slowly begin to tremble. Scalding hot coffee dripped down his hands and onto the dilapidated porch. Somewhere behind the shack a dog whelped uncontrollably.

When he finally realized I had drawn up alongside him and was staring into the distance with him, he added: "Beg your pardon, sir, but that no storm. No storm like you thinkin'. Sky may be shakin' but that no storm."

Only when he turned around from the porch's edge did I receive the full effect of the cloud's impression upon him. Only then did I realize that I had never before seen the face of fear. Not really. Not on his daughter's face an hour earlier as she tore during birth. Not even on the face of my wife as she held a monstrous child in her arms and realized her own death was imminent.

"Sir," he said humbly, yet firmly – all the while looking down and to the side while addressing me – "please sir, it best you be getting home now, sir. We 'preciate your help, sir. God bless, sir. You been a blessin'. I can't never repay. But best leave now 'fore the weather turns. You don't want to get caught on the road in these parts. Mean weather we get in these parts. Not like up East. It's best you get home to your family 'fore it gets bad. Lock up the house. Lay low for it to pass. Stay put until the last dog stops its hollerin'. And stay clear of your door and windows, too. God bless sir."

I informed him I had no family to get back to and that it was probably best if I checked on his daughter again before heading out, but it was no use. Before I could finish a sentence or even realize what was happening, he had relieved me of the mug of coffee he had given me minutes earlier and, bowing his head, walked past me and into the shack. After a minute I collected myself, figuring his strange behavior might be attributed to the color of my skin, for it all struck me as unaccountable. When I knocked at the door to check on the baby there was only silence. From the porch I patiently explained my final obligations as a doctor but received no reply. Then I demanded entrance on terms of liability and the Hippocratic oath, but no one stirred. There was no crying. Only in the distance, the sound of thunder rumbled across the barren fields. I had no alternative but to leave. I stepped down from the porch, walked out to the dirt road where I'd parked my car, and left. As the shack disappeared from sight, two sounds like the crack of cannon fire reached my ears. I continued on, dreading the prospect of driving home through the rainstorm.

It had been just past noon when I'd delivered the baby, and no later than one when I sighted the clouds. When I arrived back at my house at about two, the faint cloud bank that had barely broken the horizon from the porch of the shack had gained in density and depth, seemed as dirty as the bed of the Red River itself. By late afternoon the sky to the north was bruised and yellowish brown but strangely unlike most storm clouds I had seen since arriving in town a few months earlier to set up my practice. These clouds seemed to have their origin not from the skies above but from the ground below. In addition, a chalky, stinging wind had kicked up. The temperature had dropped some ten degrees as the sun was slowly blotted out. Trees hissed at the approaching storm and a hum like locusts filled the air. By six o'clock the sky was pitch black. In the distance, dogs whined fearfully.

I felt sure a tornado was upon us and heeded the advice of the new grandfather, who seemed to know something of these matters, or at least spoke with the conviction of one who did. Though I was tempted to snatch a glimpse of the twister of the plains which I had heard so much about while growing up, I thought it imprudent to do so. This old man had knowledge I didn't possess, and

though as a man of science I preferred relying on my own pow-
ers of reason and was wary of indulging in superstition, I thought
at this early date in my country practice it would be wise to heed
the advice of a local. Though part of my mission among these
benighted poor was to subdue ignorance through the wonders
of science, I did not think this required me to act in a foolhardy
manner. And so I hid under the bed for the better part of an hour.
The winds picked up their intensity. It seemed as if, somewhere in
the distance, desperate voices—almost human in tone—cried out.
At some point during the early hours of evening I must have fallen
asleep, unaware of how exhausted I had become from the events
of the preceding two days. Only adrenaline and coffee had kept me
awake during the eighteen-hour vigil I kept while my patient was in
labor.

When I awoke an eerie calm had descended on the countryside. I rose from beneath the bed. It was early morning of the
next day. The sky was still yellowish brown. I surveyed the outside
of my house for damage but saw none, though a coat of chalky
dust covered the entire countryside, including my mailbox, car, and
even my porch. Most strange of all, I thought, was that it seemed
not to have rained.

When I went to my office later that morning, my questions in
town met with reluctance. No one wanted to discuss the storm. It
was as if the townsfolk did not want to acknowledge the mysterious phenomenon of the previous night, as if their silence on the
subject were intended to convince me it had not occurred or was
hardly unusual. My honest inquiries seemed to be making folks
more uncomfortable than usual. And though some of this can be
attributed to my having been born, raised, and educated up East,
it was clear to me that much of the reticence was related to the
storm. My questions seemed to be making people uneasy, and
even, in one case, hostile, so I chose a different course of action.
It would not be good for business, I figured, to make townsfolk
angry at the new doctor, even if he was the only one in a sixty mile
radius. Though few families had cars, I had been made aware by

several suspicious natives that the local trains ran into Fort Worth and that quality medical attention could be found there.

That afternoon I drove back out into the country to check on the newborn and young mother but found the house deserted. As no neighbor lived within a mile, I could not inquire about the family's whereabouts. No one answered my knocking at the front door. More peculiar than the silence within the shack was the complete absence of noise that surrounded it, for the previous day my concentration during delivery had been repeatedly disturbed by a well-meaning dog that the grandfather had eventually had to tie up out back to keep from interfering with his daughter's labor. I went around the back of the shack to check on the beast and saw it reclining peacefully on a grassy patch beside a large oak tree. I whistled playfully as I approached the animal, but the dog did not rise and wag at my approach. I knelt beside the beast, patting its back and rubbing behind its ear soothingly to wake it up, but the dog felt cold and rigid. I rolled the animal toward me and stared into its face. Never before have I been more certain of a diagnosis; no cause of death had ever been more definite to me. A mask of fear was frozen on the face of the stiffened corpse: this dog had died of fright.

I recoiled, stood up slowly, then ran back to the house. Pounding on the front door to no avail, I decided it was my duty to seek entrance and check on the health of my patient. To my surprise, the door was actually unlocked and the house deserted, as if abandoned in great haste. Though the kitchen was in perfect order, the bedroom was in disarray. Two dresser drawers lay on the bed, their contents scattered. In the corner of the room leaned a shotgun which I had not seen the day before. Confused, I ran back to the front door, staring hard up the dirt road in either direction, for the family owned no car and I figured that as flat as the land was, I might be able to make them out in the distance. Nothing I saw surprised me, though something I felt did.

Standing in the doorway in the afternoon heat, the unmistakable sensation of a cool drop splashed against the back of my neck.

It was not raining and the porch, though in ill repair, was entirely covered. I wiped at the sensation then turned and looked upwards to discover the source of my unease. There above the front door, upon the lintel, was smeared a band of reddish clay, a stripe I was sure had not been there the day before, for it glistened and appeared freshly painted. I stood on my toes and wiped two fingers across the dark smear and drew them to my nose and then to the tip of my tongue. Though fifteen years have come and gone, I cannot forget the sensation, the strangeness of the realization— one for which no medical school could prepare a student—of finding myself standing in the doorway of a squalid shack, in the middle of prairie waste land, beneath a stripe of blood.

As strange as the events of the preceding forty-eight hours had been, the life of a country doctor is so hectic and so filled with the unaccountable that I soon forgot about the events surrounding the storm, the delivery, the dark stripe of blood. They were replaced by the quotidian affairs of the rural family doctor: the midnight house calls, the countless deliveries, the broken bones from the saloon brawls, the gored sides of cowboys, and the infant deaths. Soon, my medical duties were added to as well, for the townsfolk quietly had grown to respect my skills and sought out my services in a civic capacity. As a member of the town council, I had to plan budgets and vote on matters involving education and taxes. But though I was beginning to feel myself an indispensable member of the community, I still felt, at times, like an outsider.

Not that people were unkind or distant. On the contrary, they were pleasant and grateful for my work, but seldom did a day pass when I did not feel like they were privy to knowledge into which I, by virtue of my Boston birth, could not be initiated. This grated on me somewhat, for after having to leave the northeast, I hungered for community. I wondered if they had learned about my troubled past and were only indulging me until a doctor with a more stable history arrived. But at the same time I knew that if I could not escape my past in this barren waste land, then it could not be escaped. I would be doomed. All would be lost.

Finally, as months became seasons, and seasons years, it began to strike me that the citizens were genuinely warming to me. But with this new sentiment came an unsettling suspicion: it seemed less like they were keeping something from me and more like they were keeping me from something. Something terrible, perhaps. I did not suspect the source of this mysterious distance until some three years into my residence when the yellow, bruised sky returned, this time appearing southwest of town.

It so happened at this time that a certain elderly lady of substantial means had come into my care. Long known as the town eccentric, the woman was bereft of loved ones, her only son—I pieced together from an improbable source—having preceded her in death. Absent relatives in town, and without any close friends given the peculiar nature of her manners, her situation had become desperate, even—almost—pathetic. A relative in Galveston telegraphed the mayor asking if someone, for a considerable monthly fee, would agree to provide a living arrangement and basic care for this old, senile woman. Sympathizing with her condition as an outsider, I responded to the announcement the mayor had made at a town meeting, not knowing at the time that I had been the only one to do so.

Though she was eccentric, I had to allow she possessed a certain charm. She dispensed ginger snaps and profane oaths with equal aplomb and was quick to correct me when I addressed her as "Miss," insisting—to my surprise since I had not heard townsfolk refer to her as a widow—I call her "Mrs." I wrote this peculiarity off to the same delusions that inspired her to maintain, in the face of all reasonable opposition, that she was a first cousin of Queen Victoria. She was odd. Odd in an endearing kind of way. But for the most part she wasn't bad company. I might add that the monthly stipend allotted for her care was not disagreeable, either. As I early on suspected she would not outlast winter in her advanced state of dementia, I agreed to terms with the relative and took her into my care. In truth I felt sorry for her, and I made her comfort my calling. I became fiercely determined to ease her suf-

fering, no matter what the cost. Hardly a month into the arrangement her condition worsened, and I took her into my house while
her relative made plans to sell her house and land.

So it was that one fine spring evening, after I had fed her and
was administering her nightly dose of morphine, the wind chimes
on my porch began tinkling in an uncharacteristically violent manner, and as if wakened by the ethereal sounds, she stirred from her
groggy condition and motioned me close to her side.

"Yes, Mrs. Shallcross, what is it you want?"

"I want to die," she mumbled.

Believing her remark related to the sudden change in weather
I assured her that tomorrow would no doubt be a beautiful spring
day. "According to the Almanac," I offered soothingly, "this next
week's supposed to be beautiful. We could use some rain, though.
The land's awfully dry."

"This land's haunted."

I was silent. I did not want to indulge her hallucinations
further but did not want to appear insensitive to what might be the
last bit of conversation she could muster in this world.

"It's beautiful countryside," I remarked, trying to steer her
away from unpleasant thoughts.

"No, it's not. It's terrible. And it's damned."

"Mrs. Shallcross, it's just windy outside. You get some good
rest and tomorrow I'll pick you more flowers for your vase."

"There won't be flowers tomorrow," she said.

"Of course there will be. There are always flowers in the
spring."

"Not tomorrow," she replied, gesturing toward the window of
her bedroom.

I followed the crook of her arm to the window and sky beyond and caught sight of a hue I had seen only once before in my
life. I left her bedside and went to the window. The incident of
three years earlier sprang back upon me. Staring out the window
into the bruised and swirling sky, I recalled the stormy night, the
abandoned shack, the strange behavior of the old man that I had

never seen again. I turned back to Mrs. Shallcross and went to her side.

"Mrs. Shallcross, do you know something about this weather? Tell me, please Mrs. Shallcross," I said, shaking her arm, but the morphine had taken effect and she had descended into her mad dreams. I returned to the window and watched the strange portent. In the distance, trees hissed softly and farm animals hooted. But the cloud did not come toward town, instead moved off slowly to the northwest, toward Worlf Ridge.

The next morning, enough chalky dust covered the country-side and hung in the air to droop flowers and cake in one's mouth. I went about my normal duties. A fire in the next town, likely caused by the storm, required I attend to the injured of several families, three of whom eventually died. These events were suf-ficiently distracting to keep me from thoughts about Mrs. Shall-cross's unusual remarks.

Toward the end of May, however, as her conditioned wors-ened, and I felt certain she was on the verge of death—a blessing I thought, given the frequency of her hallucinogenic fits–she repeat-ed the magic words I had not heard, or even thought of, in years.

She pulled me close to her during a thunderstorm, looked at me with crazy eyes, and grumbled insanely for over an hour. Just when I had grown tired of her hoarse rantings and was determined to give her still more morphine to ease her suffering, she fixed me with her eyes and prophesied, "You wait. Holy Ghost Man. He coming."

I was frightened by this dark revelation. But my fear was lost upon her for she quickly shifted her topic of conversation and soon descended into her drug induced slumber. It was that night when I realized, however, that though she suffered terribly, I could not let her die. I had to keep her alive, no matter what the cost. And not just for the source of income she provided, but because she had become to me a sort of high priestess, an oracle, my only hope for community. My pride in my own self-reliance had led me astray. I had begun to suspect that reason itself had failed me, alienated me in my search for happiness. My faith in it had cost me my wife, led me to medical school with false promises, sentenced me to exile. Here in this virtual wilderness, I had found science wanting. Countless nights I had drifted off to sleep suspecting there had to be something more. And then I met Mrs. Shallcross. She alone, in her weakened and dependent state, had provided me community. She alone, with her cryptic mutterings, seemed privy to knowledge all others lacked. And so as the months wore on, I became more and more convinced that she alone could make me whole, anoint me with the meaning I so desperately sought.

I did not fully realize it then, but my hunger for mystery had completely subdued my thirst for healing, for service, for decency. And so the next evening after I had fed Mrs. Shallcross, I changed my routine. I did not give her morphine. Though she begged and pleaded with me, I did not give her morphine. Though she cursed and swore at me, I did not give her morphine. I told her I would never again give her any morphine, but that I would do all in my power to sustain her and prolong her agony. At first she was con-fused, then overcome with insane anger as she realized that what I was doing, in effect, was sentencing her to the hell that was her present condition, the hell that was her life.

I let her consider this fate for twenty-four hours before I revealed to her that there was a certain action she could take that would restore her morphine, but that the terms of this agreement were not negotiable. She damned me to hell and said she'd do any-thing, but I left her bedroom before giving her either her dinner or the chance to strike a deal. I let my words soak in for another day before returning the next evening. All that night she moaned and screamed and if I had had neighbors in close proximity they surely would have called the sheriff and had me arrested. When morn-ing came, I was refreshed and pleased. That day at work, though, I made a terrible decision: driven by a wicked impulse, I decided I would neither feed Mrs. Shallcross, give her morphine, nor visit her room. For an entire week. I left a single pitcher of water and a small glass by her bedside. That was it. To this day, I can still hear her cries.

My plan had been simple, really: a week of unmitigated, unspeakable pain would break the seal, cause her to spill the secret I was sure she possessed. But during those unbearable seven days, something strange happened. One night in the middle of the week, I awoke to silence. Previously, I had had no trouble sleeping through her howling, but the silence…the silence unnerved me. Try though I might, it was now I who could not go to sleep. Still, I did not want her to dictate to me the terms of my plans.

Yet as I lay in bed, unnerved, something odd happened, though exactly what I can't say for sure. It became clear to me that at some point in the early hours of the new day, perhaps just prior to my waking, her screams had ceased. My first thoughts were that she had died, that my plan had backfired. I got up from my bed and went to the door of her bedroom and listened. She had not died, I learned with relief, for I heard faint mumblings, as if the crazy old woman were conversing with herself. I did not wish to disturb her and risk resurrecting the screams and returned to bed, but still I could not go back to sleep. That entire day at work the thought of the silence distracted me. By midmorning, in between appointments with patients, I determined I would return to her room that nightfall. So I did.

Entering her room silently at about 9:00 PM, I stole up to her bedside and knelt beside her. Though her eyes were shut, she smiled darkly at my presence; I had not fooled her. Unshaken, I informed her that if she told me everything she knew about the storm, and about this strange Holy Ghost Man to whom she'd made vague reference, I might consider restoring her morphine.

"Now tell me truthfully, Mrs. Shallcross, have you decided to speak to me of this Holy Ghost Man, or do you persist in being a stubborn mule?" My remarks, however, did not produce the desired effect. I cannot forget her reply.

"You should have asked him these questions yourself last night, good doctor, when you listened at my door."

I was confused. And frightened. Did she mean this man had entered my house without my knowledge or consent? Did she mean that it was he who had been speaking the previous night, and not herself or some imaginary fiend? Or was she merely hallucinating again? I was determined not to be outfoxed. Composure was essential to the success of my plan, and so I chose my words with great care.

"Will you ask your friend back to your room tonight for another visit, Mrs. Shallcross? Tell him I will bring him some tea, if he like."

"The doomed don't take tea."

I was perplexed, and this time my face betrayed my fear. She had outmaneuvered me.

"Doomed, good doctor, doomed to wander. He can't find his way home. Seeing the candle in my window, he stopped to ask me. But I can't undo his fate, for he doomed himself. Long, long ago. Doomed himself to bring storms. Careful 'lest you do the same. As it is, you'll meet him soon enough."

I left the room hastily, not thinking to snuff the candle I had set on her sill the night before. I was afraid and confused. I locked all the doors and windows in the house. I did not sleep that night but paced nervously across the living room, a butcher knife in hand. Had she been hallucinating? Had I been hallucinating? Was this a prank? A burglar? A ghost? I was a man of science, in the vigor of early middle age, and yet I had been cowed by an octogenarian, let a shriveled hag of a woman frighten me. I was ashamed and knew I could not petition others for help 'lest my treatment of Mrs. Shallcross be revealed. I paced the floor in anguish, cursing myself beneath my breath, then aloud. "Why don't I just kill her," I thought to myself, breaking the very oath I had again sworn to uphold after my failures in Boston.

At three o'clock in the morning, I sat down in my reading chair, exhausted. Apparently this Holy Ghost Man would not be returning that night. As I began to drift off against my will, I was disturbed by a cacophony issuing forth from Mrs. Shallcross's room. But this particular noise did not consist of curses and screams. No, this noise was unmistakable: this noise was laughter. I did not move from my chair all night long.

The next day at work I was a wreck. I ended up closing the office early and walking the streets in town. Passersby looked at me strangely. I did not want to risk their suspicious inquiries, and I realized that as much as I dreaded it, I had to force myself to confront Mrs. Shallcross once more. Three times I stopped on the way home before summoning the courage to return.

Even then I ended up standing on the porch an hour before entering. Once I entered, though, I was resolved and moved with haste to execute my plan. After checking that the doors and windows were still locked, I made coffee, lit several candles, and barricaded the doors. I resumed my vigil, but sometime around midnight I foolishly sat down again in my reading chair, tired from the constant pacing of the previous five hours. I must have dozed off for some time. A slight pinprick on the arm awakened me. I rubbed near it for a moment, still half asleep. A good half-minute passed before I realized what sensation it was that had stirred me.

When I opened my eyes, it seemed I saw Mrs. Shallcross seated across from me, smiling insanely. Hovering over me like a dark angel. Apparently, she had somehow summoned the strength to rise from her bed, leave her room, and rummage through my medical bag until she found the stash of morphine I kept hidden. The syringe still hung from the crook of my arm. In hindsight, I suspect she had given herself a shot too, for the sheer madness of what she then confided to me could only have come from the mind of a mad and senile addict.

"You only think you want to meet Holy Ghost Man," she said smiling at me, rocking back and forth like a prophet in the midst of a vision. "But what do you know, good doctor? What can you really know?"

I had no answer. She smiled and nodded. She knew my ignorance. In truth I can't attest if I dreamt what followed—if in some desperate fit I myself had taken morphine—or if in fact she'd somehow risen from her bed, drugged me, then proceeded to augur forth her grim revelation. All I know is that the story remains engraved upon my brain, burnt there by the intensity of her mad gaze. Having fixed me in her sights, she let words flow freely from her foaming, toothless mouth.

"He came from Mississippi after the war, a preacher man with his son. He'd tried savin' souls all during the war. Wandered the south apreachin'. Followed Yankees 'round Mississippi and 'Bama. Got word of Sherman's march and beat him into towns by a hour, preachin' 'bout the doom that would be upon 'em, tryin' his best to save 'em all. But a man can't be saved don't wants savin'. The march nearly killed him. Broke his heart. Lookin' over his shoulder he saw Atlanta burn, saw the fields burn, heard the women cry, the rebel yell. Watched his wife killed. Shot in the head by a renegade Yankee, on Christmas day outside Savannah. And his little boy at his side the whole time, just a kid, cryin' for his mama. And that's the day the boy knew he'd be a preacher. Daddy knew it, too, knew the boy'd been touched."

"And when the war ended, he took his son and headed back to Ruggsville, where his daddy's people lived. For his daddy was a preacher, too. The son tried to get the old man to move west, but he said he'd stay put. Try to rebuild his town and church and make peace with the past. Try to obey the new law. But the son became difficult. Said he'd got the Ghost. That the Spirit had filled him, and he needed no law. Said you can't make amends with the likes of Sherman. Right then and there, he swore a violent oath against his father. Much as that war hurt him he did not learn its lesson, and he pays for it now. For though no man I ever met was more filled with the Holy Ghost, that man was proud. And pride brought him ruin. You see, he was a good man. Some would say he was a great man. But he could be a bad man. And one day he finally up and took his boy and headed west, the two of 'em—to Louisiana… then Texas."

I distinctly remember, about this time in her rambling, that I had become convinced that either she or I was insane. Which one, I could not say, but I felt that by concentrating perfectly on her story I might demonstrate my sanity, and so though high on morphine, I fixed her in my gaze and listened intently.

"It was no wonder when the young boy took to preachin'. Ever so often his daddy'd let him preach in the small church he built near Gainesville. The congregation grew. And that's when I met him. No man could preach with more passion. Folks came from ten counties to hear his sermon. That man was beautiful. A voice that could bring the winds to heel. Eyes like burning coals. Two months later we were married. It was not easy, for his son had a troubled soul. I did right by trying to raise that boy, but he was difficult, never took to my care. But I loved him. I knew his lot was hard. As he got older he started preachin' more, demandin' that his daddy give him the pulpit. He was skilled in God's secrets and could speak in tongues like you never heard. He won many souls for God's service, but he grew restless in the process. Soon townsfolk met him in secret and he would prophecy for them."

"We all knew the day would come, just not when, but that boy'd leave to start himself his own church. And it was so. Before he turned seventeen he took the train out of town. Town to town he'd preach, though a man can't rightly preach from a train. A man needs roots. But this man was on fire and would not relent— not for home, not for a wife, not for family. And all the while his daddy's heart ached, missin' his only son. But then, as the months passed, the sadness turned to anger, and a violence come upon him. Not long after, he lit out for his son, to teach him respect and the rite of repentance. For he saw in his son his own rebellious nature, and this sight he could not bear. He stalked him, caught up to him in the Arbuckles. A mining town. And he told his son, said—'You can't take no train to escape your father. Can't hide no place your father won't find you. Can't run so far your father won't see you. Can't speak so soft your father won't hear you. Get back, man! You're become unclean. Renounce your sin. Return to the church of your birth. Serve the faith of you fathers.' But his son was in a bad way, and he answered in defiance, 'I will not.' And the two took to fightin', the son and the father. The boy struck first, struck in desperation and the foolishness of youth. But the father struck with anger. Anger and the hatred of injured pride. He killed his son in an argument. Killed him with bare hand. In front of a crowd of witnesses. Killed him dead. And then he dropped to his knees and cried. Pulled his hair out 'till sunrise."

"And then he began to roll. Rolled out of camp. Rolled on his side down the road. Holy roller. And he's been rollin' ever since. Forty years that man's rolled. Forty years he's haunted ten counties. And that cloud—that's him, him and the dust of his forty-year penance. Forty more remain. That's his cloud. Holy Ghost Man's."

"Maybe he'll stop for a night and rest, eat locusts or cobweb, maybe a grub he's kicked up. Maybe feed on grass like the cows, banished as he is from his fellows. But then he roll. Roll 'till he grinds himself away. Sputtering and thundering and speaking in tongues. Haunting crossroads and creek beds. Rollin' across the countryside, praising God for his mercy when he comes upon abandoned campfires and burnt mesquite. Diving into ashes, bathing in soot. Rejoicing when the embers still hot enough to sting."

"And the highwaymen themselves tremble and turn. Maybe he'll come on a traveler unawares, ask the way back to Mississippi, to Ruggsville, for he wants to find his daddy and make amends. But his daddy's gone. And Ruggsville was never rebuilt. So he rolls, rolls across the land. The road's his rod. His penance. For he cursed his father and killed his son and now he can't never have a place in this world."

"Sometimes a sinner will boldly approach the cloud. Seek shelter in storm. Thieves and deserters, injuns and rebs. It don't matter who. There's no shortage of sinners out west. For this land's lawless—no Buffalo Bill show. But the cloud's his. His alone. At first folks saw in it what they wanted. Halo. Inferno. Whatever suited them best. Old folks fasted at first sight of the cloud. Kids took to memorizing Isaiah. Widows fashioned hairshirts. The men took to bickering, claimed it was a sign of the times. But all were agreed on one thing—all were agreed the pews were more full come Sunday. Most folks, though, they let him be now, for they learned. All real debts you pay alone. And rollin"s his lot. His from the moment he struck his son. His from the moment he cursed his father. It's a hard ransom. And so he rolls. Rollin' sinner. Rollin' saint. And he won't stop 'till the debt's paid. Can't. For his sin is bad. His debt big."

This was madness, sheer madness. Though I was full of morphine and on the verge of unconsciousness, I knew her story for what it was. I tried to utter an oath of protest but my strength failed me, and the last thing I remember is looking into her eyes as she smiled at me warmly like a mother tucking in a wayward child.

When I finally came to, I was disoriented. It took me a good hour to stir from my chair. I was crying and knew immediately why. Still I had to wonder: Had I been dreaming? Had I succumbed once more to the addiction I thought I had beaten? Had I been visited by a ghost who revealed mad truths to me? I knew I must speak to Mrs. Shallcross, but she was not seated across from me. Though my legs were wobbling, I managed to get myself to my feet, and then to Mrs. Shallcross's room. I collapsed upon entering, then crawled to her bedside.

She lay peacefully upon the bed. Dead. I pulled the covers over her, sat down on the bed next to her, and cried. I prayed to God for the repose of her soul, begging forgiveness for my selfishness. In denying community, I had killed my only companion. In pursuing my own ends, I had killed my benefactor.

I could not have been seated there more than a half hour when the wind chimes on the porch began to stir once again. It took me a good while to figure out what this might mean, but when I did, I made my way slowly to the window. I could not tell how much time had passed since my interview with Mrs. Shall-cross—if it were the darkness of the same day, or evening of the next. All I knew was that the sky was yellowish brown, the trees hissed, and in the distance, on the outskirts of town and headed my way, brooded a grim cloud. A thunderclap shook the house. I felt faint and again collapsed. When I came to, the darkness was upon me. The primal dust storm had found me. The pillar of cloud had called my nameI ran to the front door, for my car seemed the only means of escape. And there on the porch I bore terrible witness. Though the night was confusing and dark, I could discern that the winds were out of order. The moon shone a sickly yellow. The constellations seemed either snuffed or disjointed from their assigned station and wheeling madly through space. Night had been undone, the sky pulled back from the earth, revealing a black beyond. I was overcome by the chaos when my eyes were drawn down to a gaunt shade in the middle of the road, standing motionless amid the smoking cloud.

In truth, I could not tell where the figure ended and the cloud began, for from his person seemed to emanate the entire swirling conflagration. He was still some way off and had stopped rolling. His shape was bleeding, skinned raw and emaciated. So few were the clumps of flesh and earth that clung to his broken frame that it was possible to count his bones. When he saw me, he just stood still and stared at me. And gestured. At the motion of his hand, the winds leapt forth, answering his summons, whistling with the agony of a thousand ruined souls. We had not had eye contact for more than a minute when I thought I heard the cry of a vaguely familiar voice rise above the turmoil, a cry from a voice I'd forgotten but whose lips I'd once watched form a forbidden name. And I knew whose voice it was and why blood had been painted above the door of his shack. I bowed my head and went to join the cloud of penitents, then fell to my knees. But the shade motioned me back. Seemed to command me to rise and go, point the way for my return.

And so, as if spared for another witness, I ran. Ran to my car. And fled. By some miracle, for I could hardly see the road before me, I escaped. In three hours I was in Fort Worth. And a few days later I was back in Boston. There I confessed my acts to the authorities, who were lenient—in part because the statute of limitations had expired and in part because no witness could be secured, no reasonable cause found, to testify against me. In two years I was freed. I never resumed the practice of medicine, and I have chosen to live humbly and in seclusion. I do hope, someday, to start a family. But I know I'm not ready. I do not want to be visited again, and though I do not know if the life I lead protects me, I do know the storm has not found me. Not yet. I have come to think it won't, that such was not my punishment. That the visit, instead, was mine. And that this fear is my penance, my hell. To work out the purpose of this visit in fear and trembling. And the fear is great, I assure you. The penance, I pray, an admirable hell.

And as for Holy Ghost Man, I find myself compelled to respect his commitment to settle accounts. To pay the last copper. Though his witness confounds me, I believe it born of an authentic faith. So I do not doubt but that the cloud still wanders a waste land many miles away. Still lost. Still doomed. But doing what needs to be done: Rolling. Roll, Ghost, Roll.

Five Mississippi

Coach chuckled at the thought: "*Five Mississippi*. What kind of fool way to count time is that? Who could say?" He shook his head, barely containing a grin, and looked up at the scoreboard. The season had come down to this. Ray was right about that much. Any hope Fort Griffin had of making the playoffs for the first time since the Carter administration would be decided in less time than it takes to count Five Mississippi.

Yes, Ray Henry Burleson had been right. In Five Mississippi, it would all come to pass. "But how much time was that?" Coach J.R. Widtmark wondered as he watched his seventeen-year-old quarterback jog back to the huddle after the final timeout of the season had ended. Maybe four or five seconds, he mused to himself? Six would seem a bit much. It was tough to say because it was different than seconds. The unit of measurement was different—the time itself was different. This was so on a playground or a football field, which were really the same thing. Coach tried to recall where he himself had learned to count time that way—to count Five Mississippi—but he couldn't pin it down. Either in the backyard with his two older brothers while growing up or at school during recess. Probably from his brothers, he figured. But where had they learned it? From mom and dad? Maybe. If not, then from others on the street, the older kids? It was impossible to say other than that it seemed to have grown naturally out of those afternoons long ago, from the hardscrabble terrain of West Texas, from the play-grounds, backyards, and empty lots—a way of reckoning time that was maybe awkward sounding but functional and indigenous as the mesquite. What Five Mississippi *was* was *not* five seconds. There was time and then there was *time*. That much Coach knew. And what was remarkable was that it had taken a seventeen-year-old quarterback to remind him of this fact at such a crucial moment.

As Coach watched Ray step into the huddle to call the play, he allowed that Five Mississippi may not be right for folks everywhere. If you'd grown up in a different time and place and not spent your springs playing baseball or your summers skipping rocks into Hubbard Creek Lake, but had maybe played video games or lived in a big apartment building somewhere, then "Six Potomac" would probably do. Or "Four Chatahoochie." Or maybe even the more generic "Five One-thousand." But if you were from Shackelford County and grew up playing football, it was "Five Mississippi." Seconds just wouldn't cut it. Because the passage of time on a play-ground is not the passage of ordinary time.

Initially, it had surprised Coach to hear Ray mention this, given the particulars of their situation. Ray had been standing beside him during the timeout, dutifully waiting while Coach was talking things over with Coach Rusty up in the press box. The situation was grim. Three points down. No timeouts left. There was maybe enough time for two plays, but if they chose that route then one would have to be a quick out pattern. There was not enough time for a first down. The illegal procedure penalty had set them back far enough so that by the time Tony could get twenty yards down field and make a catch, the clock would likely have run out. That meant you couldn't work the middle of the field, only the sideline.

If they could pick up seven or eight yards on an out pattern, then they might be within field goal range. It would still be a forty-three yarder, and that was no done deal. The alternative was to get the seven or eight yards and then go deep after that, but that would mean Breckenridge would know what the last play would be. No element of surprise would be left. In his gut, Coach felt the field goal was out of the question because Duane had been inconsistent with long snaps and Billy had had a terrible week of practice kicking the ball. The kid just wasn't poised. Fortunately, Breckenridge didn't know this. But they did know Coach JT Widtmark and his tendencies.

Coach figured that when he sent the offense back out there, Breckenridge was likely to think they'd be playing for the tie and so likely preparing to throw an out. That was the safest thing to do. If you got the field goal and sent the game into overtime, your chances were pretty good because you were at home, and it's tough to win in overtime on the road. After fifteen years of conference duels, the Breckenridge staff knew Coach Dub, and they knew he was not a gambling man. The chances were good he'd play it safe; the whole stadium expected that, including his wife, who'd married him because of his dependability. The only other option was going for broke now. There'd be some element of surprise in that. Going for it all at once when they thought you were going to squeeze two plays out of the clock.

What Coach knew more than anything, though, was that he wanted his best player to decide their fate, and his best player wasn't his kicker. He knew that at the end of the day, you want the game in the hands of the kid who's earned that right. Billy and Duane were out of the question. They'd been inconsistent showing up for summer workouts, and he suspected they occasionally slacked off during conditioning drills. They weren't bad kids; they just weren't the right kid. Hadn't earned the full respect of their peers. Hadn't earned the right to make this last play. Only one kid had earned that right. Only one kid could take that heat, and that was Ray. Coach finally nodded his head, as if in agreement with a voice from the beyond, then he took his headset off, and looked at his quarterback.

"We're all in, Ray. Right here, right now."

Ray smiled.

"Shotgun or five step," Coach said, thinking aloud, though he knew the answer already. "Gotta be a five step. I don't want to put too much heat on old Duane, so let's go with a five step."

"Sounds good, Coach."

"Yeah, let's just go with a five step. Let's keep it simple, too...'Right, 528.' Don't forget to look the safety off. Go on a long count, too. Five yards never hurt no one. And tell Tony to sell them on the out. He's faster than the corner. He'll be expecting Tony to run an out anyhow. But you gotta freeze the safety first. Got to"
A moment of silence passed between them.

"This is it. Make sure the boys up front realize that. No excuses. There won't be any time after this. It's all we got right here," he said, suddenly wiping his brow and then looking around him and checking his pockets as if he'd misplaced his car keys or something. "They got to give you enough time to air it out. We're all in—right here, right now. What do we got left again?" He turned to check on the scoreboard, but Ray firmly placed his hand on Coach's shoulder, completely stopping his motion. Coach was a little stunned by the sudden act, and even more so when he saw that Ray was smiling at him. And that was when Ray Henry Burleson uttered the words Coach would never forget, the words that would be told around the Fort Griffin Coffee Shop and locker room for years to come. The words that would never fail to bring a smile to Coach's face. Words that were much more than mere words.

"Five Mississippi, Coach."

At the time, Coach looked at him confused. "Huh?"

"Five Mississippi—that's all we need. All anyone can ask for." And then Ray was off, jogging back out onto the field. He was halfway out to the huddle for the last play of the game before his words registered with Coach. And that's when Coach started chuckling.

"Five Mississippi," Coach repeated to himself again, as he

watched Ray drawing the huddle in tight, giving special directions to Tony, just like Coach had told him to do. Coach caught himself shaking his head and trying his best to rein in a laugh. He didn't want the other coaches or players or even the fans to see him chuckling while the first chance for a playoff birth in a generation hung in the balance.

The truth was that Ray's words deeply pleased him, convinced him he hadn't coached in vain. He knew that now. It didn't matter how the game ended. Ray understood. He'd learned what really counted. Knew that whatever happened during this last play of the game, all would be well. What mattered most had already been decided. Had already been won. What mattered the most was implied by those two simple words: "Five Mississippi."

Waiting for the huddle to break, Coach caught himself getting philosophical, something he normally averted. He figured you could tell a lot about a person from the way they told time. His dad, for instance, still used military time. The Sarge woke at 0500 and didn't leave the office until 1900. You could tell a lot about the way he viewed the world from that little bit of information. A lot about his attention to detail. His belief in the need for order and discipline and duty. And you could also probably figure out how he'd vote on certain issues. There were other ways to tell time, too.

Coach knew some folks didn't use B.C. or A.D., and though he thought it was odd, he knew it to be true. And it had been Becky who'd told him about the railroads inventing time zones to improve business efficiency. She'd learned that when studying for her Teacher's Certificate, which she'd started pursuing after they'd learned they couldn't have children. She'd dived into her studies then, and they both started to read more than ever before to get their minds on other things. Coach himself remembered hearing somewhere— on the History Channel, he thought—about the Mayans and how they used a whole different calendar of months and years. That had stunned him, but the more he thought about it, the more he figured to each his own. He reckoned if it worked for them, then fine.

Because he knew one thing for sure—Five Mississippi had

worked for him when growing up and playing football on the fields and backyards of Childress and Cross Plains and Moran. It provided enough time for the receiver to get down field and test the limits of any young quarterback's arm. Enough time for the action to develop and showcase each kid's ability. Plus, you couldn't hurry the count or you wouldn't be saying it right, and that wouldn't do. The play would go over. Those were the rules on every playground across the state. Who was to say how they came about? And at the end of the day, who cared? The rules may be arbitrary, but the intricacies and order and fun they helped create wasn't. In the final analysis, the rules worked. And that's all that mattered.

The thing was, Coach thought, as he watched Tony nod at Ray's direction as the huddle prepared to break, you had to actually say "Five Mississippi," annunciate every single syllable, and that made it different than seconds. "Seconds" wouldn't do. Too quick. It had to be "Mississippis"—"one Mississippi, two Mississippi, three Mississippi, four Mississippi, FIVE MISSISSIPPI!" The last one was the loudest, because who could contain the excitement of finally being able to join in the activity around you and rush the quarterback? It was tough not to rush in early, but the rules required strict observance. The beauty of this rule was that everyone got to oversee its enforcement because each kid on the playground could hear the time being marked as it was called out. There was something democratic about it. And something mysterious.

Yeah, Coach knew his young quarterback was right, and he watched with pride as Ray finally broke the team from the huddle and slowly walked them to the line of scrimmage, eyeing the defense's personnel and alignment. Ray had been right about a lot of things; in Five Mississippi, their lives would be changed. But in truth, it had been the nine years preceding this last game of the regular season that had really changed their lives. It was the thought of those nine years that brought it all into focus.

And in an instant, Coach remembered the first time he had met Ray. He'd been subbing a PE class at the elementary school. He hated getting that call, but he'd negotiated with the School

Board for his mornings to be free during the season because he put in so much work on the weekends. The only catch was he'd be the lone sub available in town for elementary school PE. And so he found himself on a Friday morning nine years ago, before the game against Coleman, trying his best to organize a bunch of ten-year-olds into a game of kickball. Not a week after Becky's first miscarriage. He'd tried hard not to dwell too much on this bad news, and it was just as well that he got the phone call to substitute teach. That was when he first met Ray.

He could tell right away that this was the kid who would lead them to the promised land. Ray was marked from the start. In truth, his whole grade was full of good athletes. Though the Mc-Coy kid was bigger and had a stronger arm, he wasn't QB material. But Ray, Ray had it, and Coach knew he'd found his future leader. Problem was, Ray was in 3rd grade at the time and in the middle of a fight, hitting the McCoy kid's fist with his face, bleeding everywhere but still standing tall. Eventually, he backed the kid up until he was exhausted and then pinned him against the gym wall. Young McCoy collapsed, buckled under Ray's determination. But Ray didn't punch him—it wasn't in his nature to be violent. It was in his nature to endure. To be stoic. A ten-year-old Roman senator. But in Keds and a cap. It was in Ray's nature to outlast any sort of adversity and be the one left standing, composed and in control. Ray had endured and won. The consequence was now his to issue— and he chose grace. So Ray stood over the whimpering McCoy, fists clenched, and then he turned and walked away. He'd made his point. The fight hadn't been pretty, but surviving isn't about looking pretty. Neither is winning. It's about being the one who answers the bell, who's left standing with dignity and perspective at the final whistle. It's about being the one your teammates know will be there, come hell or high water.

And Ray was that guy. He exerted the silent gravitational pull on his peers that all good West Texas quarterbacks have. A resolve and poise and toughness that made them good ranchers and husbands and fathers but miserable car salesmen. Which was fine with Coach, because he wasn't in the sales business. He was in the football business.

And he knew that if the Fort Griffin Broncos had any hope of making the playoffs, it would be on the shoulders of Ray. But that would be years down the road. Somehow, Coach would have to survive until then. He sensed that a half dozen .500 seasons separated him from that future date, but he too was willing to endure. The School Board wanted to win, but they also knew how to tolerate a losing season or two. Just so long as the kids were learning teamwork and manners and sportsmanship and having fun and not getting suspensions or thrown in jail. Coach knew if this little kid could endure the fight he'd just gone through, then he himself could endure angry boosters and administrators. And as he made his way across the crowded gym floor to separate the two, he thought he might have a kindred spirit in the little ten-year-old with the bloodied nose.

He put the two boys in quiet time, but toward the end of gym class he called Ray over.

"Say, son, why'd you get in a fight with that boy? Don't you know he's bigger than you?"

Ray was silent for a few seconds.

"I'm sorry, sir."

"Well, listen, that's all right. I just want to make sure you're not hurt and all. Are you ok?"

Ray nodded his head. "Yes, sir."

"You're Ray Burleson, aren't you?"

Ray nodded.

"I know your folks from church, and I know they don't want you fighting and neither do I. I just don't understand it, Ray."
The boy looked down.

"Well son, did that boy say something mean to you? You can tell me."

"No, sir."

Coach was confused. He could tell Ray wasn't the kind to start something.

"Well, what happened son? What did he do?"

Apparently struggling mightily with whether or not he should 'fess up, Ray finally answered.

"He said Annie couldn't play kickball with us, sir."

Coach was confused. He wasn't sure he'd heard him right.

"Now, what did he do?" he asked, leaning in closer to make sure he got it right.

"He said Annie couldn't play kickball with us."

"He said Annie couldn't play kickball with you?" Coach repeated, still not sure he'd heard correctly.

Ray nodded his head.

"Is that all, son? I mean, that's not nice of him, but did he say or do anything else?"

"No, sir."

Coach mulled this over.

Though he was a bit quiet by nature, Ray sensed he needed to explain in more detail.

"And she always plays kickball with us, sir. She's always center field 'cause she's fast and can throw."

This didn't make any more sense to Coach, but he thought he could respect the little fella's loyalty. He bit his lower lip, a tad confused but half aware that he was in the presence of a loyalty unusual for a ten-year-old—or an adult, for that matter. Looking down at his watch, he realized it was time for class to be out and so he blew his whistle and dismissed the kids. Ray's nose had stopped bleeding, but Coach thought he might call his dad to let him know what happened. He wasn't sure if he'd call the McCoys, but he thought he might since Bobby had cried the rest of PE class even though he'd started the whole thing. Coach had another class to sub, but after that he made a bee-line for the principal's office to fill out his paperwork and make his calls. He knew he'd be coming back down after football season, maybe sooner, to watch this little kid who was defending his friend.

As fate would have it, he was back down that next Monday, after an ugly Friday night loss to Coleman. And that's when he'd decided to start grooming Ray. There was no time to lose. Flag football was the order of the day, and he made Ray one of the quarterbacks. Each team had four downs to make twenty yards, and you could only rush one player, and that only after counting Five Mississippi.

"What happens then?" Ray asked, while his classmates milled about, giggling and tugging on each other's flag belts. He was full of questions, and most of them good ones.

"Well, for you, if you haven't thrown a touchdown by then, you'd better tuck the ball with two hands and run for the hills. 'Cause they'll be coming after you."

"But is that enough time?" he asked Coach earnestly.

The other kids had finally stopped horsing around and gathered around to hear Coach's answer. He read their sudden attention as a sign of some skepticism about how important Five Mississippi was to the success of their endeavor. He felt compelled to make a strong case.

"Yes, sir. It's enough time for a lot to happen," Coach said, putting his hand on Ray's shoulder and smiling at him and then out at his audience. "Yes indeed, it's enough time for anything to happen, and don't you forget that."

"But why not seconds?" one of the kids asked.

"Oh, no. Seconds wouldn't do. That's for clocks. Let me ask you something, do you see any clocks out here?" Coach swept his arm around the playground. The kids followed the motion of his arm, a little confused by the question, eventually shaking their heads no. "Let me tell you why. Clocks are for your classroom. For the hallway. For inside. They're for places like banks and things. Now don't get me wrong—that's fine and all. All I'm saying is that they're not for out here. No, seconds just wouldn't do out here. That's why there's Five Mississippi. It's the perfect amount of time to let a play develop. It's all anyone could ask for. It's like the nine months a baby's in his mama's belly. Who knows why it's right, but it just is."

The crowd of kids seemed satisfied with his explanation, as if he'd reaffirmed what most already suspected while managing to convert the rest. Ray nodded his head and smiled, and Coach wasn't sure but that he thought Ray was about to chuckle. Ray spent the better part of the period waiting for the rusher to count off his Five Mississippis before taking off for big yardage. Coach figured the future franchise was a work in progress and that he had plenty of time to get him to think to throw first and run second. He just wanted him competing for now. He had an inkling the little fella might like to be a ball boy for the varsity when he got to middle school.

The truth was that if he'd have known more at the time, though, he might have thought of putting Annie at quarterback because she did have the best arm in the grade. Annie was the best friend Ray ever had, and it might have been a good thing for the McCoy kid that Ray had got to him first because her temper was a thing to be feared.

She might have ended up quarterback, Coach mused—as he watched Breckenridge settle into the alignment he knew they'd call after fifteen years of playing against them—if it hadn't been for that day during a sixth-grade Y.M.C.A. baseball game. Coach had taken over for the team when a parent asked him to step in one day after a Rotary meeting. The previous coach had lost his thumb and index finger in an oil rig accident, leaving the kids in a bad way. Coach agreed to help out—he felt terrible about the situation. More than anything, though, he wanted Ray and his group of friends competing at some sport that spring. He'd gotten to know Ray's family, too; they were at practically every sporting event that occurred in town, even though his mom worked full-time in the pharmacy and his dad was a ranch foreman. Coach was coming off of a 6-4 season, and he knew he'd have the support of the parents, so he accepted the offer to fill in for the rest of the baseball season. It had proven every bit as challenging as his high school duties. But he could not have anticipated what awaited him on this particular day.

It was the fifth inning and Annie was playing centerfield, and Ray was in left. They were up by a run, thanks largely to a double

Annie had hit in the third. It had been classic Annie. The other team had been making fun of her while she was on deck, screaming about how a girl shouldn't be playing on a boys' team. Coach had expected this might happen and told Annie not to let it bother her. She didn't.

When she finally got up, she fouled one off toward the opponents' dugout and nearly hit their coach. She stepped out of the box and stared over at the other team, adjusting her batting glove. Then, as if to make her point, she fouled the next ball off in the exact same place. This scattered two of the smart alecks who had gotten off of the bench to holler at her after the first foul ball. It was dead silent after that—dead silent until she crushed the third pitch into deep left center. Ray just shook his head and smiled.

But he wasn't smiling in the fifth when, with two outs, she hollered over at him "Cover for me!" and took off her glove and started running off toward the parking lot. "What?" Ray had shouted back, confused. But she was off. No one knew what the hell she was doing. No one except Ray, who was finally able to put it together after a dozen or so seconds of confusion. He'd seen the butterfly at the end of the fourth inning when they were jogging back to the dugout after retiring the other side. A beautiful Monarch. Huge. He'd had half a mind to chase after it himself. And he knew then that if Annie saw it there might be trouble. His worst fears were soon realized; trouble fluttered into view with two outs left in the bottom of the fifth.

No one in the stands knew what to think; they just saw her running and jumping and apparently swatting after something in the distance. Chasing after something beautiful that no one else could see. She could have been dancing, and in fact, some in the stands swore she was. But in half a minute she had disappeared behind the parking lot beyond center field. Her dad went after her the moment he saw her drop her glove. He sensed the act portended something ominous. It did.

She and her dad were waiting for the team in the parking lot after the game, which they ended up losing. Coach told the other kids he'd talk to them at practice on Tuesday night, and then he called her over. Most of the kids had already loaded up into their minivans or trucks to head home with their parents when Coach finally sat Annie down on a picnic table and spoke with her. Tears were in her eyes. Coach had asked Ray to be there to lend her moral support because he knew she wouldn't take it well.

"Annie, hon," Coach said, "you know we love having you on the team. You're one of our best players. But you can't do that. Can't just run off like that. Your teammates are depending on you. Do you understand?"

She nodded her head, looking at the ground.

"I'm just not sure what to do about this. What do you think is the fair thing to do?"

Coach didn't want to bring up the squirrel incident that had happened at the beginning of the season, which was before he got on board with the team but which a few kids had repeated for his benefit in the dugout after they'd watch Annie disappear chasing the butterfly. Fortunately, that incident had not resulted in a loss but just a triple. Annie had stopped to feed a squirrel part of a Nestle bar she'd hidden in her sock and sneaked out to center field, leaving Ray to field a ball not ten feet from her. Another time she'd apparently tucked one of the Narnia books into her glove and tried to smuggle it into the outfield to read between pitches, but she'd been caught. Coach knew that neither incident required mentioning—they went without saying. The truth of the matter was that Annie had so many different passionate interests that it was impossible for her not to explore as many as she could fit into the course of an afternoon, even if the afternoon included a baseball game. But Coach had raised a fair concern. They both knew it, and Annie shrugged her shoulders, deep in thought over his question.

"We want you on this team. You're a heck of a player. But, well, I just don't know."

Coach was at a loss. He really didn't know what else to say. Ray put his hand on Coach's shoulder and gestured that he would handle it from here. He deferred to the judgment of his future quarterback, the first of many times he would do so over the next several years. Coach never once regretted doing so.

"Annie," Ray said gently. "Are you all right?"

She nodded her head.

"Annie, we'll always be friends. You know that. But you just can't do that anymore. I mean, you just—you can't do that."

He didn't know what else to say.

"I know," she finally said, deeply saddened by her action and even confused by it. She couldn't explain it and didn't even try. After a minute of silence, she took her glove off and handed it to Ray, wiped her eyes once, and walked away. And from that day on, she never played on the boys' teams. Something had happened. She wore dresses more often after that and threw the ball less and less at recess. No one ever talked about it or really put it into words, but everyone seemed to understand it somehow. Ray was sad, too, because it was the last time he ever played on a sports team with his best friend. He was down the rest of the season.

Coach knew he had to do something to help get Ray excited about 7th grade football, which was right around the corner. He'd spoken with all the junior-high coaches about Ray, and most of them had already heard about his grade school exploits. Still, Coach felt like he needed to do something special, given the situation. So at the beginning of the summer, he called the Burlesons to ask if Ray could visit him in his office one day. Mrs. Burleson drove Ray to school and waited in the gym lobby. Coach sat Ray down in front of his desk and asked if he'd like to be ball boy for the varsity football team. He spoke sternly of the commitment, describing in details what it would take and speaking little of the fringe benefits that might appeal to a kid. To seal the deal, Coach took down his prized possession from his shelf and handed it to Ray.

"It's Chuck Moser's book. Ever heard of him?"

Ray shook his head from side to side. "No, sir."

"Moser's the greatest coach in the history of football. There's Lombardi, there's Landry, and there's Moser," Coach said, not sure if the names meant much to Ray but willing to give it a try. "But most are agreed that Moser's the best. Won three straight state championships for Abilene High in the fifties. Practically invented football. And this was his manual. My Uncle Ross started for Moser's '54 title team, and he left me this book in his will when he passed on a few years back. And I want to give it to you for the summer. Are you interested?"

"Yes, sir." Ray was as nervous and excited as he had ever remembered being. He could hardly speak.

Coach scooted the book across the desk to Ray but stopped halfway. "But, there's one catch." Ray looked devastated with fear that the book, so close, might be out of reach.

"And this is it. You gotta promise me you won't miss any Varsity games, home or away. You'll travel with the team. Same bus and all. And you'll be there on the sidelines for all the action. The official ball boy. Filling water bottles. Keeping track of the game ball. Fetching the tee after kickoffs. But you gotta be ready to take a test on this book on the day the Varsity reports for two-a-days. Think you can handle that?"

"Yes, sir." A tear was running down Ray's cheek, and Coach knew he'd found the program's savior. He finished pushing the book toward Ray, who grabbed it in both hands and stared at its simple cover—"Abilene High School Football: Organization"— then clutched it to his chest. Coach stood up, stalling for time to figure out what he should do next, for he'd been making up most of the interview on the fly and only now realized how solemnly the proceedings were being received. Finally, he reached into a desk drawer, pulled out a ragged old varsity jersey, and threw it to Ray. "Now you report to me here, in my office, at 6:30 am on the morning of August first. I'll be handing out equipment to the varsity, and you'll sit here at my desk and take the test then. Ok?"

Ray nodded his head in terrified delight.

"All right, then," Coach said, fishing around in his mind for a dignified way to wind down the interview, something official sounding that would leave an impression in Ray's mind. "Case closed. At ease. Uhm…you are dismissed. I'll see you on the first.

6:30 sharp."

"Yes, sir," the young quarterback managed, gulping out his response.

Ray was there on the first, book and pencil in hand, wearing the jersey Coach had given him. At 6:00 am.

He'd be early for every single one of the meetings he ever had with Coach, even stumbling into some impromptu, like the lunch meeting on the Monday before the last regular season game of his senior year—a meeting which for some unknown reason had sprung to Ray's mind at the very moment while he was settling in under center and staring out over the Breckenridge defense while Five Mississippi remained in the game. On that Monday at lunch, Ray'd eaten his sandwich with Annie in the cafeteria and then become so distracted about the game that she finally told him to head over to meet with Coach.

"Go meet with Coach. And tell him 'hi.' Tell him I won't be chasing down any butterflies Friday night."

Ray smiled. "Are you sure?"

"Positive."

"I'm sorry," he said.

"That's all right." She squeezed his hand. "I'll talk to you after school."

He smiled, amazed at her understanding, and headed over to Coach's office to finish his chips and cookies. When he arrived, he quietly took a seat. The whole staff was present. They'd half expected he might show up, as he often did. Coach was holding forth. "Well, Ray, good of you to join us." Coach winked at him, clearly pleased he'd stop by. "I guess even a blind hog'll find a acorn every now and then."

Ray smiled.

"Ray, you're just in time," Coach Rusty said. "Coach Dub here's been telling us how after we win this one, he's gonna do that dance he promised."

"Hell, Rusty, I'll dance naked at midfield if it means we make the playoffs."

"Good Lord, no!"

"That just ain't right!"

The whole room laughed.

"I'm just kidding. I don't get naked. Not anymore. Except maybe to shower. Or take a crap. Nah, I don't think much of getting naked anymore, but here's what I do think."

They all began to hunker down and take notes, for his voice had changed its tone with the last sentence.

"Here's what I think, and y'all tell me if I'm wrong." This was Coach's way of saying *Shut up and hear me out, 'cause this is what we're doing.* "I think a ten yard out is a long handoff. I think we're that good. We can throw on 'em all day."

"All day and all night," Coach Turner chuckled, nodding his head.

"That's right. We'll throw in a little ground and pound, some iso.s to soften up their belly, and a lot of play action and roll out. But mainly it'll be our short passing game. Lot of three steps. They'll have seen the Throckmorton film and be wary of Tony getting deep on them. I'm thinking they'll play a loose cover three. Not wanna give up a big play. I'm expecting them to adjust to our twins and trips look. Coach Scott is nobody's fool. They'll be all over our combo routes, too. They always are. We can't run the wheel this week—sorry Rusty. But that still leaves us a lot."

Coach Rusty nodded at this assessment and jotted something down in his notebook.

"They'll figure if they're close late in the game, they can pull it out. Hell, they got nineteen senior starters this year. They expect to win these types of games. What they'll worry about are flukes. Flukes and big plays. They'll want to eliminate the big play, which is fine with me."

Ray nodded. The other coaches grunted in agreement.

"Nah, what I'm worried about is their offense. So Ray, listen up. You'd better buckle up your chin strap this week and come ready to knock heads. You may get as much work at free safety as at quarterback."

"Yes, sir. I'm ready." He loved these meetings and was glad

the coaches didn't mind him hanging around while they discussed strategy.

"That's good. 'Cause I tell you what, if there's one thing I've always hated, it's the triple option. Damn pain in the ass because not enough teams run it anymore. It's a nuisance to try to prepare for 'cause you don't see it any other time of the season. And it's tough for the scout team to give you a good look. The freshmen on scout team, hell, they're lucky if they can chew gum and piss at the same time, much less run a triple option with precision. It's tough to duplicate in practice, and it's even tougher to defend. That's why I want to keep it simple. I know we've given them some different looks in the past, but this time I want it simple as can be. I don't want to slow play it or change assignments on it. I want to defend it the same way every single time. I want every one of our guys to know exactly what he's doing before the snap of the ball and not have to wonder about changing his technique or assignment depending on the formation."

Coach Marshall made a gesture of concern about this, but he remained silent.

"My philosophy is to turn that option into a toss as soon as possible. That's how we've had most of our success against them in the past—making it a toss. To do that, we gotta smoke the QB every time. I mean every single time. It'll pay dividends in the fourth quarter. If you get punched in the mouth enough times, you're gonna put the ball on the carpet. I don't care who you are. But the longer the ball's in the quarterback's hands—the longer the play stays an option—the more pressure there is on us. Indecision creates mistakes. We need to keep the assignments simple. Make sure that what our boys do on game day is what they've been doing all week. It's all about repetitions—it's like shooting free throws. It's no time to get cute. Football ain't about cute. But if the football stays in that guy's hands, and he turns that corner, then the indecision will multiply, and it's Katy-bar-the-door. They'll be off to the races. They'll have us where they want us. We'll be asking people to make plays they haven't been practicing to make. Plays they're not capable of making. But if we light up that QB and turn that option into a toss, then it's 'Welcome to my wheelhouse.' Game over. Play-offs here we come. This is what I believe."

Ray nodded his head. The other coaches were grinning at Coach Dub's excitement. They might not all have agreed with his tactics, but they all agreed with his heart and spirit a hundred per-cent, and they loved when he got on a roll like this. It was why they coached.

"So, Ray, what that means is this. The pitchman is yours. No matter what. I don't care if the QB runs by you with the ball. You attack the pitchman. Even if he runs up into the stands to go get himself a hotdog, you're following his sorry ass up there and get-ting him the relish. You understand? And don't be dilly-dallying around talking to Annie or none of them other cheerleaders on the sideline when you're following him around, you hear? Think pitchman. Though while you're at it, you might tell Annie not to go chasing after no more butterflies, too. We'll need all the cheering we can get."

Ray just nodded and tried not to laugh. The whole staff knew the butterfly story by now. In fact, Annie babysat for most of the young fathers in the room, and they practically thought of her as their oldest kid. Coach had never forgotten that baseball game, and he was secretly pleased that Annie and Ray had stayed close all these years.

"Yes sir, you tag that pitch man," Coach continued, "'Cause Cael's got the quarterback. That's his only assignment this week. I reckon he can handle that. He's gonna engage the tackle, jam his outside shoulder, shove him into B Gap, and then step down the line to smoke the QB. Travis will work his way inside/out, from fullback to quarterback, and if there's any gas left in the tank, he'll chase after the tailback. We'll put him deep—five yards if need be—to help his angles. But that tailback's yours, son. And he's mighty quick. Hell, he's more than quick. He's sudden. And you're not, Ray, so make sure you take a good angle and break down when you get in striking distance. Use the sideline as a defender—funnel him out of bounds if need be. It's as good as a tackle, though you don't get your name in the paper for it. But if you get in a footrace with him, you're gonna lose. I ain't saying that to hurt your feelings, now. It's just true. But that's ok. 'Cause you got brass ones. And brass ones trump speed every day of the week."

Ray could barely contain a smile at the confidence Coach had in him. He just nodded his head. He was excited about the game, as happy as he had ever recalled being, and the excitement only built up as the week progressed, reaching a fever pitch on game day. In fact, that Friday afternoon, while Coach was painting the end zone for the big game, Ray was in his AP Chemistry class trying his best to stay focused. It was tough, and his mind skipped around from reviewing the game plan to writing Annie's name in his binder and drawing up plays for the big game. He spent lab time running through his audibles and checks, Breckenridge's tendencies and personnel. He even plotted out what he'd say to the team before the game.

But as much as he was trying to concentrate on the game, Ray couldn't help but think about Coach. About how much he'd given to the school over the years and how good he was to all the kids. About how he checked up on everyone's grades. Went to the musical if a player was in it, and sometimes even if a player wasn't. About how he insisted Tommy Greg play the tuba in his football uniform at halftime of Homecoming because Tommy'd given his word to the band director he'd do so before the season started. About how he'd gone to Ray's granddad's funeral in McCamey, and even stayed for the wake, though he didn't know anyone. How he lined the field every Sunday afternoon and then again Friday in the early afternoon and collected and washed uniforms after every game and would stay late after practice to break film down with kids. About how he always asked how your family was and really cared and knew their names and ages. About how good he and Mrs. Widtmark were to host Thursday night team dinners and how Coach loved to work the grill in their backyard. And mostly, about how Coach'd shown up one day nine years ago to sub for 3rd grade

PE and changed the course of his life.

Even the goofy stuff cracked Ray up—how Coach would always make them listen to Johnny Cash in the weight room and say stuff like. "You think some rock and roll punk could have written that stuff? That's poetry, boys. None of this rap or heavy metal junk. Michael Jackson couldn't carry Johnny's jock, and neither could that Mick Jagger clown."

Ray realized he couldn't focus on chemistry or the game plan, and after a while he quit trying. Instead, he decided to try to make a list of Coach's sayings and rules. He wondered if this would be the last football game he'd play for Coach—the last game he would ever play, period. He jotted down the list in his quadrille. When he finished, he silently read back over it, smiled, and tried to contain a chuckle.

No horseplay in the locker room.

Desire wins games; turnovers lose games.

Be respectful to your opponents and your parents.

No dates the night before games.

Polish cleats the night before games.

Be on time.

Never sit on the field.

Take care of your body—shower after practice and dry between your toes.

Drink lots of milk.

Call the ref "sir."

Remember that football players get blocked, but champions don't stay blocked.

Never show fatigue—fatigue makes cowards of us all.

The harder you work, the luckier you get.

Walk humbly.

Gang tackle.

Make the world a better place.

Play to the whistle.

And it was the sound of the referee's whistle, Ray thought, that shook him out of his daydream to find himself beneath the center, staring out over the Breckenridge defense, for the final play of the game. A hum had filled Bronco Stadium as the crowd waited expectantly. In the distance, the cheerleaders began a chant. The band started to play the fight song. And before Ray knew it, he was in the middle of it all. Dropping back to pass. And in a few moments it was over. The ball was released from his hand and into flight. Nine years of work had been released into the night sky above Fort Griffin.

Annie had paused to watch the ball and was overtaken by a feeling she hadn't known in years. She couldn't exactly express it in words, though days later her best friend Patti would say she'd yelled out "Cover for me!" and then dropped her pompoms and taken off down the sideline, much to the confusion of Patti and the other cheerleaders. She was a blur sprinting down the field, and just barely perceptible in the peripheral vision of Coach, who had begun to count Five Mississippi to himself and move slowly toward the end zone at the start of the play.

One Mississippi…

Soon, all were eagerly following the flight of something beautiful. And because beautiful, something that had to end. For much more than just the football was descending from the night sky upon Fort Griffin. As if sensing this, the entire crowd was rising out of their seats. Now, both Annie and Coach were moving fast toward the end zone pylon, and even Ray found himself inexplicably jogging toward something in the distance.

Even the opposing coach nodded his head approvingly at the pass for it was a thing to be admired. Ray had properly planted his feet and redistributed his weight, rotating his shoulders and snapping his arm down through his hips. The spiral was tight, and the trajectory perfect. In fact, the whole play was a thing to be admired. Twenty-two, pimply-faced teenagers had executed an intricate choreography of maneuvers with precision and poise and courage. An entire season, and years of sound coaching, had been distilled into a single play. It was a tribute to all involved. To both teams. Both coaching staffs. Both towns.

Two Mississippi…

The backside cornerback had timed his blitz perfectly with the snap count, not moving up until after Ray had checked off at the line of scrimmage. The safety had slipped into place to cover for his teammate only at the snap of the ball, playing a loose man scheme. Meanwhile, the fullback had stepped up—his hips low and ready to strike—checked the playside edge and moved to the blindside to pick up the blitzing corner; the two butted heads like rams and fought to a standstill.

The playside offensive tackle had drop stepped into position to engage the defensive end, keeping his shoulders square to the line of scrimmage and punching his open palms toward the breastplate of his opponent, both thumbs up. The end had fired out low and hard and gotten upfield quickly, then faked an inside move before dipping his weight and ripping through the tackle's outstretched arms, delivering an uppercut to the space behind the blocker's outside armpit and then trying to use leverage to pivot around him at a hard angle, as the arm of a compass might rotate about its fixed center.

Three Mississippi…

After snapping the ball, the center immediately stepped to his right to help the guard control Breckenridge's All-State tackle, who had tried a spin move to the inside. With sound technique and workman-like precision, he helped bring the two hundred and fifty-pound stud under control, sealing off the inside and stopping his momentum until the guard could regain his balance and base. Sensing they had him under control, the center directed his attention back to the middle of the line, eyeing the second level defenders as he'd been taught. And indeed one of the linebackers was on a delayed blitz. He barely had time to collect himself and prepare to meet this new opponent, who had a full head of steam. Not liking his odds in this circumstance, he stepped up to attack the blitzing foe but at the last possible moment dipped down and exploded into the linebacker's left thigh and knee. The defender hadn't expected this, but struck his arms out, palms downward, at the new plane presented him, attempting to protect his legs and evade the block with a sort of lateral skip to his right. But the center sensed this shift in weight and rolled his hips around to his own left, taking the linebacker down hard.

Four Mississippi…

Meanwhile, the playside cornerback had taken a read step and then backpedaled, hesitating at the receiver's first move. But film study, the dire down and distance, and the persistent shouts from his position coach on the sideline before the snap had told him to expect a double move. His eyes stayed focused on the receiver's waist, and he did not commit to the feigned route—an out whose seven-yard stem had been run to look identical to every other pattern the receiver had run all day so as to disguise his intentions. The defender's hunch paid off as the receiver accelerated out of his hitch. The cornerback opened his hips at the right moment, turned and ran stride for stride with the receiver down the field, riding him slowly toward the sideline to limit the quarterback's target area and interrupt his adversary's ability to break inside for the ball. But Ray had thrown a beautiful pass, and it was heading to the far pylon of the end zone and would be arriving there at the exact same moment these two athletes would be. As they crossed over the goal line, both were nearly out of bounds. But before they went out, they rose together, gracefully reaching for the ball, shoulder pad to shoulder pad, as the crowd itself rose to its feet. As the better part of Shackelford County rose to its feet.

Yes, everyone rose, all in tribute to the contest. To the months of practice and sprints and film that had made this moment possible. And a wave of noise rose with them, a cacophony of voices somehow understood by all. Yes, the people rose to their feet and swayed and shook like flame as the action unfolded beautifully before them. All elements of the communal spectacle—fans, band, coaches, and athletes—rose in a crescendo for the fullness of time was upon them, and the short-lived play revealed itself to be the beauty of the entire season of sacrifice rolled into maybe half a dozen seconds. Into the time it takes to count Five Mississippi. Yes, the season had come down to this, and the people would have had it no other way. Yes, they all seemed to say. Yes

WIVES OF THE DEAD

Once again, a cacophony erupted from the residence at 1630 Winthrop Court. The brownstone on this quiet, sleepy Beacon Hill cul-de-sac was growing accustomed to the confusion of snide remarks, vicious glances, and shrieking outbursts that rang through its hallways as a war was waged for the soul of the house by parties who, had they been less splenetic and more knowledgeable of the matter at hand, would have realized the mutual benefits of entente. But the home of Nathaniel Winslow Storey, America's most accomplished second-tier novelist of the nineteenth century, would not know such peace. And so the house's foundation was being shaken, as it were, by this most unlikely gaggle of devotees.

But anyone who knew the house's four tour guides would not have been surprised. Fortunately for the house and the surrounding neighborhood, no more than two of the guides were ever on duty at any one time. Except for today. Today was different. Today, the house was to be the beneficiary of a gift from the sole living descendant of Storey, a gift that promised to bump the brownstone up in stature, moving it past two other Storey residences in the hierarchy of tourist sites associated with the author. There had even been talk among the giddy that the gift might push the seldom visited house closer to that most coveted status of National Historic Landmark. For today, 1630 Winthrop Court would receive into its care the slopjar of Storey's youth, and not since the days of the grail romances had so many imaginations been enthralled and transfigured by the thought of an empty vessel.

In truth, Storey's family had a fascinating history. A Storey had sailed for New England with Endicott and suffered through the worst of those early winters, losing a leg to chilblain and three infants to pneumonia. One had prosecuted a heretic for antinomianism and sentenced the misguided soul to exile among the benighted colonists of Rhode Island. Another had been a confidante of Jonathan Edwards when his fiery sermons were fueling a religious awakening in western Massachusetts, later editing the works of the great divine. Hardly a generation later the family resurfaced again in our nation's history: a branch of the Storeys had provided occasional shelter to cousin Abigail Adams and her children while her husband served abroad as a diplomat. And when, after the Revolution, Salem became one of the wealthiest cities in America, it was due in no small measure to Storeys, who had captained and later owned schooners and privateers that traded molasses, rum, and lumber with ports of call as distant as China. The family's fortunes had faded somewhat in the nineteenth century when the shipping industry in Salem declined and the nation pushed west, yet the clan managed to meet with some further acclaim as a few of their number had served the Bay State with distinction as members of its Lower House.

And though it was generally assumed the line had suffered a slow decline—or at the very least achieved more prestige than they were rightly due—none could deny that in the final account they still had accomplished much, and in fact a good deal more than most. So it was not surprising that in the latter half of the nineteenth century a son could be born into this noble race who would go on to win small renown. What would be unusual was the field in which that fame was achieved. Though never explicitly stated, the impression the family of statesmen had long given the public was that affairs such as literature were beneath it.

Yet by 1873 it had been a generation since the clan had produced a figure of note, and so it should perhaps be forgiven if one of their ranks abandoned Boston and the family hearth in the name of adventure, striking out boldly into the world beyond the Berkshires. For it was in the spring of that year when Josiah Winslow Storey, much to the disdain of his relatives, moved west with his young wife to make his fortune and grow up, as it were, with the country. But Josiah never found the mythic abundance of the frontier which he believed he had been promised. Though a healthy son would be born to him in a town on the Texas frontier, the family would soon depart for the Sawtooth Mountains. Within two years of the move Josiah was, for all intents and purposes, bankrupt. And in the third year of this self-imposed exile his lovely, young wife left their house one morning—after preparing her husband his favorite breakfast, seeing him off to work, and nursing her newborn for an hour—made her way to the outskirts of their sleepy frontier town, entered an abandoned mineshaft, and hurled herself one hundred and fifty feet to her death. Her body was not recovered for weeks.

Josiah was devastated, but his pride was sufficient to confront and come to terms with even this trial, and he persisted in his schemes and remained out west. He refused offers of monetary aid from relatives in Boston and would eventually settle in California and open a general store that did well for some years. He scratched out a decent living, earning enough to pay for a graduate from Andover Seminary to tutor his only son in the classics, reading to him Homer, Cicero, and Dante. But within a decade the cheap source of newly arrived immigrant labor had driven his store out of business, and the very year that Turner declared the frontier closed, a broke, disillusioned, and bitter Storey returned to the east coast and threw himself at the mercy of his Beacon Hill relatives.

By then they, too, lacked the energy and material resources which had once distinguished the line, and in order to save money to pay his son's college bills, Josiah was forced to accept a job working for the import retailer J. Leopold Gatzki, serving in a position whose degrading effects on him did not go unnoticed by his son. Josiah's prospects improved only after the death of his own father, at which point he and his son moved into the family house at 1630 Winthrop Court, a residence which the two shared for exactly one summer, before young Nathaniel Storey enrolled for his freshman year at Harvard College.

Nathaniel won his earliest acclaim before graduating from school, publishing poems in the <u>Harvard Advocate</u>, and by the time he went off to fight in Hay's "splendid little war" against Spain, he had married, produced a son, watched his wife deteriorate into neurasthenic depression, and written three novels. His fiction had caused a minor stir in Cambridge, one that still persisted in some circles. And though he never became an author of the first order, dying tragically young at San Juan Hill, there were those who would insist his best works did not compare unfavorably with the worst of the young Henry James.

Four such critics regularly volunteered their services to 1630 Winthrop Court, and they had gathered with great anticipation to meet the grandson of their beloved author who was, according to an obscure missive received by a Mrs. Barrister, the President of the local chapter of the Storey Society, to donate to the residence the slopjar Storey had used as a youth on the frontier. The house was also to receive various grooming articles employed by the author over the course of his life. It mattered none to any of the tour guides that the assortment of belongings hailed from different periods of the author's life and were of disputed origin; in fact, all were agreed that a single room could hold the variety in pleasing juxtaposition. The general belief was that the addition of the slopjar, tweezers, comb, vanity mirror, and filing board would complete the house's toiletry exhibit in the bathroom, considered by all of the guides to be the weakest room in the brownstone.

"The slopjar," mused aloud Mrs. Barrister, who doubled as the head tour guide, "must be reserved its own shelf. Such an intimate artifact deserves special care."

Tiffany Oapsy, the youngest of the four tour guides by some thirty years, blushed at the mention of the word, refusing to speak it in connection with Storey. Though this was the third summer break she had worked at the residence, there were certain familiarities she refused to take when conversing about the figure she would only refer to as "Mr. Storey." The fact that she must return for her senior year at Wellesley in only two weeks made the attention to decorum only more necessary, for she was writing her Honors thesis on Storey and did not in any way want to compromise the integrity of her project before it got underway. "Mr. Storey would want it so," she said in response to Mrs. Barrister's suggested placement of the item. Her voice trembled like the flame of a votive candle, its tone wholly sympathetic with the intimacy implied by a toiletry article from the author's youth. "Perhaps we can place it by the window to take advantage of the natural lighting."

Mrs. Tinkerton, who did not quite understand what a slopjar was but good-naturedly wanted to be included in the conversation, nodded her head in full agreement while munching on the stash of Snackwell Devil's Food Cake treats she perpetually kept in her purse.

Ms. Grumpelli did not hear any of the preceding comments but interjected in her harsh voice while gazing down at her watch, "Say, when's this grandson supposed to show up, again?"

"Half seven," replied Mrs. Barrister.

"What?" Grumpelli responded, confused.

"Seven thirty," Barrister explained, only half trying to conceal her contempt.

"Seven thirty, humph…" Grumpelli repeated, clearly impatient. "Where's he coming from again, New York? It doesn't take that long to get here from New York. I went there once, and it didn't take me that long."

"The apartment is in New York. He is flying in from the estate in Devonshire. His plane was to have arrived at five o'clock, and he will head here after refreshing at the Four Seasons."

Miss Oapsy gazed raptly into the distance at the thought of a descendant of her beloved Mr. Storey freshening up. Her heart quivered at the thought of the life of this lonely bachelor, for she knew his story well. So it was that she sympathized with how intensely he must have felt betrayed and harried by his homeland and its lack of appreciation for his literary talents, a neglect so insulting that it had forced him to publish his own works and then forced him—against his will, she imagined—to settle abroad. She knew that her decision to constantly wear black as a token of mourning for this exile was appropriate. And she was equally certain that she alone could restore his faith in his homeland, nurture him back to strength. And if the friendship they struck up after today were to develop into something more intimate, then she thought that yes, she could bear him a child, revive the noble Storey line. She lost herself in a daydream of a summer in Devonshire, thrilling with the recent rumor she had heard that this last of the Storeys had been speaking with American publishing houses about a brilliant novel he had in manuscript form and for which he was attempting to find a press. But Oapsy's visions were abruptly dashed by a grating voice at her elbow.

"Is he gonna have his wife and kids with him?" asked Grumpelli.

An awkward silence fell upon the room.

"Mr. Storey remains a bachelor," answered Barrister coolly.

"He's not married?" asked Grumpelli, cocking an eyebrow, feigning surprise. "How old is he again?"

"Mr. Storey was born in Brookline in 1927. He will be seventy-three in late July."

"Doesn't he have any kids or anything?"

"Mr. Storey has never been married."

"Hmm," mused Grumpelli, pleased she had once again been able to tease out into the open facts known by all the tour guides, but facts from which they each drew different conclusions. She was silent for a pregnant moment before continuing her train of thought. "And you're sure he's not, you know, uhm…."

Barrister lifted her chin and, as if poised atop a stairwell staring down at the filth huddled in steerage, sized up her antagonist.
Embarrassed, Oapsy looked down at her shoes. Tinkerton, unawares of anything at the moment save her Snackwells, crumpled
up one small green cookie bag and fetched another from one of
the bottomless recesses of her purse.

"Ms. Grumpelli," Barrister intoned, "you are nearly seventy
and not married, are you not?"

Grumpelli looked confused, and just when Barrister's remarks
were beginning to register, Tinkerton began to cough violently
and spit out crumbs of chocolate devil's food cake. Grumpelli
was about to protest Barrister's dig when the chief tour guide shot
her a glance that communicated much, reminding her that while
Grumpellis were herding swine in Sicily, Barristers were throwing
tea into Boston Harbor, storming Ticonderoga, and helping draft
the Massachusetts Constitution. Before the situation could escalate,
Barrister marched off to resituate a flower arrangement, and Miss
Oapsy rushed to the aid of Tinkerton and immediately ushered her
over to a seat, gently patting her back.

"Mrs. Tinkerton, you must be careful. You should be sitting
down anyway. You know the doctor does not want you standing
for more than ten minutes at a time. Have you taken your pills this
afternoon?"

Mrs. Tinkerton gave in to the good sense of her young friend.
What she had said was true. Tinkerton had difficulty standing for
any amount of time, a disability that hindered her effectiveness
as a tour guide. The circulation in her feet was poor, leaving her
ankles perpetually purple and swollen. Her brow was always damp.
Her blood pressure was absurdly high. Frequently, tourists on her
shift found themselves worrying so much about her health—about
whether or not she would keel over and die mid-tour—that they
forgot they were on a vacation. Miss Oapsy had sensed these
anxieties among the clientele, and before each of Mrs. Tinkerton's
tours, she would very discreetly ask the sturdiest member of each
party to carry a folding chair from room to room for her older colleague so that she might sit and deliver her script.

But lately Mrs. Tinkerton had had to abandon at least one tour a day, telling confused parties they would have to lead themselves through the house, handing out a profusion of literature as she shooed them out of the parlor before collapsing on a sofa, wrenching off her shoes, and elevating her grotesquely misshapen feet. She dared not let the other tour guides know this, though. She especially did not want Grumpelli, whom she viewed as her chief and bitter rival, to have this satisfaction. Miss Oapsy, with whom she was paired on Thursdays and Saturdays, had suspected Tinkerton's deteriorating condition for some time, however. A week ago a tourist had threatened to call an ambulance for Tinkerton. Only the accommodating and skillful diplomatic instincts of Oapsy had saved the day. She calmed the angry tourist and gave her a free pass and a "Save our Storey" commemorative pin. Oapsy cared greatly for Tinkerton, yet at the same time felt obligated to uphold the sanctity of the office. She took her duties to Storey deadly seriously and wanted the shrine attended with due reverence.

After Ms. Grumpelli had silently smouldered from Mrs. Barrister's reprimand for a minute and Miss Oapsy had tended to Mrs. Tinkerton, Barrister left the flowers to tend to final preparations at the small buffet she had personally paid a caterer to provide and set up. Much to Barrister's chagrin, there were few other guests at the reception. Over two months ago, she had hand selected and mailed out beautiful rice paper invitations—complete with calligraphic script and souvenir stamps—sending them out to esteemed Cambridge philanthropists and scholars and select members of the media. Alas, she had received little response to show for her efforts.

"The Event," as she had lately taken to calling Storey's reception, was to have begun at six o'clock. It was seven o'clock now, and there was only a handful of guests present: Barrister's son, a wealthy lawyer, had called from his cell phone to say he was en route; Mrs. Tinkerton's aging mother, who herself was ninety-seven years old, had been wheeled in from an area nursing home in Scituate and sat silently in a corner with a blanket in her lap; Miss Oapsy's college roommate—the editor of the Wellesley school paper—

was present; so were Thomas Grout, a used-book store owner, and his wife, a librarian from the local public branch, an assortment of curious and condescending neighbors, a few precocious high school students from Milton Academy (cousins of Miss Oapsy), and a Harvard professor whose continuing education classes Mrs. Barrister had taken for three consecutive years and whose company she had gone to great lengths to cultivate so as to give legitimacy to her intellectual pursuits. He secretly feared she might be stalking him, but since she regularly offered him her opera tickets he figured it was an arrangement he could risk, though this particular evening he was beginning to wonder if his love for Puccini could justify this humiliating association.

None of the guests was mixing, and Mrs. Barrister had begun to worry. She went over to where Professor Morrison was standing—drinking a glass of wine and discreetly making a regular note of the time on his watch—and offered him a water cress sandwich. He declined, adding apologetically that he would have to depart by 7:45 to make it to the opera on time, neglecting to mention that his date for the evening would be an attractive young coed in his graduate seminar. This apology was enough to send the usually composed Barrister into a mild, though well-concealed, panic. She silently cursed herself, for indeed they were her tickets that he planned on using, and she even momentarily considered insisting he return the tickets to her on the spot. Though this would have the desired short-term effect, it would likely expose her real ambitions and destroy her long-term goal of acquiring intellectual respectability, and this had of late become the driving force in her life.

No, she thought to herself, she must cultivate the professor. She smiled, pressed his hand warmly, and assured him that she understood, adding that she was certain that Mr. Storey would arrive momentarily. She then hurried off to the other side of the reception room and tried to appear busy rearranging the cheeses and sampling the Beluga, whose price alone managed to console her somewhat. By herself for a few moments, she wondered if the evening would be a failure. She took great pride in being the president of the local chapter of the Storey Society, the first of its kind. In truth, her interest in Storey was fueled at least in part by her younger sister's presidency of the Medford Chapter of the Daughters of the American Revolution, an honor bestowed her in a controversial ballot four years ago. As she could find no other such presidencies available at the time, Mrs. Barrister set about to fashion her own such office.

She liked to fancy she shared something of the pioneer spirit which had inspired the earliest arrivals to the Bay State. She could not imagine that their errand had met with any greater resistance than hers. And if they could set about to found a new world, then she could, too. She even imagined her task more daunting; the Puritans had only had to contend with famine, winter, and plague, whereas she had to grapple with the forces of ignorance and vulgarity. Indeed, she knew her mission had not exactly been aided by the supporting cast she had managed to assemble about her. Nonetheless, they would have to do—for now. She herself had first heard of Storey three and a half years ago while perusing the shelves at Grout's Bookstore and had set about shortly thereafter restoring this misunderstood writer to prominence and securing both Storey and herself places within the Boston literati. Her charges had arrived at 1630 Winthrop Court through very different, but no less circuitous, paths.

Tinkerton's involvement came about quite accidentally. Her cousin had been a longtime maid for the Barristers. Three years earlier, while dropping off a Christmas present at the Barristers', this cousin had been made to witness an uncomfortable family confrontation: an argument between Barrister and her son about her plans to buy and restore the residence at 1630 Winthrop Court. Though sympathetic with his mother's situation after the death of Mr. Barrister, the son did not like the idea that his inheritance was being spent on such a venture. But Mrs. Barrister was adamant. Tinkerton's cousin took note of the conversation, and leaving the gift in the vestibule, let herself out quietly. The next morning she called up Mrs. Tinkerton, who for years had written a local history column for the <u>Revere Gazette</u>, a platform from which she had argued the importance of reconsidering the Irish roots of American literature. That very night Mrs. Tinkerton called up Barrister and asked if she might help out at the house. Desperate for help, Barrister had agreed.

Lately, however, Barrister had become suspicious that Tinkerton was seeking to remake Storey in her own image. The hunch had begun when Ms. Grumpelli informed her that she had overheard Tinkerton's odd introductory remarks to a party of tourists, remarks that could only have been meant to suggest that the great-grandfather of their beloved author was the bastard son of Rebecca Storey and the family's Irish, indentured servant, Thomas O'Riordan. Barrister had found the news disconcerting. Yet she knew, too, that Grumpelli was not an altogether trustworthy informant and was insanely jealous of Tinkerton's superior command of Storey family history and her ability to recite her script with modest proficiency. Mostly, she was furious that Tinkerton had uncovered the fact that she had never finished reading any of Storey's novels. She had started them all. But she could not manage to finish a single one. Recently, she had attempted, and failed, to force herself to read Storey's most celebrated and difficult novel: <u>Brokario</u>.

Storey's reputation as the foremost of America's second-tier novelists who wrote at the fin-de-siècle had been won largely upon the acclaim of this novel few had actually read but which many took the liberty to discuss. <u>Brokario</u> was a work of highly wrought fiction that elaborated the history of one of the most obscure characters from <u>The Divine Comedy</u>—a figure so obscure, in fact, that he does not even appear in the final version of the poem but only in an earlier draft whose authenticity was in doubt as early as the Renaissance. The draft would disappear and resurface several times a century, finally vanishing for good in a fire popularly attributed to Mussolini's Brown Shirts. Only a handful of legitimate scholars ever saw the work. One such figure was Longfellow, who came across the manuscript while working on his translation of

Dante, and it is Longfellow whom most credit with assigning the mysterious document its infamous moniker: "The Lost Canto." Though many today maintain that such a canto never existed, the mystery surrounding the work took on a life of its own. What is certain is that no more unusual tale exists in literature than that of Brokario, the aspiring, vain, but touchingly incompetent Italian poet of the thirteenth century whom Dante had once tutored and whom he encounters on the path toward redemption, not a stone's throw from the top of the mountain of Purgatory—at a penitential wayside, literally within sight of paradise.

Dante stops briefly to speak with Brokario, an actual contemporary who died tragically young in 1310, preceding the Florentine poet in death. When Brokario learns of Dante's success writing in the vernacular, he becomes enraged, inexplicably descending into a fit of blasphemy, ultimately earning himself a place in hell with those treacherous to their benefactors. In a mad fit high atop the holy mountain, he begins to verbally assault Dante, cursing the divine plan that allowed his own toil on earth to go uncelebrated by the vulgar masses, until he finally—in one of literature's most disturbing displays of blasphemy—rejects the promise of grace amid a barrage of profane oaths, insisting he is too good to labor amid the pedestrian sinners on the holy mountain. The astonished Dante can only watch in horror as Brokario pushes him aside and breaks away from his assigned station, storming down the mountain path toward the gates of hell, howling blasphemy with every step. Eventually he stumbles down a steep, rocky outcropping, and while in the act of falling, manages to turn and make final eye contact with Dante, who had given chase and was committed to rescuing his friend.

Storey's journals reveal that he based the scene upon a sailing accident he had witnessed in his early manhood. While rounding Nantucket on a foggy autumn night in his great uncle's sloop, Storey watched a trusted deckhand get knocked overboard by a rogue wave. He had quickly thrown hawser to the sailor, a lifelong family associate. The unlucky mariner had initially grabbed the line, and

Storey began pulling him to safety through the choppy and freezing waters. But then, driven by a perverse impulse, he released his grip on the rope, smiled darkly into Storey's eyes, and let the waves pull him gently away into darkness.

The scene from <u>Brokario</u> had caused Charles William Eliot's wife to faint. Upon awakening from her spell, she insisted her husband withdraw Storey from consideration in Harvard's <u>Five Foot Shelf of Classics</u>, a slight for which Storey's relatives had never forgiven the Eliots. More than one cousin would occasionally remark, during late night conversations after cocktails, that the move had cost the family untold fame and royalties. Barrister herself suspected as much. But it hadn't.

Not that most readers of Storey knew this much about <u>Brokario</u>. Certainly the residence's four part-time tour guides did not. Grumpelli herself had never gotten that far in the novel. As of late, a new ambition had captured her imagination.

Ms. Grumpelli had committed herself wholeheartedly to a campaign designed to ridicule, undermine, and assault the integrity of Tinkerton, by any means necessary. This ambition required she wear clothes that accentuated her slim figure and Easy Strider shoes to emphasize her good health and devotion to fitness, even going so far as to walk to work. This appalled Barrister, who offered to have her picked up and driven to work, or—at the very least—supplied with a bus pass (as she had arranged for Tinkerton). Even Oapsy, whose father dropped her off for work, offered Grumpelli a ride. She resisted all such overtures.

On her off days, Grumpelli secretly stopped by the house and waited in the alley until tourists left, then quizzed them as to the contents of Tinkerton's script, taking notes on family facts and even inquiring about her rival's tone of voice and style of performance. On days when she worked alternating shifts with Tinkerton, she would hide important artifacts from each room so that her coworker's tour would suffer. Lately, she had taken to swapping the locations of paintings in an effort to embarrass Tinkerton and upset the rhythm and delivery of her script. Once, in mid-July of the previous year, she even turned off the air conditioner while

Tinkerton was with a party of fifteen in the attic, and then feigned ignorance of the matter when paramedics arrived and wheeled Tinkerton off on a gurney.

Tinkerton eventually caught on to these ploys, however, and was aided at fending them off by the thoughtful and diplomatic Oapsy. One day Miss Oapsy tactfully suggested to Barrister that she hire a security guard to roam the house during hours to protect against the possibility of tourist theft. Barrister was flattered at the suggestion that the house merited such measures and immediately hired an off-duty policeman. This seemed to temper Grumpelli's designs. But she was resourceful.

The fact of the matter was that Grumpelli had had no idea who Nathaniel Winslow Storey was until she responded to an ad in the paper seeking help at the Storey gift shop barely a week after Barrister had opened the site. This venture involving the past proved much more complicated than Barrister had expected. Realizing that acquiring and training tour guides in the niceties of history was going to be more difficult than she had initially supposed, Barrister soon offered to train Grumpelli to give tours during off-peak hours. She accepted, but not without reservations. Her reluctance was fueled by her past experience in the Louisa May Alcott Society. Years ago she had been a member in good standing, reading <u>Little Women</u> some dozen times (though actually finishing it only once), until one day she stopped receiving the <u>Alcott Newsletter</u>. She was devastated. Her phone calls to the President were never returned. Yet had she been entirely honest with herself, she would have confessed that the unfortunate situation might have been caused by her repeated attempts to advance her thesis that all the members of the Alcott family were gay. Recently, a similar insinuation had won her the ire of Barrister.

Grumpelli would not cease from her crusade, however, and while waiting for the arrival of their guest from Devonshire, she recalled the confrontation she had had with Barrister only a week ago. Barrister had loaned her an edition of the collected letters of Storey, and she remarked to her employer how odd she thought his letters were.

"What sort of man signs his letters to male friends 'With respect and affection'? And you know, for that matter, what sort of man writes letters to other men, period?"

Barrister was dumbfounded. "What?" With a glance she appealed to Miss Oapsy to intervene. Oapsy dutifully complied, repeating her explanation of the previous week.

"Oh, but Ms. Grumpelli, it was not uncommon for people living in the nineteenth-century to write letters. It was the accepted practice, before the phone."

Grumpelli cocked an eyebrow as if hearing an absurdity for the first time.

"There is nothing unusual about Mr. Storey's letters," Oapsy continued gently. "He's just using a polite, conventional closing to his letter. We mustn't judge it by our standards today. It means nothing."

Grumpelli continued, undeterred.

"Everything means something. Are you saying that doesn't strike any of you as weird? 'With respect and affection.' 'Affection.' What sort of man has 'affection'? Or at least admits to it. I've never heard of such a man!"

Now both Barrister and Oapsy were stunned.

"What kind of man does that? Not a real man, I tell you. Now I can't say for sure, but the evidence looks pretty good to me—" but her rationale was mercifully interrupted by another one of Tinkerton's coughing fits as she tried to inhale another Snackwell. A debris field of devil's food cake crumbs lay scattered about the helpless Tinkerton, who was wheezing and lurching forward every few seconds in a violent cough. Oapsy moved quickly to help her friend, and even Grumpelli stopped talking for the moment, though less out of concern than out of the fact she'd lost her audience.

Barrister shook her head. She did not have the time such considerations. She was only happy that such a tasteless comment had not been uttered in the presence of tourists during hours of the house's operation. She cast another look in Miss Oapsy's direction, another silent appeal for her to defuse the situation (and which was already being attended to by her trustworthy young aide), then hurried off to check on the wine, all the while making silent plans in her head about how she could arrange for the dismissal of Grumpelli and increase the subscription base of The Storey Journal, a scholarly periodical which she was to edit but that as of yet had not published a single issue.

Miss Oapsy once again came to the rescue. In a dozen or so seconds, she had dislodged the offending wedge of snack cake and restored her friend's health. The truth of the matter was that without Oapsy, Barrister's dreams would have floundered long ago. The Storey Society would have been lost without her energy. As it was, the house suffered enough during the school year when she could only work part time. This greatly pained Barrister and Oapsy, for of all the members of the society, her devotion was the most pure. Only Oapsy came to the job with true knowledge of, and passion for, her subject. In fact, of late she could not get enough of the house at 1630 Winthrop Court.

She had taken to visiting the house in the early hours of the morning. Using an extra key Barrister had cut for her the previous year, Miss Oapsy would enter the back courtyard at the postern, unlock the kitchen door, and wander through the rooms, fingering family heirlooms, lingering at thresholds and gazing dreamily out the gauzed windows onto the moonlit, cobbled-stoned streets of Beacon Hill. Storey had become a passion for her, and she had been researching his life diligently for the past year and a half. Yet as much as she enjoyed the reading and detective work of the archives, she enjoyed the house even more. During these quiet hours, she thrilled at the idea of the house, barren of human activity and other distractions. She quickened with the thought that her beloved author had once roamed these passages when he had been about her age. These secret visits sustained her. So far as she knew, no one had suspected her midnight meanderings. And it was the thought of these intimate visits she was indulging in when Mrs. Barrister, desperate for moral support, stole up behind her near the buffet table.

Miss Oapsy sensed her presence and turned. For the first time she noticed the exhaustion on Barrister's face, where bags like black bunting drooped beneath her eyes. She immediately knew what was worrying her mentor.

"Don't worry Mrs. Barrister, I am sure Mr. Storey will be here soon."

Barrister smiled at Oapsy's kindness.

"I hope so, but I don't know how much good it will do. Professor Morrison left five minutes ago, and the Grouts are leaving now, too."

Oapsy turned in the direction of Barrister's gaze and caught sight of the Grouts making a discreet exit. She tried to ease her employer's now visible distress.

"Well, I know they had to get back to the kids. I overheard them say to someone that they couldn't find a babysitter for tonight."

Barrister bit off a smile at the cruel irony of Oapsy's well-intentioned remark.

"I know," she said, touching Oapsy's shoulder in a gesture of true gratitude. "I of all people know how hard it can be to get good help. Thank goodness I was lucky enough to find you."

As if on cue, a bickering Grumpelli and Tinkerton lumbered over, the former inhaling a croissant sandwich and the latter, now recovered, dragging her folding chair behind her like a child with a security blanket.

"That professor and those bookstore people left, Mrs. Barrister," Grumpelli managed between mouthfuls as a hint of a smile broke across her face. "The rolls and cold cuts are gone, too. There's some of that water cress, but it smells rank. What do we do now? Should we leave or something?"

Barrister was tempted to respond viciously but checked herself.

Tinkerton didn't wait for her employer's reply, but barged in on a completely unrelated topic. "I wonder what this slopjar thing looks like," she said, while unfolding her chair, plopping down in it, and nibbling on another Snackwell cake. Unconsciously, Miss Oapsy began to fan her with one of the programs Barrister had had printed for the night's event.

"I bet it's beautiful, but in a simple sort of way," Miss Oapsy said hopefully. "I wonder if it looks like some sort of spittoon. Maybe it's brass, even, with some gold leaf or mother of pearl trim…."

"Dear," said Barrister, patting Miss Oapsy's arm affectionately, "there's no doubt Nathaniel is worthy of such a slopjar, but I fear it won't be quite that extravagant. Remember, Miss Oapsy, it dates from our Nathaniel's years on the frontier."

"What she's trying to say is it's just a piss bucket," interjected Grumpelli.

"It's decidedly not a piss bucket, Ms. Grumpelli," corrected Barrister.

"Ok, a crapper."

"Not a crapper, either." Though Barrister was saddened by the dismal turnout, there was still enough fire in her belly to mount a final assault against her tormentor. "Ms. Grumpelli, you will refrain from using such vulgarity in my presence."

"Well, it ain't no grail."

"No, it's no grail, or a chalice, either. Nor is it an urn adorned with heifers lowing, dressed in garlands, following pipers to a green altar in some distant meadow." Her allusion was lost on her company.

"I bet it's ceramic. The Irish favored ceramic pottery for all things in the nineteenth century," said Mrs. Tinkerton, as she wiped a sleeve from her period outfit across her mouth. She had rented a nineteenth century pioneer outfit to recreate the atmosphere of Storey's frontier youth, but the expense had gone for naught. With her red nose and baggy dress she looked very much like a homeless rodeo clown. And as Barrister was about to correct her, she caught sight of the last officially invited guest slipping out the front door. A silence stole over the large parlor-room, disrupted at intervals by Tinkerton's mom, snoring in her wheelchair in the corner of the room, the heavy blanket now partially covering her feet after having fallen from her lap. The only conscious guests who now remained were the students from Milton, and they were present only to escape dorm food and eavesdrop on the strange behavior of these senior citizens. No one else was left. The sadness of this realization was about to bring tears to Barrister's eyes when her antagonists resumed their squabbling.

"How do you know they liked ceramic things? And what does it matter anyway, the Storeys weren't Irish," Grumpelli insisted.

"Aren't," Miss Oapsy stated, insisting desperately on the family's continued relevance.

But Tinkerton blasted back without hearing her younger friend's words.

"And what do you know about Mr. Storey, anyhow? You haven't even read one of his works."

Grumpelli gasped, as if she had been dewigged in the company of hundreds.

"Why look at you, you old fool," Grumpelli rallied, "dressed like a cowgirl. You can't even stand up!"

"Ms. Grumpelli, control yourself," intoned Barrister, who still had a sense of decorum about her, as she nodded over at the bewildered high schoolers, now huddled nervously by the buffet tables.

"This is what they wore back then," stuttered Tinkerton, lowering her tone of voice momentarily. "I know all about it from my research. Maybe you should do some before you try to give a tour."

"Maybe you should do less research and more living, you shriveled up geezer. You can't even walk around the house. Why just yesterday you told a family to tour themselves around," Grumpelli said, now making circuits about her foe's chair while poking a finger out at her. The stationary Tinkerton took swipes at Grumpelli, who was circling just out of her reach. Barrister tried to separate the two, seeking to correct them at every possible opportunity. The efforts were useless, and now every gripe and source of contention that the group had managed to keep in check over the past several years were unleashed upon each other: whether the guides should wear contemporary clothes, the dresses appropriate to the frontier, or the style of the fin-de-siècle; whether the house should be redecorated, updated, or restored; whether admission to the house should be free, graduated, or a flat fee.

Only Miss Oapsy did not engage in the spat. She had removed herself a short distance from the fracas, and was gazing intently out the window. Had she not been lost in her thoughts, she might have seen the ominous clouds that had gathered over the Cape to the east. A storm would be breaking soon. But this was of no concern to Oapsy, for in her mind she was already in Devonshire not Boston. The squabbling continued for several minutes more, barbs flying and voices shrieking, when at the most pathetic moment possible, a glimmer of hope broke in upon those assembled.

The front door was suddenly thrown open, and a beardless, bronzed man entered the house from the blustery evening beyond. He was not much older than Miss Oapsy. Though he spoke with an English accent and was dressed in a tweed jacket with a crimson ascot, he resembled nothing so much as a shepherd youth torn from the pages of a child's book of Greek myths.

"Mr. Storey regrets that he has been detained and that his arrival will be delayed indefinitely," he announced before the astonished audience. "He called from in flight to relay that his jet was forced into a holding pattern over the Atlantic. He begs your pardon, hoping you'll indulge his absence for it has been with long-suffering patience and great expectations that he has entertained this day of homecoming."

There was silence. They had been waiting for the triumphant return of the sole surviving member of this once great house, but there would be no Storey. The four women were unsure what to make of this strange figure and the news he brought. The truth of the matter was that they were unconcerned at the moment and had forgotten the cause of their gathering. Yet in their frenzy, they sensed this absence was no longer relevant to the matter at hand. They believed this visitor inconvenient—felt as if he were an intruder. After some moments of awkward silence, the argument resumed, and the golden messenger, after sampling the Beluga, stole silently away. The cacophony resumed at 1630 Winthrop Court, continuing unabated into what was promising to be a long, bitter night, an atmosphere entirely unfit for the return of even this Storey.

The Secret History of a Secret History

The sound momentarily unnerved him, resembled, so he imagined, the sound of human teeth scattered across cold marble floor. A smile curled to his lips as he realized he must have kicked the sound into existence. He fumbled about in his pockets until he found what he was seeking. Taking out a candle and a matchbook, he produced a small ring of light and began his search.

In little more than a minute, his suspicions were confirmed. He found the first tooth toward the back row of the chapel. Small, coffee stained, and surprisingly sharp; it nicked the pad of his forefinger and drew forth a tiny dot of blood. He held it aloft for inspection, apparently pleased, and then placed it in a pocket. The others he found just off the center aisle, near where the chapel and the narthex met. They resembled less teeth than bits of gravel. He let them be. It would take another minute before he found the body in a far corner of the narthex. Crushed to death beneath the large, oak pedestal that had once held aloft a bust of Tolkien.

Despite the grim discovery, the figure remained preternaturally composed. After surveying the scene, he undertook a peculiar course of action. He blew out the candle, returned it to his coat, and donned a pair of lambskin gloves. Retreating from the chapel, he silently closed its heavy main door, and then produced a handkerchief with which he then wiped down the knob and brass fixtures. Carefully skirting the range of the one security camera in the Front Quadrangle, the shadowy form made its way toward the Great Hall's undercroft, the subterranean pub and gathering place whose doors remained perpetually unlocked and whose musty vault contained the lone payphone on the grounds of Exeter College. In the damp dark of the crypt, he sat in a booth near the phone and stared out through the ground level window, across the quad, apparently waiting for something or someone.

The records would show that the police fielded a mysterious call from the college at exactly 4:51 AM, approximately the same time Jonathan Mims had entered the chapel. It was a ritual to which the college janitor frequently succumbed, though he spoke to none of it and likely would have denied it if confronted about the practice. In truth, he was a bit ashamed of the habit, even though it was innocent enough and born of an authentic piety. It was something he could not explain but merely did.

On this particular morning, he had been on his way out of the chapel after several minutes of silent prayer, when he made the unpleasant discovery of the body. After having made his way to the far corner of the narthex to leave ajar a window to provide circulation to the otherwise muggy precincts, he came upon the fallen pilgrim. Not half a minute later, the police entered the chapel, flashlights ablaze. And so early one summer morning, Mims, longtime and loyal employee of the college, found himself surrounded by officers of the Oxford Police force while at his feet lay a lifeless body, whose peculiar manner of dress suggested it was a female American, though this information could not have been gleaned from its face, which was a crushed and bloody mass. And next to this frightening heap lay the enormous brass head of Tolkien, which seemed to stare up at Mims: cold, indifferent, immortal. And wearing, so he thought, a dark smile.

Nearly a century had passed since the author of <u>The Lord of the Rings</u> had been a young scholar at Exeter. Much had changed at Oxford since then. Now close to a third of the university's students were foreign born. And though dead Americans were a bit unusual to find in Oxford, living ones were not. Especially in the summer. Early each June, thousands of Americans, with education degrees from colleges sprung from small prairie towns, descend on Oxford to drink of its rarified atmosphere. Desperate for inspiration or experience that might mark them as unique, these teachers enroll in one of the university's many summer school programs geared specially for this clientele and designed to package one thousand years of prestige into a three-week vacation. There is something touchingly pathetic in the scene, as hordes grovel for a taste of old Oxford, its tradition, and a way of life their colonial forebears had renounced by way of revolution. Most know little of the ancient town, only that it might anoint them with an experience that their housewife sisters and their middle manager husbands can not readily access.

More often than not, the opening scene unfolds the same way. The arrival at the train station is hectic, as dozens of confused pilgrims clad in Bermudas and Easy Striders roll their suitcases off the train, mind the gap, skirt the row of taxis outside the front entrance and, map in hand, begin the fifteen minute walk up through the old town and toward the patchwork of thirty-nine different fiefdoms known as the colleges, which collectively constitutes the nearly nine-hundred-year-old university.

The clever sort might think it a subtle form of revenge the English were visiting upon the upstart colonists. India had long ago won independence. Nearly a decade had passed since the Royal Yacht Britannia set sail from Hong Kong Harbor. But the ghostly power of empire continues to cast its spell over the easily awestruck provincials, whose world of strip malls and on-line diplomas has not equipped them for daily encounters with inconvenient facts such as a cathedral that took a century to build or a cobblestone street that has known medieval moonlight. History has not yet been laid low. The past has not yet been subdued. Not in Oxford.

It is here, in this ancient university town, where Charles Stuart set up his court and sought sanctuary, fleeing the mobs of Roundheads who held sway in London, that this strange touristic phenomenon has most firmly taken root. For several years, the exiled king kept the righteous Huns at bay, but they eventually captured him and lopped off his head. Nearly half a millennium later, the middling have returned. The cheeky student of history might remark that this was inevitable, for there was business to finish. Merely a king had been killed; there remained a way of life to extinguish. These latest visitors have arrived to complete the task.

But something is different about these guests. That these are the children of ranters and levelers, tinkers and shopkeepers, none would deny. However, they hail from the states: desperate outposts like Texarkana and Scranton and Mobile. And though these summer program students might imagine themselves empowered with the prerogatives of the customer, such convictions are delusions. Subtler forces are at work in this exchange of goods. Usually broken, often divorced, invariably starved for meaning and a whiff of something authentic, these consumers yearn for order. Their earnest faces plead silently for something their vocabularies can't quite articulate but which an earlier age would have called *tradition*. They are dying to be subjected. And in June of 2006, one of the eager pilgrims found accommodation.

The students who arrived early for breakfast in Exeter College's Great Hall that morning were already trying to explain the unexpected appearance of police within the college grounds. All traffic between the chapel entrance, the college nurse, and Staircase 8 had been rerouted by the presence of neon orange construction cones. The door to the Middle Common Room had a sign on it that said it would be closed until further notice. A lone bobby was stationed discreetly just inside the chapel door, where a forensic pathologist had already set about his macabre duties. The occasional flash from a police photographer's camera illuminated the cavernous narthex as lightning a benighted landscape.

Though no students had been awake early enough to see the gurney wheel the corpse out to an ambulance waiting on Turl Street, a student out for a morning jog through Christ Church Meadow would later report having overheard a uniformed person refer to "removing the body," presumably a dead one and ostensibly to a morgue. But this knowledge was partial and incomplete. There was some speculation that the chapel might have been broken into because it had hosted a concert the previous evening, but it seemed agreed that the audience for a chamber quartet was unlikely to include a vandal. Though perplexed, most students nonetheless felt secure and were confident the police would sort the matter out. Even among the summer crowd, it was common knowledge the chapel was generally left unlocked; it was also well known that the Porter's Gate was bolted at midnight and closely monitored throughout the day and evening. The curious who disembarked from the red, double-deck tourist busses which endlessly circulated about Oxford, popping in for a quick look at the perfectly manicured quad, were greeted by the unapproving and watchful eye of the Porter, who brusquely turned them away and made them seek out the less closely guarded quad of Jesus College, just across the street.

Access to Exeter was tightly guarded; once gained, though, a degree of freedom reigned. Anonymity, however, did not. Four cameras scanned the grounds; one a piece at the Porter's Gate and the Steward's Gate (which seemed always to be locked), one that rotated slowly across the Front Quadrangle, and one with poor reception in Margary Quadrangle, separated from the Front Quad by the chapel, which extended out into a space that otherwise would have been the size of several tennis courts. Only the Fellows' Garden lacked such oversight, but it was perhaps the most difficult place to access in the college. In addition, any who crossed the Front Quad in the middle of the night fell within view of the Porter's post. Obsessively vigilante, the lanky Mr. Vere was a guardian of routine: he wore the same college blazer every day, drank from the same coffee mug, and vacated his window only when his bladder required him to do so. Physically, he was something of a caricature of English types. He could have stepped from a page of Dickens into a frame of Hitchcock without drawing attention to himself. He greeted each passerby, at seemingly all hours of the day, with a silent but courteous nod of the head. Though several of the American students had taken to calling him the Ichabod Crane of Oxford, all appreciated his presence and attention to detail. Not a single student could recall entering or leaving the grounds without encountering him or being cognizant of his gaze falling upon them. And yet strangely more than one late night reveler, returning in the early hours of the morning from a night of pints, swore to himself that as he passed the Porter's post he caught a glimpse of a distinguished figure—the Lord Mayor of London, the University Rector, a member of Blair's cabinet—through the lodge window. All were too embarrassed to make mention of these suspicions, fearing looking the fool. Nonetheless, the students' perception of Oxford as a place of spires and dreams overshadowed their ability to imagine it as anything other than a safe space, an impression that assured that the breakfast conversation would not dwell long on the activities that apparently had taken place in the chapel the previous evening.

"I guess we'll know something when someone does not show up for class," one early riser remarked to a table of classmates while gingerly setting a saucer and coffee cup down next to a plate of scones and easing herself onto the bench.

"Surely no one died. Maybe it was a heart attack or something. Most of the people at the concert were pretty old. A lot of locals."

"The police wouldn't still be here if it was just a heart attack, though."

"That's probably true."

"I bet something was stolen from the chapel. After the concert."

"Maybe."

"If that's the case, then you know Ichabod saw who it was. Nothing gets by him."

"That's definitely true."

"I'm not going to worry about it. We'll find out soon enough," Kathy resumed, focusing her attention back on her coffee cup, which a pimply teenage servant, in black slacks and a white blouse, had just refilled.

Somewhat uneasily, the four returned to eating their breakfast, an act that seemed to signal a general agreement between the four students at the table. Some one hundred students, the majority Americans, were enrolled in Exeter's first summer session. All attended the same morning lecture before breaking off into the smaller, specialized classes of their choice in the afternoon. Though all were generally pleased with the quality of the program, mealtime had quickly become as popular to the students as the classes themselves. Not even the mysterious events of the previous twelve hours could eclipse the pleasure of a scone or a good cup of coffee.

"So what's the lecture on today?" asked Tina, changing the subject. She was a middle-aged AP English teacher with twelve hours toward a Master's. She was extremely well-read on Dickinson and Whitman but had never been abroad before.

"Let's see," Jim answered, taking his program schedule out from his jeans pocket and unfolding it. "Tuesday, June 15. Here we go. 'Nigel St. Hubbins. Noted scholar of Elizabethan England, author of the Booker Award Finalist <u>Shakespeare's Wife's Dog</u>.' His lecture is titled 'The Secret History of Secret Histories.'"

"What? 'The Secret History of Secret Histories'? That's bizarre. What does that even mean?"

"That's it?" asked Kathy. "Is there any more information to go on?"

"None. Not a thing."

"I have a tough enough time with regular history, much less secret history," Kathy offered, a wry smile curling across her mouth before it opened to receive the remainder of a scone. "I wonder what it'll be about," she managed to add before swallowing.

"All I know," Parker said, while pouring a large amount of cream into his coffee, "is it's got to be better than the Marxist we listened to yesterday."

Jim nodded his head and smiled.

"And where is it?" Kathy cut in. "Is this one in the Sheldonian, too, or the lecture hall?"

"Let's see….It's in the…" Jim returned to the schedule again. "It's here at Exeter. The Quarrell Lecture Room. So we have an extra ten minutes. We don't have to walk across town."

"That's good. I still need to get my ticket to Stratford. Barry said if I didn't get it by noon they'd be sold out. Do you think I should run down to High Street and try to buy it now?"

"Probably so, if that's what Barry said. He should know."

 "Do I have time," she asked, looking at her watch.

"Yeah, if you hurry,"

 "But don't let Barry see you," Parker said, smiling smugly.

"You don't want to piss off Barry."

Tina had heard none of Kathy's dilemma. She was experiencing a moral crisis, contemplating skipping both the lecture and the Shakespeare performance in Stratford in order to go look at some crop circles she had Googled the previous evening. Barry was the furthest thing from her mind.

Yet she was very much on Barry's mind. Barry was the Program Assistant, an uptight Exeter undergrad who needed to remain in town during the summer in order to research Waugh and Forster. Though most of the students in the summer program assumed he was gay, he was not. He had taken the job on the advice of a fellow student who had worked the program the previous summer and claimed the opportunity to hook up with impressionable cougars was tremendous. Barry began the program a wealth of information on the local scene, providing directions to the nearest Boots, instructions on how to use the college computer lab, and advice for how to treat the deferential servants in the dining hall: though most of the American students initially felt awkward with the serving arrangements, by the fourth day of the program, hardly a one would have thought twice about sending back an overdone egg. This quick transformation—from embarrassed tourist to relentless guardian of propriety and standards—had been the only thing about the Americans that had impressed him. That and Tina's relatively well-preserved middle-aged figure, to which he had taken a fancy. By the end of the first week, though, his patience and desire to charm had worn thin. He was now entirely convinced that access to higher education should not be a right guaranteed to all. Parker had sensed the condescension in Barry's comportment, while most of the women in the group continued to find him charming if quirky. Kathy was oblivious to Parker's disdain and, apparently still ruminating on the events of the previous evening, returned to the matter of the police investigation being conducted not a stone's throw from their conversation.

"I was at the concert last night and didn't see anything unusual. Do you think someone could have had a stroke on the way out? Maybe it was a local. There were lots of old people there."

"I don't think it happened during the show. Or after it. I think the cops showed up in the middle of the night."

"Do you think someone broke into the chapel then? To steal something?"

"Isn't it usually unlocked?"

"I think so. It would be dumb if you tried, anyhow. You can't get anything by Ichabod," Jim repeated, repeating his remarks of a few minutes earlier while nodding at the dining hall's entrance, where the slender sentinel had suddenly appeared, apparently to refill his coffee. His hooded eyes scanned the tables while he refilled his mug, apparently taking mental inventory of all present at such an early hour. He left without saying a word to anyone.

"I don't mean to sound morbid or anything, but with all the ghosts that are supposed to haunt this place, it is kind of creepy. Have y'all heard about the ghost tour that is supposed to take you to every well known haunted place in town? Tracy was telling me about it."

"Between ghosts, the Inklings, Alice in Wonderland… there's a tour for just about everything."

"They know how to milk this atmosphere for everything it's worth."

"Anywhere you go, ghosts are always gonna be a cash cow."

"But especially here."

"Yes—especially here."

"Have you seen where the martyrs were burned to death? It's on Broad Street. Right in the middle of it. A stone 'X' set into the pavement. People walking by it—even on it—every day without knowing what they are doing. It's incredible."

"That was Cranmer, right?"

"Yep—walked right into the fire."

The simple statement brought their breakfast to a halt. They stopped to contemplate such an act. Each could imagine walking right into a Border's or a GAP. But not a fire. An uncomfortable silence settled upon the table. The anxiety was general. An unspoken accord seemed to require a change in the topic of conversation, or at the very least a lightening of its tone.

"Now that's a ghost story."

"I'm more interested in the kind of tour with ghosts and goblins. Chains rattling in the attic. Famous dead writers and stuff. Who'd you say went on that tour again, Tracy?"

"Yeah—she could tell you about it. When it leaves, where it goes. I think she said there's an information booth. It's on Broad Street, too, across from Blackwell's. It has brochures on all the tours. Ask Tracy, though, she has all the details."

"She's a character."

"No doubt."

"I saw her at the concert last night. She tried to get me to take pictures of everything afterwards. She wanted a shot of her with the cellist. Then one of her in front of the altar. She even wanted me to take one of her mugging with the statue in the entrance— like one of those shots you get in a booth at the fair."

They all chuckled. A plate was dropped at the head of the

hall, by the pastry table. It shattered and broke the warm hum of breakfast conversation among the two dozen students in the great hall. By the time they had all turned their heads to see what had happened, two servants were on the scene cleaning up the mess. A supervisor issued quiet commands as the attendants knelt before the table, then turned her attention and an icy glare to the offending party, a summer program student who, clearly embarrassed, was doing his best to contain a nervous smile as he continued down the line of scones and buns. They each registered the tension but said nothing, returning, in a few seconds, to their previous topic of conversation.

"She asked me about that yesterday, too. In the Porter's Lodge. She's a hoot. She actually asked Greg if she could get on his shoulders so she could put her arm around the statue as I took a picture. He declined, if you can imagine."

"Greg's the guy from Cleveland? With the moustache?"

"Yeah."

"I'm sure Ichabod would not have been pleased, either."

"Probably not a good idea."

"True. But I'll tell you what is a good idea—those double-deck busses. Tracy and I rode around in one of those on a tour. It was great, looking down on all the sights and people. You can eavesdrop on conversations at stoplights, just sort of hovering there above people. They're so used to the busses they forget you're there. At any rate, she's the one to ask about the tours. She's gotten me to go on a few with her. Last Saturday, we went to Christ Church, where they make the Harry Potters. The hall in Hogwarts—that's at Christ Church. It's amazing. And do you know they have their own clock tower there? I mean, it tells their own time. It's called Great Tom. I love the way they name things—Big Ben, Great Tom... Anyhow, it's a degree west of Greenwich, and that translates into something like ten minutes. So their clock strikes ten minutes later than the one in Greenwich, even though it's in the same time zone. Isn't that cute?"

"I don't know if it's cute, but it's something."

"Inefficient. Dangerous," Jim offered with a sarcastic grin.

"And don't forget just plain dumb," Parker interrupted.

"I know. I love it. So eccentric."

"That's the English."

"Now there's your 'salutary neglect,'" Parker smirked.

"Makes you wonder how they ever managed an empire," Jim mused, taking a final sip of coffee.

"Well, there's no doubt that's how they lost it," Parker concluded, leaning in to the table so that the servants passing by didn't hear. Tina was growing tired of Parker's cynicism. Kathy was entirely oblivious to it.

"Wait—now explain again why it rings ten minutes late."

"Well, I didn't get it all, but Tracy can explain it. She was taking notes. She should be down for breakfast soon. She always eats early," Tina offered, happily returning to her scone.

But Tracy would not be down for breakfast soon. At that very moment, Tracy was on a slab at the morgue.

While breakfast was winding down and the four students waited for the arrival of their friend, Detectives Bean and Mansel were making their way to the Porter's Lodge from the chapel. They had just surveyed the scene and taken several pages worth of notes, speaking with the one remaining member of the forensic team who was collecting the last bits of evidence. A young officer, newly minted from the academy, had recently arrived to tape off the premises and was turning away the curious.

Bean and Mansel found the Porter where they had been told they'd find him: in his office, his attention moving back and forth between the gate to the college, the window (which overlooked the Front Quad), and an old monitor which rotated the grainy images shot by each of the security cameras. The three engaged in a quiet conversation for a few minutes, during which time Bean did most of the talking. Finally, the Porter reached a bony finger out toward a nail on the wall, from which hung a large ring of keys. He then escorted the policemen out of the Lodge, making a right out of the doorway and then a left before the intensely green and closely cut lawn of the quad. Staircase 8 was the first doorway on the left. The wooden floors creaked as the three began their ascent up the narrow passage. At the top of the stairwell was a small landing upon which a cramped bathroom opened. The door was ajar, and Mansel peeked in. A toilet was somehow wedged between a sink and a wall. The gabled rooftop overhead cut into the full height of the room and would have required an average-sized adult to hunch over while shitting. Mansel's back tightened up at the mere thought of such an arrangement. On the south side of the landing was a solid oak door with a number 9 painted on its front. The Porter procured his dark iron ring, inserted a key, and with a sudden violent jerk, opened the way into the room. He stepped aside for the detectives, leaving the key in the lock as they entered.

They found the scene hardly extraordinary. Mansel himself had always wondered what a room at Oxford looked like, and as he entered the quarters he became half aware that his touristic curiosity was getting the better of his sense of professional duty. He was shaken back to the matter at hand by the brisk approach of his partner, who brushed by him on entering the room and immediately began a systematic study of the space. The Porter leaned silently against the threshold while Bean and Mansel went quietly about their work, Bean muttering occasional details to his partner while making a thorough investigation of the rooms. Both were oblivious to the Porter's presence and his careful attention to their observations. In fifteen minutes, their work would be complete. They would lock up the room, securing what they assumed was its only remaining key, deciding against sealing it off with police tape so as not to draw more attention to the room.

What they had found was not exceptional. The subject of their investigation knew no extravagances. The quarters were small and immaculately maintained. A small study looked out over the quad. It was in good order, appearing not to have been lived in. The tiny bedroom that was attached to the study overlooked cobblestoned Turl Street and neighboring Jesus College. It was equally well-kempt. Clothes hung neatly in the small wardrobe, one inch between each hanger. A toothbrush, toothpaste, and a hairbrush were precisely laid out on the counter of the small sink in the bedroom. The only unusual detail had been the content of the book satchel, which rested at the foot of the desk in the study. In it, they found a stack of <u>Cliff's Notes</u>, a laptop, and four DVDs, all movie versions of texts on the summer syllabus. The program novels themselves were still in her small suitcase, apparently untouched during the two weeks of her stay. Their stiff bindings and bare margins confessed they had seldom been opened. What had been opened, and literally read to pieces, was a set of <u>The Collected Tolkien</u>. Bean flipped through the pages of <u>The Silmarillion</u>, whose binding was in a state of decay and which was held together only by a green rubber band. He was impressed by the marginalia and underlining, which appeared on many pages in a variety of inks. He turned to the title page and found, in the handwriting of a junior high girl, the following: "Tracy Moore, 1971." He flipped to the table of contents and noticed that a middle-aged Tracy Moore had added a color-coded legend at the foot of the page. In green ink was written "2-94, The Journey." In red ink there appeared "8-99, see The Golden Bough" and beneath that, in blue ink "4-01, see Campbell."

Laid out on the desk was a map of the city and a brochure on a walking tour of the Inklings' favorite haunts. A half-dozen sites had been highlighted with a neon orange pen: the Kilns, the Eagle and Child, Christ Church Meadow, Pembroke College, St. Cross Church, the Lamb and Flag. A journal on the desk revealed the difficulty the deceased had encountered while trying to remain on the Atkins diet during her stay in Oxford, as well as an impressive assortment of notes on ghost tales she had rousted up from locals.

"Never ceases to amaze me what the Yanks find of interest," Bean finally said, flipping through the journal without bothering to sit at the desk's chair. "Even I haven't heard of half of these ghost stories. And I've lived here twenty years."

"Like what?"

"Well, let's see," he said, eyes scanning the journal and try-ing to decipher the handwriting. "You know of the ghost in the Eastgate?"

"The hotel?"

"Yes."

"He the one who roams the hallways? An armored sentry or something? From medieval times?"

"Yes."

"Heard of it."

"Did you know that the crossroads of Turl and Brasenose is the most haunted place in Oxfordshire?"

"I heard something like that once, though I'm not sure what it means. How do you measure that, anyhow? And isn't that near here, by the way? A block or so over?"

"Yes, it is."

"Now there's a cheerful thought."

"Well, how about this. It gets even better. There's apparently a headless specter who makes his home on Staircase 6."

"Headless specter—here? In Exeter?"

"Yes. Right across the quad, it looks. She even drew a little map of the college." His partner leaned in for a quick glance of inspection. The Porter smiled but said nothing.

"Bloody hell."

Bean continued, with the clinical interest of a pathologist. "You couldn't invent this shit. Not in a million years. Fascinating, really."

Mansel's silence suggested agreement. He had a habit of deferring to his older colleague, who had a degree from university. He looked at the map and found himself impressed by its detail and scale, for it resembled the proportions that he'd observed while working in the quad that morning.

"Look—there's the chapel," Bean pointed out, and then moving his forefinger along the map, "and here we are. Staircase 8." Mansel stared into the map, lost himself amid its intricacies, found himself roaming its dark hallways and peering into its corner rooms.

Bean continued: "Listen to this. It gets even better. Down at Magdalene—"

"Why do the Yanks come here for vacation?" Mansel uncharacteristically cut in, interrupting his superior after shaking himself free from the map. He was suddenly genuinely confused and almost indignant. "I mean, I know this place is beautiful and all, but there's so many good beaches in Florida. I'm dying to get there."

"Good question. The romance, I suppose."

"Romance? The beach is where there's romance."

"Well, wait till you hear this," Bean said, finally pulling the chair out to have a seat. He read on for several seconds in silence. "Christ, this is insane. According to this, one of the buildings at Magdalene was built on the site of a medieval hospital. Then, twenty or so years ago—back in '85 or '86—a student was awakened in her room in the middle the night and found herself surrounded by a half dozen monks, ready to operate on her. She ran screaming down the halls and woke everyone up. She withdrew from school the next day. And ended up being committed the next week."

"Jesus—that is insane."

They both shook their heads.

"Who records this stuff anyhow?" Mansel continued. "Doesn't she have anything better to do? She needs to get a life," he finally added, though in his heart he regretted the words even as he said them.

"She needs to get more than a life. She needs to get a man."

Mansel grunted in a sort of primitive affirmation.

"All these lonely old maids. We ought to tax the Yanks for shipping them over here for their silly summer school and getting themselves killed."

Mansel tried to chuckle a bit, and his partner, perhaps encouraged, continued.

"Did I tell you that last week I had to wait thirty minutes at Boots just to get my prescription refilled. Bloody half hour. Queue of Yanks getting pictures developed. And one towel-head, who argued with the chemist for about five minutes over the price of something."

His partner shook his head in a gesture of disbelief. The Porter observed in silence.

"But they buy our shit and hire out our coaches," Bean rolled on, unimpeded. "They're the reason why we can pay the bills. Maintain our old haunted castles. Our Queen mum. We're their fucking Disneyland, mate. Their haunted, fucking Disneyland."

Again Mansel shook his head, but this time with a combination of amusement and deep concern about what these words suggested about his homeland.

"One thing's certain," Bean said, finally closing the journal and standing up, "if you go looking for ghosts long enough, there's a good chance you might wind up one." The two were pleased with the sentence's polish; it seemed a good way to end their investigations into the room. In fact, they were so pleased that they did not notice the Porter had taken his leave with these words. As if on cue. Had they seen this, they might have observed a dark smile flash across the pale face for a moment as he turned and went silently down the staircase.

Bean and Mansel found their next appointment with no trouble. Jonathan Mims was exactly where he'd told the early response officers he would be after his initial questioning. He'd been allowed to return to his tiny office next to the undercroft as it was determined there was little chance of his leaving the premises unseen and likely no additional information he could give after his interview early that morning. Though it was clear, he had little formal education, his responses to their questions did not lack punch or firm opinion. Mims had definite beliefs.

"Mystery?! There's no mystery, mate. No real one. I've seen her sort for years. Since the summer programs began. There's been Yanks coming out of the woodwork ever since. For at least twenty years. Oxford's full of them in the summer. More Yanks than Brits come June."

Bean and Mansel nodded their heads in agreement with Mims. Regardless of one's feelings about this particular case, this point, at least, could not be contested.

"Strangers in the house, I say," he continued, shaking his head

and emitting something between a cough and a sigh. "There is
no England anymore, is there? I'm not a racialist, mind you, but
between the Yanks and the Pakis, the place is been overrun. There's
dark days ahead, mate. Dark days."

He paused again and stared off as if into a great distance.
As if he were a lone watchman, abandoned to face unfathomable
odds. Bean and Mansel took this moment to size up their charge.
If not for the knots and welts on his face, a quick glance at Mims
would have given one the impression of looking at a distant cousin
of Churchill. There was a similar shape to the enormous head. An
impression of grave responsibility was etched upon the face and
brow. Though short, Mims had thick wrists and hands and powerful shoulders. One could easily have imagined him a mason present
at the construction of Westminster or perhaps even an archer at
Agincourt. Except for the fact he was black.

"At least the Yanks go home," he continued, returning from
his imagined watch. "And they stand with us when there's a row.
They draw the easier lots, mind you. You won't hear of a Yank
flying missions like our boys in Afghanistan. But the Pakis…they
get on our councils. And they change things. They've never tried
to become British. They're quite clever, really. There's your tragedy.
But this woman, she's no tragedy. I don't mean she was a bad sort,
only that she got herself killed by rubbing on a statue. It's quite
odd, isn't it? Rubbing yourself, that way, I mean. And so the statue
fell on her. It's a shame, really. But there it is," he said, as if pointing to a hidden piece of evidence that resolved a great dilemma.
"So you see, there's no murderer roaming the streets. No headless specter. Just a lonely woman who read <u>The Hobbit</u> a time too
many. There's your mystery."

Mansel nodded his head again. If there was one thing he had
learned after years of observing tourists from the states, it was that
they loved magic and mystery. They'd find romance in a leaf of
grass if you'd let them. Though he and his partner found Mims's
words convincing, both left the interview knowing the chief would
want more to go on. A name, perhaps. A profile of a suspect at

the least. A specter would not due, of course, but neither would a woman rubbing herself off on a statue of a beloved author of children's tales. A villain would have to be found. A suspect with a dark past. A secret history. A summer industry was at stake. They needed a plausible story. The mystery would have to be laid bare. The case would require to be opened up as if it were a bit of clockwork, the gears and cogs labeled—the mechanisms explained—before a curious public. Only then could it be pronounced closed. Though neither Bean nor Mansel was sure exactly what had happened or how the investigation might be resolved, each had decided in his own mind what he'd have to do even before they had gotten back in their car. They would offer up, for the chief's consideration, Jonathan Mims.

And yet as they drove in their car back to the station, even Bean had to admit to himself that there was something mysterious about the events. Pathetic, yes—but mysterious nonetheless. The deceased's apparent devotion to Tolkien was irrational. And in some ways, the very crime scene itself defied reason.

What struck the two as most curious was what the evidence suggested about her final seconds, for she had apparently shimmied up the shaft that had for decades held the bust of Tolkien, himself a student at Exeter in the 1920s. Perched some eight feet above the floor of the narthex, the grim mask of the immortal author stared down upon all who entered the chilly space, a number which had markedly increased since the recent release of the successful films. It was a totem that had struck more than one tourist as a sort of gigantic Pez dispenser.

Mounting this pedestal was indeed a formidable undertaking. And yet, both Bean and Mansel felt there was perhaps something noble in the very idea of the effort. For this had been no easy feat for a fifty-year-old woman who was, by even conservative estimates, some sixty pounds overweight. It had been, as far as the two detectives were concerned, the herculean effort of one obsessed. The crowning, if bizarre, moment of a failed and disordered life.

All evidence suggested she had climbed to the top of the shaft—an effort that must have brought intense, perhaps even pleasurable, sensation—before the additional weight had rendered the object top heavy and sent it crashing down on her. Upon inspection, Bean determined that a pair of screws was apparently missing from a bracket at the base of the pedestal, though whether these would have secured the object was doubtful, and at any rate, it would have been virtually impossible to determine if the screws had been recently removed or forgotten upon the pedestal's installation some forty years ago. Regardless, the object fell. Tolkien's brass nose drove through her skull, whose backside had shattered like egg-shell upon the cold marble floor. Her teeth were knocked loose by the author's chin, scattered like die across table. Yet curiously, her thighs had not released their grip on the oak column. Not even in death. Forensic evidence recovered from the bust suggested her last moment had been spent kissing the eternal, lifeless brass lips.

But then she fell back to earth. She died on the instant.

Mansel could not sleep at all that night, and Bean did not sleep well. The next morning, neither one could articulate to themselves the cause of his insomnia. They were consumed with a feeling that resisted words and made them feel deeply uncomfortable. For-tunately, they were greeted at the station that morning with clear orders from the chief.

By ten o'clock that morning, the sun was shining brightly all across Oxford. The streets and walkways of the old town were filled with students and tourists and even some locals. Scattered throughout the medieval town, a dozen red busses were already belching their way down cobblestoned streets, and the cameras of a few hundred tourists were already clicking.

Bean and Mansel found Mims outside his office, repairing a switch box in the undercroft. He offered no resistance when hand-cuffed. He seemed either stunned into silence or long ago resigned to the idea that his life would inevitably take such a turn. Escorting the squat suspect out of the subterranean crypt and into the bright daylight, Mansel was thinking less about the person whose life he was about to irreversibly change and more about what Bean had written in the Cause of Death blank while filing his official paperwork: "Death by Oxford"—an answer that had amused his superiors but required he rewrite his report.

They both doubted the arrest would lead to a conviction. It would, however, provide a distraction and end speculation until the summer program was ended and the tourists had returned home or moved along to another amusement, perhaps one on the continent. The chief knew he had to stall, intuited that time and space were strong allies and that both were in his favor: that advocacy for a divorced, childless woman would be difficult to muster and maintain across an ocean. No less than George III had failed for similar reasons.

So Bean, Mansel and Mims made their way across the Front Quadrangle without a word between them. Had they chanced to glance through the open door of the chapel, they would have spied the wispy form of the Porter, barely visible in the shadowy vestibule. He appeared to be in conversation with a young tour guide, who was diligently scribbling notes in a pocket-sized journal. With the sweeping, deliberate gestures of a conductor, the pale figure seemed to trace the fall of the pedestal and mimic a final moment of terror. A casual observer might have thought that some sort of account was being drafted, or a petty conspiracy hatched.

In the Great Hall across the quad from the chapel, a small army of mute servants was setting out linens and silver and preparing for lunch. Just across the way, Barry had cornered Tina by the passage to the Fellows' Garden. Somewhat to his surprise, he found his advances greeted favorably. And in the tiny office next to the Porter's Lounge, the cleaning woman was busy dusting. She stopped for a moment to look at a curious object on the corner of the Porter's desk, behind a well-worn copy of <u>The Return of the King</u>: it was a small yellowish pebble that upon closer inspection could have been an animal's tooth. She set it back down next to two old, rusted screws, which she then examined. Apparently finding them useful, perhaps for a long-neglected household task, she took a quick look about her, swept them into a pocket of her apron, and continued her dusting. Beyond the walls of Exeter, hordes of students, with bags of trinkets purchased from High Street souvenir shops, scurried across cobblestone, for school was beginning. In classrooms and labs all over the medieval university, tutors were stifling yawns, clearing their throats, and shuffling their lecture notes.

In the midst of this activity, Bean and Mansel escorted Mims through the Porter's Gate. Their strides magically fell into step with the vaguely audible toll of Great Tom, whose time answered neither to Greenwich Mean nor to the immutable laws of physics, but only to Oxford itself. And for good reason. There were secret histories to recount, pilgrims to seduce, and a shadow empire to run.

Never No Inkling
Or, The Ever-present Danger of Praying a Lie

I was going to hell, I just knew it. I must have been the only guide in the history of ghost tours who'd never had a paranormal experience. I was a phony and a liar. Worse than that—I was a fraud. Of course, you'll do anything for a dollar in grad school— even risk perdition, apparently. The truth is the job wasn't something I had actively sought out. In fact, I kind of stumbled into it, though I guess I should have figured that of all places, Colonial Williamsburg would have been a hotbed for such activity. As it turned out, Carla had told me about the ghost tours, not a month into classes. My life would never be the same again.

"Dear, your TAship isn't enough to live on. Not in this town. Listen, everyone does them," *them* being the ghost tours and *dear* being her preferred means of addressing her fellow grad students even though she was half a foot shorter than me and maybe two or three years older, tops. It was just about the time I'd received my first batch of papers to grade, and I was beginning to feel like the exploited laborer all graduate students are. I was vulnerable to her sales pitch. "It's a good way to make extra money," she continued in earnest, her hand reaching out to momentarily touch mine in a sort of motherly fashion. Her fingernails had been painted black about a month previously and bore evidence of her chronic nail-biting. The rest of her hands were concealed by the fingerless, knit black gloves she wore each day. She was a strange amalgam of styles, a sort of Peppermint Patty goes Goth, complete with freckles, Birkenstock, and generous swathes of mascara that had the effect of funeral bunting. "It's the only way to make extra money in this town. And it's so convenient. But the best part about it," she said, lowering her voice as if on the verge of revealing some secret knowledge to which those outside the TA's universe must never have access, "the best part…is that the tour is yours—it's your own private class, your own captive audience."

Here she grabbed my hand again and pressed it firmly, as if channeling knowledge to me through her very touch. "It's a moveable feast, and you are the host! The teller of the tale. There is no gatekeeper." Her eyes watered and shimmered with excitement. I honestly thought she was about to lose herself in some weird moment of ecstasy. This was doubly uncomfortable for me because I barely knew her and because no one wants to see Peppermint Patty that way. Some things just aren't right. "It's history from the bottom up," she explained, finally collecting herself. "You alone are the author of the story. It's *guerilla history*, dear, and I think it's time you join the revolution. "

However awkward the scene was, her words appealed both to my curiosity and my frustrated sense of self-importance, especially because as a TA you are in control of so very little. Your advisor tells you what discussion group to lead and when to post office hours and then has the audacity to dump a batch of 50 papers on your desk every third week, expecting them returned within

48 hours. Your class schedule is restricted by your concentration and your social time is eliminated by the fact you have to read the equivalent of a Dickens novel each night to keep up with the workload. Sentenced to a book-laden limbo and the very good chance you might never know the peace of tenure, many once proud grad students succumb to the machinery of academia and drop out. In its own mysterious way, it's a dark satanic mill, a system geared to overwhelm the naïve and aspiring scholar, producing ABDs and not PhDs. Many gladly embrace this doom, wandering the halls of academia teaching entry level history surveys to business majors until decades pass and a lukewarm retirement party is thrown that not even half the professors in the department bother to attend as the long-suffering instructor is gently ushered out to pasture. I had an aunt who'd been teaching freshman rhetoric at Emory for thirty years—I knew this could happen. So the idea of immediately having the chance to author my very own guerrilla history, as Carla phrased it, excited me.

Implied, too, in Carla's secret knowledge was the promise of fellowship with select grad students. In hindsight, I think this appealed to me perhaps most. For in an instant, I conceived the invite was one not extended to all the other first years. It was the thrill equivalent, I imagined, to the one the former cheerleader experiences when receiving the bid to join her desired sorority. The fact that Carla, president of the History Department's Graduate Student Association, had recommended me—a lonely first year—to become a tour guide had to mean something. Apparently, I'd passed some sort of test, it seemed, and was poised to become an initiate. Don't get me wrong, I loved the idea of being a rebel historian—of sticking it to The Man and fighting the power—but what I became half-aware of at that moment was that what I really wanted most in the world was what Carla seemed to promise: membership in a tribe, and few tribes are as narrow and difficult to crack as the world of graduate students. When you grow up the nerdy, only child of a divorced mother in Huntsville, Texas, are the only girl in your high school's BC Calc Class, and love Jane Austen more than Miranda Lambert, you jump at the chance for community. So not more than a month into grad school, I was ready to join this exclusive club, thumbing my nose at the establishment in the process, provided it didn't offend Carla, who'd sort of turned out to be my well-meaning, if severe, guardian angel. What I did not realize at the time, though, was that the 21st-century establishment was more likely to be a lesbian from Vermont in a Subaru than a WASP from Greenwich in tweed. And it was every bit as oppressive. Meet the new boss—lame as the old boss.

At any rate, Carla had barely released my hand when I had already begun to imagine myself giving a tour in a beret and Doc Martins, GI Jane style. What Carla had promised was, very literally, history from the ground up—from the grave up, actually—and nothing is as subversive or democratic as the grave, for it overthrows everyone. There, royal governors and widows, planters and slaves, were all equally worm-eaten. Through the magic of the ghost tours, I wouldn't have to wait for some process as arbitrary and loaded as tenure to start producing history. I could more or less throw up a shingle, post on Facebook, and get to work. Of course, not literally anyone could do it. The Board of Overseers had to approve, but the college's history department was in good with the Board, and all tacitly agreed that the nightly tours were just another way to wring revenue from the restored colonial village. The hours were undeniably terrible—no professor wanted to work 10:00-midnight twice a week—but a grad student in need of grocery money would jump at the chance. At the end of the day, I figured it was just another way for the company to sell bandwidth after hours.

It actually surprised me how quickly I justified my actions to myself. In a matter of days, I had worked out an elaborate backstory for my charade, claiming that as I was exploited during the daylight hours—paid peanuts to TA in a system geared to cultivate a sort of learned helplessness, producing perpetual grad students and ultimately customers for shrinks—I had a right to defy The Man in all his many guises: administrators, professors, Board of Overseers. They might rule college and classroom, select the textbooks and govern the historic district. But I owned the night. Lucky for me, the Ghost Tour Industry is even less regulated than Wall Street.

If I were to be totally honest, I must confess that in those early weeks on the job I dealt pretty fast and loose with history, as did my colleagues. Not that I neglected my research. Under Carla's guidance, I dug through colonial deeds and wills and church records, uncovered letters and diaries from the 18th century onward, scoured newspaper clippings from the distant past on into the present. All in an effort to identify intriguing candidates for ghosthood: "stories with a hook," as Carla was fond of putting it. What she meant, though, was "stories that would sell." Early in the course of my training, which consisted of following her around on tour for a few nights and then listening to her pontificate about research one evening at a local watering hole, she imparted to me the industry standard: each tour should relay the ghost stories of at least one woman, one slave or servant, and one ward of the state or beneficiary of the almshouse. The presence of such poltergeists did not need to be verified, she added, merely confirmed as reasonable conjecture. The deceased had to have been an actual person who once lived in the area, and reference to them had to be skillfully woven into one's script, preferably with one of the stock phrases Carla herself had signed off on: "some are sure these noises are the work of______," "locals apparently maintain that ______," "the reasonable would not be amiss in imagining that ________." Her attention to rhetoric was sophisticated, contained a scholarly ambiguity that would be difficult to prosecute. In short, she taught me how to say things without saying things.

Though I sensed she favored me over the other young recruits, saw in me a sort of protégé, we all received the same strict instructions not to color our commentary with a value judgment about the ghost's former life—under no conditions were we to explain why they were denied eternal rest and thus doomed to walk the night. Carla was firm in explaining that we did not want relatives of the ghost "lawyering up" over charges of slander. She even hinted that she'd once been deposed over just such a matter, though none of the other guides knew the specifics.

Even though I was from a small East Texas town, new to grad school, and overwhelmed by the workload, I was attuned to the ideological color she was imparting to the tours. A part of me was afraid to object. I'd seen Carla break down more than one grad student whose tours did not meet the criteria, guides who had loitered with their customers at Peyton Randolph's house or the Royal Governor's garden instead of taking them to the gaol or servants' quarters. And though I've always been pretty much between the forty yard lines when it comes to politics, I figured out soon enough it was wise not to share this publicly. Not in grad school. Carla could be brutal when it suited her—it was not a pretty sight. Though I tended to find the Randolph and Wythe houses the most interesting, I resisted the inclination to linger there in my tours. Eventually, I came to view the tours more as performance art than scholarship, anyway. And if my colleagues too often drifted into polemic, and encouraged me to do so, I reminded myself that my goal was less to resurrect the life of a downtrodden gardener or forgotten blacksmith than to rout anything supernatural from its hiding place, forcing it to reveal its mystery, if only as an angry rebuke to the absurdity of my tour. I had my own reasons for such spiritual aspirations, reasons which I will explain later. All that need be said now is that I sought neither historical accuracy nor retribution for past wrongs: I sought money for rent and, hopefully, vague confirmation of a beyond. But I would soon learn that the beyond answers to no one.

Still, I must confess that more than once I awoke in the middle of the night, fearful that I had betrayed the sacred duty of the historian and would be visited by the avenging shade of Von Ranke, Lord Acton, or even Thucydides himself. At these moments, a very real fear gripped me, revealed to me that though the system had indeed exploited me, it was I who was now exploiting the dead, fashioning a new sort of supernatural servitude, enslaving ghosts to do my bidding, transforming the deceased into a sort of commodity in service of an ideology, and glorifying myself in the process.

If I sound a bit confused or perhaps even resentful, I apologize. I have no right to feel that way. I made the decisions of my own free will. No one put a gun to my head to go to grad school or start giving tours, and the truth is mine was and is a topnotch school with a great history program. The support they offer graduate students is better than most. Yet there were surprises to living in Williamsburg, including a dearth of adolescents from wealthy families in need of tutoring or SAT prep classes, a source of income large metropolitan areas inadvertently provide their grad students. Some academics would no doubt be shocked to learn of Williamsburg's ghost tour phenomenon—Cambridge, Berkeley, and Princeton have no equivalent industry. But anyone with knowledge of Virginia knows the peculiarities of the state, is aware that something strange happens to it just north of Richmond. Somewhere along a mysterious latitude, no one knows the exact location, C-SPAN gives way to NASCAR, and guns and ghosts become viable industries and even respectable dinner talk. This isn't mentioned on the school web page or in the brochures they hand out at college fairs. But it is true nonetheless. So what would be laughed out of the board rooms of Fairfax or the parlors of Georgetown might be treated quite seriously 80 miles and a hundred and fifty years to the south.

Overall, my professors were very good, and their work was of high quality, even if I found myself disagreeing with some of its political bent. I must say I enjoyed my classes and learned a lot. The hidden benefits of the TAship weren't bad, either—it provided me insurance, including dental. I also got to intern at the <u>Quarterly</u>, one of the best colonial journals around, as well as spend 3 weeks each summer on an archaeological dig at Jamestown, which made it all worthwhile. But the monthly stipend didn't provide much in the way of money—archaeological digs, no matter how much fun, don't buy toothpaste.

What the outside world of muggles fails to realize is that grad students, though generally passive and unassuming, are by nature drawn to the margins and all things subversive. They wouldn't be in grad school if they weren't. They usually seek to create, and if possible inhabit, fantastic realms far from reality. In this manner they are self-selected exiles, and a grad student who moonlights as a ghost tour guide is the exile of exiles. A sort of fifth column only apparently aligned with the professors and institution. Through the help of Carla, I learned a whole different way of being in those first few months. Soon enough, I knew what sources to cite in discussions (yes to Howard Zinn and a resounding no to David McCullough), what indie bands to reference over lunch (Vampire Weekend somehow established immediate street cred), and what spots in town to avoid (Bruton Parish Church and its Cemetery—eternal resting place of colonial founders—were universally scorned and deemed unfit for all but right-wing elitists and the most vulgar, bourgeois tourists). Armed with such knowledge, I could bear to wake up each morning and face the day knowing that I was fighting the good fight in my own clandestine way.

I must confess, however, that the general condemnation of Bruton Parish somewhat deflated me—it had been my preferred place of reflection during my first lonely weeks on campus, and the one spot I had enjoyed visiting with my mother when she had helped me move in. Such moments of shared enjoyment had been few in our relationship over the years. Regardless, I knew immediately that if the parish church had to go in order to secure me a place in the community of tour guides, then go it must. Thus was I transformed: a paper grading automaton by day, I underwent a startling metamorphoses at night, changing into a sort of Buffie the Establishment Slayer armed with a pen and tour script, channeling the stories and voices of the dead in order to lay claim to a Revolution and, ultimately, the future.

The only problem—and it was a big problem—was that I'd never been visited.

❧

The truth of the matter was my fascination with ghosts and the underworld began much earlier, when my parents divorced and my grandparents died in the same year. The same month, actually. Mimi and Pawpaw had been coming to spend Thanksgiving with mom and me after dad had run off with his secretary, but they never made it. They got sideswiped by an eighteen wheeler just outside of Nacogdoches. Mom was in a state of shock. She still is. She pulled herself together enough by Christmas to decide that what was needed was a vacation, and the only one she could afford was a New Year's weekend in Galveston. Her intentions had been noble: to distract her 13-year-old daughter from an awful start to junior high and the orthodontic work she'd just learned would have to be extended another year. The plan was to stay at a Days Inn for two nights, touring Moody Gardens and the Pleasure Pier by day. Mom had even saved up enough money to treat us to lunch at the Galvez, a grand turn-of-the-century hotel overlooking the Gulf. It didn't take me long to figure out that this holiday gift was only an elaborate attempt to distract me from the void that had opened up in my life. And hers.

We had not been in the lobby of the old hotel more than ten minutes—mom peppering the concierge with questions about tourist sites, the weather, restaurants—when I told her I needed to use the restroom and wandered off while she tried to flag down the waiter to order another hot toddy from the beautifully restored bar. I'd seen a group of eccentric, disheveled people gather around a short, plump Creole woman at the far side of the lobby, near a collection of ancient white wicker furniture. Sensing kindred spirits, I went to investigate. This woman turned out to be the guide for a ghost tour, a wielder of mysterious and unimaginable power. She was much shorter than I, but she spoke with an earnest energy usually reserved for the pulpit. The Galvez nametag she wore identified her as "Miss Cleo." I was charmed by the combination of her awkward delivery and the absolute confidence she had in the importance of what she was doing. I had been standing on the outskirt of the little group no longer than a half minute when I heard her speak the words that irrevocably altered the course of my life, three magical words that still boggle my mind: "haunted toilet stall."

It was inspired—I knew it even then as the precocious, little foreign-film-loving teenager that I was! Her words were charged with a mysterious power: *ironic, absurd, banal.* Ironically, absurdly banal! The words were a game changer. Hers was a coinage worthy of a Beckett or a Bergman—but only a Beckett or Bergman at the very top of their games. I doubted the three words had ever before been lined up just so in all of history. It was an immortal line uttered by what turned out to be a lovable, touchingly incompetent ghost tour guide. Even my tender ears realized the unique moment in human history to which they'd been made a witness. I'd heard the magic spell and was now an accomplice, a co-conspirator. I knew at that instant—was confident beyond all reasonable doubt—that I'd been chosen for a special and high destiny, one which I could not then avoid.

"Without further ado, ladies and gentlemen," she said, as genially as any rosy-cheeked cherub, "please follow me to the haunted toilet stall." Miss Cleo's words forever cut the tether from my past. I looked back over my shoulder only once before beginning the tour, catching sight of my mother, now at the bar, beginning a flirtation with the bartender that she no doubt hoped was sufficiently disguised as a sort of innocent inquiry about the best ice cream parlor on the seawall. Then I was gone—off on a journey with Miss Cleo and the dozen or so misfits on the ghost tour. Walking down the loggia toward the grand ballroom, I felt oddly at home with this new cast of characters. Their incompetence and complete ignorance in the face of the supernatural endeared them to me, for I had always felt similarly given my mother's preternatural conversion experience—an altar call that she'd answered when only nine during an Eisenhower era revival in a tent outside Tyler. She ended up convinced that this had pushed dad away, but I think that was letting him off the hook too easily. Regardless, I was the first in three generations of the Beaufort family to reach the teenage years without experiencing some similar conversion, a point that more than a few relatives had brought to my attention at holiday parties through the years. Miss Cleo seemed to offer me some sort of escape from this burden, or perhaps a final chance at initiation, an invitation to join the long, distinguished Beaufort line. It was an offer I could not refuse.

When she brought the motley assemblage to a halt before an enormous black and white photograph halfway down the concourse, I was just sure this was exactly where I belonged. "If you look closely here, ladies and gentlemen," she said, "you will see an ordinary picture of the hotel lobby. It was taken in 1919. Some of the furniture remains the same," she said, sweeping her hand out before the crowd and nodding at the wicker sofas and coffee tables that lined the each side of the lobby. "But if you look closer, you can see a ghost and orbs." Here, she again pointed at the photograph, and the audience leaned in for a closer look, emitting a sort of collective, affirmative "ahhhh." "There is lots of energy in this part of the hotel," Miss Cleo said, pulling out her iPhone and holding it out in front of her in the palm of her hand. Apparently, Miss Cleo had logged onto some sort of ghost-detection app. She looked intensely at her phone while turning it to and fro, as if it were a sort of divining rod. Every few seconds, her long painted nails glanced across the touch-screen. The audience began frantically snapping pictures of the photograph, the hallway, the lobby. "I am getting lots of energy now. If you see lots of orbs in your pictures," she said with a sincerity theretofore unknown to me, "it means there are ghosts present. Orbs are ghosts," she said, clarifying the matter for us as easily as a middle school science teacher might say that hydrogen and oxygen combine to make water. "Later in the tour, I'll interpret for you what the ghosts are saying," she confided to our relieved ears. "Oh, boy. I am getting lots of energy now…" she said excitedly. A general stir among the audience suggested that the feeling was shared, that a sort of community had formed.

"I am, too," a man suddenly said as he stepped forward, confirming our guide's evaluation with a confidence usually reserved for thirty-something surgeons and teenage quarterbacks. "I worked a soundboard for Kenny Chesney for years, and I know my way around electrical frequencies and static. My phone's hot. It'd like to leap out of my hands it's so hot. I was in San Antonio last week, and I can say without a doubt that there's more activity here than at the Alamo." This brought great pleasure to the ears of all on the tour, and again a satisfied stir rose among them. They nodded their heads approvingly and made gestures and noises of appreciation for their guide's expertise, convinced they were getting their money's worth.

After nearly a half minute of camera flashes and anxious giggles, the tour moved along. Everyone, that is, except for two fat, pasty-skinned, middle-aged women, who lingered in front of the 1919 photograph, as if waiting for the crowd to be out of earshot before sharing their thoughts. I do not know why, but I very consciously chose to hover behind them, so silent that they could not sense my presence.

"I don't see what she was talking about. Where is it?" The heavier one in a support girdle pointed at the picture in the general direction of where the shade was supposed to be visible, reclining on one of the wicker sofas in the lobby. "All I see is something that looks like"— the lady looked to her right and left and then lowered her voice, aware of the absurdity of the words she was about to utter—"like a dinosaur… This place couldn't be haunted by a dinosaur, could it?" she asked almost desperately, wanting so badly to affirm some sort of supernatural experience and thereby belong to the magic circle of believers that had already left her behind.

But her concern was no less absurd than the account being offered by Miss Cleo, who had walked another twenty yards before turning around to take an inventory of her audience. Only then did she notice the three of us loitering well behind the group. "Right this way, ladies. The haunted toilet stall is just around the corner. You don't want to miss the haunted toilet stall now, do you?" she said smiling and with such good will that no one wanted to disappoint her. In no time the group had returned to its complete numbers and amorphous shape. Though Miss Cleo never once explained what the made the stall haunted, it did not matter. Her calming smile brought us all to attention, suggested that we were on the verge of the tour's climactic moment.

She knocked gently on the bathroom door, soft enough to get the attention, but not disrupt the movement, of someone within. No one answered. She turned to her expectant audience, smiled, and pushed the door slightly open. In a polite, even tender voice, she said: "Hello, it's Miss Cleo. From Galvez Ghost Tours... I am leading a Ghost Tour right now. Is anyone home?" She turned to face us again. "I just want to make sure none of our guests is using the potty." Again there was silence. Satisfied that the bathroom was vacant of human activity, she held the door open with one arm and with the other, ushered us in with a graceful and practiced sweeping motion. "Wait there," she said, nodding toward the first of three brass sink fixtures mounted above a counter of dark green marble.

Like pilgrims at a shrine, our group silently entered the restroom in a long single-file line. The space was vaulted and unexpectedly large, cool as a seaside grotto or a Roman catacomb. Using her tiny foot to skillfully wedge a triangular wooden block into the gap beneath the door, she repositioned herself in front of the furthest stall door. As her congregation assembled and became silent before her, she extended her left arm and opened the stall door, keeping her eyes fixed on the visitor at the front of the line. Though I was about 10 persons back, it did seem as if a cool breeze rushed forth from the stall, and a light too, brightening the entire room though I can not begin to say how. Each tourist stepped quietly to the threshold of the portal. Incredibly, not one took a picture or referenced a ghost app—even these uninitiated vulgarians seemed to recognize a moment too sacred and intimate to digitize. And as each confirmand stood before the haunted toilet stall in silent adoration, Miss Cleo whispered some vague, apparently scripted remarks on the supernatural, not unlike a priest will do when dispensing the host. The tourists were unsure how to respond before such a space. A few tried to cross themselves, and one even knelt, though it was clear from the bungled nature of the gestures that such actions were foreign to the low church tradition into which they'd been born and which they had long since dismissed.

Though I have always been good at feigning nonchalance and indifference—it had been my defense mechanism for dealing with the jeers of classmates who mocked my love of <u>Pride and Prejudice</u>—I, too, began to feel anxious as I approached the magical door. I realized in the seconds before consummation that this moment would mean much more than my having ticked off the "ghost tour" box on my teenage ironist's bucket list. It would likely signal my full membership into the Beaufort clan—a moment for which I'd secretly prayed for years. I was about to have my very own awakening, one every bit as remarkable as my mom's prepubescent altar call. After thirteen years, I would have my very own conversion experience.

I could have reached out and touched Miss Cleo's hair extensions with my hand when I finally did indeed receive my very own religious awakening. But it did not come from the haunted toilet stall. It did not come from the energy emanating from the porcelain portal or the genial, superhuman optimism of Miss Cleo. It came to me from my mother, who had stormed into the bathroom like an avenging fury, screaming in a voice so loud that it dropped half the tourists to a knee. The other half dropped out of fear that this was the very ghost of the haunted toilet stall itself and not some half drunk, recently divorced, and tragically orphaned mother of one of the tourists. Even Miss Cleo herself was stunned—I can still hear the clickety-click of her tiny high heels as she backpedaled into the stall and landed ass-first in the haunted toilet. Mom had grabbed my hand and yanked me away from my moment of redemption, damning everyone to "high hell" for corrupting her baby with such "occult shenanigans" and "pagan nonsense," clearly forgetting that five minutes earlier she had been hitting on a bartender half her age. She dragged me down the loggia and into the lobby, whose occupants had heard the cacophony and were now as silent and motionless as the figures in the very photographs on the walls, framed antiques commemorating the hotel's grand opening a century before.

She shoved aside the doorman and horrified the concierge with a glance that promised unfathomable violence and stormed across the fifty yards of palm tree lined front lawn, somehow avoiding the midday traffic on the boulevard, out to our car parked on the seawall, where she'd been lucky to find a space not a half hour earlier. We returned to our Days Inn. Not a word passed between us until about 5:00 pm, when she said "Come on." She stuffed all of our belongings into our duffle, left two twenty dollar bills and a hastily scribbled note on the dresser (apparently payment for the room), drove through the Wendy's drive-in to get us a couple of Doubles, and headed home. We were back in Huntsville by 8:00 pm. After a few weeks of hooky, Mom resumed attending church. I did not. To her credit, she would never force me to do so.

A decade had passed since I'd been snatched away from my seaside conversion. Much of the intervening time was spent navigating the travails of the junior high and high school social scenes. Every once in a while, I'd be reminded of the haunted toilet stall and my close encounter with the beyond. Alas, the life of a teenager has immediate demands, and soon way led on to way. But as a grad student of twenty-three living in a town literally brimming with reports of the supernatural, I secretly became determined once more, in some shape or fashion, to get the ghost. But in the anxiety created by my hunger for something authentic and sublime, the exhaustive schedule of the program eventually took its toll, breaking down my circumspect nature. During dinner at a Thai restaurant with Carla and a group of ABDs that involved several too many beers, I became uncharacteristically free with my personal history and spilled the details around my grandparents' death and the aborted weekend in Galveston. I was unaware of it at the time, but the miscue served me well. I soon noticed that my fellow tour guides were deferring to me on all matters involving death, ectoplasm, and poltergeists. I had not meant to mislead them, imply that I had been visited by the beyond, but at the same time I relished my newfound prestige. I did not fully appreciate the scope of my power until one night when Carla had invited herself over to watch an old Teaching Company DVD on Foucault, which she'd just bought on eBay. I'd gone to the kitchen to get snacks and Diet Cokes, and when I returned to the living room, I caught Carla clutching the photo of my grandparents, tears in her eyes. She quickly put it back on the mantel as she heard my approach, and I acted as if I had dropped a sleeve of rice cakes and organic honey on the floor to provide her cover. I don't think she wanted me to know her great secret: that she was in love with my sadness. I could tell by the turn our conversation took that night that she was certain I had a sense for the supernatural. That I was a portal. That I was chosen.

Of course, the topic never came up when I was on the job, as most tourists also assumed I was initiated into the priesthood and had a wealth of experience with the occult. This was surprising to me at first as I expected most of the tourists were either history minors or period buffs and would want to call out the claims of the guide. Though this description was assuredly the case with the tourists who walked Duke of Gloucester Street during the daylight hours, this was decidedly not the case for those on the evening ghost tours. These attracted a unique clientele. A few were Blue Ridge riff-raff who wandered down from their trailer park meth labs to take in nightlife in the big city. A fair number were either drunk students from the nearby junior college or young parents who had spent the day at the local Busch Gardens amusement park and were trying to ease their conscience about wasting a day in such close proximity to Williamsburg, justifying the expense of rollercoaster and cotton candy by getting the kids a quick dose of history in the form of a ghost tour. Oh, a few were bonafide ghost aficionados, Haunted Highway junkies with the bogus thermal imagers to show for it. Overall, though, I would happily wager that there were more GEDs than real diplomas on each tour, and more tatts than either. It was not a hard crowd to impress, though it was a hard crowd to shepherd through the narrow colonial passages without having one, intentionally or not, wander off in pursuit of some supernatural moment.

But I digress, and so the tours rolled on, and with them, my new shadow career. Rain or shine. Soon enough, I began to prove to be invaluable to the venture, and no contribution to the cause better demonstrated my potential worth than a marketing ploy I dreamt up after I'd watched Carla relentlessly Google her name one evening between tours to see which references to her popped up first. My idea was simple: to commandeer a school computer lab for one afternoon a week and establish a "Click Farm" to move our ghost tours up in the hierarchy of search engine results. We had extra money from a grant, and I proposed that we use it to secure the lab and pay undergrad history majors to hit "Like" on our Facebook page and endlessly Google "Bold Dominion Ghost Tours" in order to overwhelm our competition. Although Carla ultimately chose not to seek the Board's permission to set into motion my plan, her unspoken reaction suggested to me that she approved of my commercial instincts. My value rose and my high standing was finally secured by a plan that actually did reach fruition. One morning in late October, in preparation for the Halloween rush, I typed up what I called a Fright Waiver and suggested we have all customers sign it before going on the tour. It released our venture from responsibility in case the tourist had a cardiac response to our tour or injured her/himself while physically reacting to an encounter from the beyond. The waiver seemed to give us a level of grittiness and street cred that the other tours lacked, and this was especially appealing to the Halloween crowds. Carla ran the waiver by a friend of hers in law school, who added the necessary legalese. The results were incredible. Ticket sales shot through the roof that season. Carla loved it, and the Overseers seemed to approve, as well. Yet I was not satisfied. For I was still living a lie.

What made the lie even worse was that it seemed practically everyone in Williamsburg had seen a ghost at some point. It's not like I was aspiring to some rarefied air. Even skeptics claimed to have seen them. I even knew an atheist psych student, a girl from Portland in my yoga class, who claimed she'd seen a ghost. I didn't think that was possible, but she swore on it. When I pointed out the contradiction between her claim and her beliefs she scoffed at me and called me a "right-wing Texas freak" and told me to "go to hell"—which, as she turned away to storm off, was a place I told her she technically could not believe in as she was an atheist. This did not go over well, and the matter was only settled when Carla intervened, grabbing me by the shoulder just in time to guarantee that the punch I had thrown at the smart ass's face would sail wide and miss its mark. Perhaps ironically, this incident only added to my clout—I was now perceived both as an expert on ectoplasm and as one who would crack the skulls of unbelievers in order to spread the good word. This may have won me the attention of my peers, but the ghosts remained unimpressed.

For in those parts, pretty much everyone had seen a tri-corner hat float above a mantle or a young girl in a hoop skirt disappear through a tavern wall. But not to have seen such a thing…that could cause problems. I recognized this early on. To allay any suspicions regarding my credentials or morbid fascinations, I'd collected rubbings from the gravestones of my favorite colonial figures, a hobby which I'd read about in a <u>Southern Homes and Gardens</u> issue, placing them around my study carrel as decorations. I even clipped a sprig of ivy from the house of Edgar Allen Poe during a visit to Richmond one Thanksgiving. I kept it in a pot near my coffee maker. It was a good conversation piece. At the same time, I took down from my fridge the postcard of Bruton Parish Cemetery that mom had sent me so as not to have any fellow students think I was a vulgar or shallow "brute," as they called such tourist types. Nor did I ever mention to my fellow students that I'd still go there late at night to think or listen to my iPod. This habit remained secret. Even with these efforts, or perhaps because of them, it was apparent to me that I was probably the sorriest ghost tour guide in history. It was depressing, but I soldiered on.

Though I had technically never been told you had to have

had a paranormal experience to be a guide, I was pretty sure that was implied in the job's expectations. I never actually lied to anyone about it—neither to tourists or my colleagues. But I actively orchestrated the misinterpretation. I played the part. And the charade was elaborate. Even my prayers, on the rare occasion I prayed, assumed a different tone than those I'd grown up hearing in the First Baptist Church of Huntsville, where my grandfather Beaufort had been the preacher as had his father before him. Alone at night, I realized that my most intimate hopes and dreams had become performances, exercises in mimicry—though my hopes were those of a confused twenty-three-year-old, my words and prayers were those of the High Church, whose records I'd been digging through assiduously for my research on the burial practices of the children of 17th century royal governors. "Oh, Lord, make speed to save us! In your mercy, hear us! In your love, remake us!" Then onto my knees I'd drop and plead: "How long, Lord? How long? If it be your will that I see, then so let it be. And if not, then teach me another witness…. I humbly accept your decision. Thy will, Lord, not mine. Thy will." But all the while inside, I was jealous and angry that I'd not been chosen for a visit. The truth was that it wasn't anything big I was hoping for. I would have been perfectly happy just to hear a deadbolt inexplicably drop into place, see a whale tooth comb nudged a smidgen across a dresser top. I didn't need the big Hollywood moment—had no desire to feel the cool presence of a poltergeist sucking energy out of a damp hallway, have a conversation with the shade of a poet or be taken captive by a chain rattling ghost as it flew me across the rooftops of the 18th century village to reveal the future to me. No, my hopes were simple. All things considered, I thought my prayers were quite reasonable.

Only once, though, did I get really desperate and suffer something of a breakdown. Sometime during the fall of my third year, I jerry-rigged a séance and tried to summon the presence of the person I'd have become if I had seen a ghost, but even this shade wanted nothing to do with me and refused my summons. I was unworthy. The truth is I couldn't blame this other, better me. What self-respecting ghost would want to haunt an ABD with psoriasis and $120,000 of debt? Not when there's a Shirley McClain to visit. I imagine even pretend ghosts have their standards. Which is all to say that by that time, I had begun to develop a contempt for Williamsburg, for the tours, for the past, and for all things supernatural, in general—not a healthy attribute for someone in my line of work. Yet incredibly, this contempt would eventually midwife my newfound confidence as a guide.

You see, I finally I came to appreciate the fact that for a few hours each Tuesday and Thursday night, I was accorded something of the celebrity power of a televangelist, only for the spiritually impoverished and new age, those children of the Boomers that sociologists loved to call the "None"'s for the box they check on religious affiliation. It was bizarre—I ended up genuinely feeling responsible for the moral and spiritual development of the tourists who gathered outside the King's Arms tavern for my 10:00 pm tour. Most bizarre was the fact that I actually *was* responsible for their moral and spiritual development. The vast majority hadn't darkened the doorway of a church in the better part of a decade and had forgotten all the stories they'd learned in Sunday school before their own parents got divorced, disillusioned, or just stopped attending. The ghost tour demographic is a strange one, neglected by campaign number crunchers and generally possessed of little spending power, political influence, or public voice. Yet this was my flock. I was determined to be their pastor for a single, one-hour period in their lives. They would be my lambs—these high school dropouts, children of divorce, and video game junkies. Not a one of them had even the vaguest notion of religious doctrine, official church positions on the afterlife or even the basics of what the Greeks or Romans had believed. Their own beliefs were a bland mishmash, a patchwork of snippets stitched together from childhood VBS programs, SyFy's Ghost Hunters, the Sixth Sense, and the latest Dan Brown novel. Lapsed Adventists, skeptical fundamentalists, collectors of crystals, runaway trans-genders, angst-ridden spawn of Appalachian Pentecostals, people for whom some vague and undifferentiated afterlife were the norm. Every once in a while, a regular family—one with a mom and dad and a few kids—would appear in the mix, and they would usually take a look around them and wonder what in the hell they'd gotten themselves into. Once or twice, I wondered the same thing myself.

I let none of these concerns interfere with my hospitality, and I made sure all felt welcome, and I soon began to relish the power, indulging in theatrics and going so far as to skip class to rework my script or practice my delivery. I felt like the Dauphin from Huck Finn, only I was actually both the Dauphin *and* Huck. This double-sense couldn't stop me. I embraced it for it alone gave me a rush.

Then one day, not long after I began this underground practice, something even stranger did happen—I began to love the tours all the more *because* I had never seen a ghost. I did not consider this unethical and took solace in the words of my dissertation advisor, Archibald Sump Stanbeck IV, himself a relic from the '60s who couldn't accept that he'd awakened in the 21st century and found himself a brick in the establishment wall he had worked to overthrow in his own student days. Discussing higher education with him was always enlightening if somewhat troubling. It was literally as if he'd awakened from a dream and found he had become The Man, and that the new generation of rebels were not merely nipping at his heels, they were calling for his head. At 70, he realized the fate of all unworthy revolutionaries: once you go down that road, there is no return. I think he secretly wanted a "do-over" so that he could become a Tory or campaign for Goldwater. His insight into the situation bore both the helplessness of this realization and his contempt for his younger colleagues, his students, and the program of higher education, more generally: "Anyone can teach a book they've read before," he once told me. "You can grab any Bozo off the street to do that. But only a great professor can teach a book they've never read before." Though I knew for a fact he was a drunk with a tendency to confuse his facts, he was a brilliant drunk with five favorably reviewed books on his resume and over two dozen pieces in <u>The New York Review of Books</u>. At first I was concerned about what his words could mean in regards to the feedback he'd been giving me on my research and papers, but I soon accepted the genius of his wisdom. It made me more comfortable in my skin and the line of work I was pursuing as a tour guide. I repeated his words to myself each night before I gave my tour. Words to live by.

Nor was it the only advice Stanbeck had given me. During my last winter in Virginia, he overheard Carla and me talking about the tours outside the grad student lounge. He was tactful enough not to say anything at the time, but later that month, during a meeting with him in his office to discuss my dissertation reading list, he asked me what had been my most interesting experience in what he termed the "ghost industry." The question totally caught me off guard, and I stammered for a response. He didn't buy my initial feint and pressed the issue. Though I could swear he'd probably been drunk since lunch, his verbal agility was formidable—he outflanked me, and I buckled under the mounting interrogation, ended up telling him what I'd never even told Carla.

"To be totally honest Professor Stanbeck," I said with some embarrassment, checking to make sure the door of his office was closed, "the only sort of experience I have ever had occurred during the first few weeks on campus. In my first year in the program. When I was spending a lot of time hanging out at Bruton Parish. Reading and reviewing my notes. It was vague—nothing definite. No flash of lightning from the heavens. But every so often, when I'd be sitting on one of the benches near the sanctuary, I'd experience a weird sensation—not scary or unpleasant, just unexpected. Maybe the sound of children playing, though when I'd look up from my reading there would be no one around. A few times it was something like a slight rumble beneath my feet. And usually then I'd feel the faintest of breezes across my face. But the surrounding tree limbs remained motionless—dead still."

He smiled and tilted back his head as if finishing off the final swig of a MacAllan 12. "I have experienced that, too," he said in a comforting tone of voice. "Your supernatural experience, of course, is from the tunnel Rockefeller dug beneath Duke of Gloucester in the '30s. It's the Colonial Parkway. It takes you out to Jamestown. It's thirty or so feet down. If I recall correctly, and I am confident I do, there is an airshaft disguised as a wishing well in the lot next to Bruton. When I first started working here, forty-one years ago, we'd occasionally hear of some poor fool mistaking the distant talk of workman repairing the tunnel's safety lights for the ghostly voices of the buried founders or perhaps some of your children at play. It's amusing to think of all those tourists buried down there, right beneath our feet, heading out to learn more about Pocahontas while the town's folk traipse around above in their silly colonial getups, playing make-believe for the barely literate." He shook his head with disgust at this last image he'd painted, then continued. "Of course, the Parkway is getting a lot more use what with the recent discoveries out at Jamestown."

I nodded my head, somewhat satisfied with his explanation, but not entirely. But before I could finish formulating my concerns about his remarks, he leaned forward in his chair and said in the most serious tone of voice I had ever heard him adopt: "Be wary of Carla. Her intentions are good, but she gets carried away. I fear she is too caught up in her quest to establish a Victims' Studies Program. It won't end well."

"I believe it's Death Studies, sir," I said reflexively, not intending to sound insolent or undermine his authority, which was, unfortunately, how he interpreted my remark. Personally, I wasn't sure if her Death Studies talk was for real or a joke. I'd hear her mention the plan once or twice but couldn't tell if it was a new course of study she was proposing or merely an attempt to institutionalize the tours, bringing them formally under the aegis of the graduate program. Stanbeck clearly saw the entire endeavor as misguided, a bogus branch of scholarship. One which he was beginning to realize his research as a young scholar had inadvertently served to midwife. He would have none of it.

"Same difference," he said, returning to the upright position in his chair, then tilting his chin up and staring down his long straight nose at me with more than a tinge of suspicion and, I sensed, contempt. I got the feeling I had just failed some sort of test, a sensation that was confirmed by his dismissive, "That will be all," which clearly signaled the end of our conversation. "You can close the door on your way out," he added after having turned back to his desk, not bothering to look over his shoulder for a response or farewell.

Out in the hallway, I was a bit shaken by the brusque dismissal. Still, I had to nod my head in recognition of the reasonableness of some of what he had said. I didn't necessarily like it, but I knew it made sense. I knew the Parkway was buried somewhere under the colonial town. I had driven it many times out to Jamestown, though to call it a Parkway was a bit of an overstatement—it was one lane in either direction. Still, it had alleviated traffic in town when the village was being restored years earlier and definitely served a purpose. I knew it had to cut through the middle of the historic district but wasn't sure exactly where.

At any rate, the words of the published sage made perfect sense. Indeed, this was why I'd asked him to be my advisor: he knew more than I did, even if his moral compass was impaired. I was certain he was right—it hadn't been the spirit of the dead trying to communicate with me. It was the poor engineering and faulty highway construction of the 1930s allowing noise to escape from the crypt of cars beneath my feet. Modernity, seeping through the crust of the earth to disrupt the colonial idyll. To shatter the spectral illusion. Unknowingly, Carla and Stanbeck—the *Rebel* and the *Establishment*—had worked in concert to destroy my faith in Bruton Parish and any residual longings I might have for a beyond. I would have been reeling had I not—that very night— realized my new calling, one which filled me with a zeal I had not known since my first childhood crush: to serve in the role of spoiler for other people's religious impulses.

From that point on in my tour guide career, I took devilish pleasure in making use of this new knowledge. The eventual course of action I settled on was wicked. On evenings when I knew the Jamestown Concert Series was holding performances and when there would be heavy traffic on the Parkway back from the venue, I would conclude my tours in Bruton Parish. There, in the midst of the dead slaveholders and the fathers of our Framers, I would ask tourists to gather in a circle in the graveyard and listen intently for a quiet minute, explaining that in recent months this spot had been witness to an unusually high number of paranormal report-ings, ranging from the low rumble of the earth to the inexplicable movement of tree limbs. Nearly half the time, an eager tourist would exclaim to the group that he'd felt or sensed something. As the anxious compatriots would ask what it was, the tourist would nervously describe what they'd experienced.

Only after the frenzy had settled down would I step in and inform them all that, alas, we were standing on top of the Park-way and that the paranormal was, in fact, very normal. I took care always to make this the final stop of the evening, and most saw the humor in the harmless little prank, and I would wish them all a good night as they headed back to their cars and hotels. But one night—only a few weeks into this new practice of mine—a devas-tated pilgrim shot me a look that I will never forget. She was per-haps thirteen, but her glance communicated much: that she'd prefer to see me buried in the graveyard rather than leading tours above it. A stabbing sensation shot through me, and I felt as if I had robbed a child. For an hour or so after the tour, the sentiment was difficult for me to square away, but I eventually did so by maintaining that I'd done the entire tour a great service by disabusing them of their wishful fantasies. They actually should be grateful to me, I reasoned confidently. I was, I told myself that night, blameless among tour guides. Indeed, my tours met the industry standard, satisfied the let-ter of Carla's law. Again and again, customer evaluations had borne this out. Requests for my tours had grown and made me the most sought after guide in the field, elevating me to the level of minor celebrity…a notoriety due largely to a power I did not have and a history that never existed: a dubious distinction in the annals of criminals, one for which not even Dante had assigned a ring. And so my final transformation was complete: I had become a celebrity scholar of a fake underworld, a guerilla historian par excellence— all my fellow tour guides were agreed. I had not only joined the Revolution. I *was* the Revolution.

Thus the announcement of my departure from the program was greeted with shock by all of my classmates, who imagined me to be the most promising and competent of future scholars. My plans to drop out struck some friends as sudden and hastily conceived. It caused others to doubt the whole enterprise of higher education. They felt certain that I, with my two published seminar papers and numerous conference presentations, was destined for tenure somewhere and thus served as a sort of validation of the program and their efforts, in general. Carla actually broke down and started to cry. Of course, it was not unusual for grad students to bail on programs. Administrators built in the attrition projections to admission figures and used them to help plot and assign course loads and schedules, but my decision had come particularly unannounced. Most discontents exhibit symptoms months beforehand, usually in the form of outbursts about mounting debt, an anemic job market, or a faltering relationship. My decision appeared unannounced as a cancer diagnosis, and it cast a similar pall over my friends, who had perceived me as particularly stable. It was cause for immediate suspicion and speculation and rumor. Most of all, it caused them to doubt the legitimacy of their own pursuits, though none ever acknowledged this publically.

Carla's questioning was relentless, and I eventually felt I needed to confide in her. In her own weird, misguided way, she'd been a supportive friend, and I couldn't let the lie live on. Not on my way out of town. I had, at some point, to speak the truth. It wasn't going to change my plans. So on the morning of the move, as I was finishing packing my little pick-up truck, I decided to reveal all to Carla. Almost all—I didn't tell her that the young tourist's reaction to my Bruton Parish pranks had me questioning myself. At any rate, I'd told her most of my ambitions and concerns over the previous two years, and she'd more or less reciprocated the confidence. I figured I owed her some sort of explanation as she was the only one to show up for my send off that spring morning several years ago. I thought it could do no harm—I'd be in DC in 3 and a half hours, my new life well underway, its course as irreversible as the tenure appointment that had once seemed my birth-rite. So when she asked me about how difficult it would be to give up the thrill of the paranormal, the one special dispensation that made so many of the grad students continue in their lives of servitude, she was astonished to learn I'd never seen or heard a ghost.

"I don't understand, dear," she said in a tone of voice that suggested real confusion or a lack of confidence or both, the first time I had ever heard either quality in her voice. "You were the one. We all just knew it—what with your grandparents' deaths and all…we thought you were the …attractor, the portal …" Her voice trailed off her, almost embarrassed at its choice of word.

I had no words to offer. None. My mind was finishing a mental checklist of items I'd need to complete in DC: call the power company, call the cable company, call for take-out Chinese.

"You mean to tell me you've never really felt anything strange? Nothing? Not even an inkling…" she asked as she rolled my suitcase across the threshold and onto the rickety porch of the old colonial that had been converted into two tiny grad student apartments. I remained distracted by the thought of the move and the work that still lay ahead of me in DC. It seemed like I'd been at it for all morning and yet the little pickup was nowhere near full. I finally came to and glanced back over at her. She looked at me with a sort of heartbroken pity. I would have found the expression deeply moving had I not been its object.

The total look of indifference on my face devastated her. She grabbed my upper arm lovingly, rubbed it with her thumb, staring at the ground. Then back up into my eyes. "Nothing? Ever?" she asked. I honestly thought she was going to have a breakdown; she felt so bad for me.

I was desperate to make the uncomfortable scene somehow less pathetic, determined not to have my last morning in town marred by any negative thoughts or tears. But I didn't want to lie at so solemn a moment—I'd done enough of that in Williamsburg. I was compelled to rip the band-aid off at once so we could actually finish moving my stuff out to the truck and let me make my escape up to my new life working for one of DC's countless nondescript nonprofits.

"Never. No inkling. Nothing." I looked in Carla's eyes and saw total devastation. It was like I had told a kid there was no Santa, Tooth Fairy, or Easter Bunny all at once. It became clear to me at that moment that she'd never seen a ghost either, and that she had drawn much of her conviction—perhaps all of it—from her belief that I had. Never in my life had I felt possessed of so much power as at that moment. But its use seemed wrong. Would have been the crowning crime of crimes. Somehow, I needed to soften the blow. Concede something, however meaningless. "The only thing I ever experienced was just the rumble of the Parkway beneath my feet, while at Bruton sitting on a bench, looking out over the graves. I even wrapped up my tours there. Had some fun with the believers."

I said this last word mockingly, but even as I finished it, I worried that she had received it differently than I intended. She released my arm, and I was unsure what to do, so I went back into the house to get another box for the truck. When I came back onto the porch, I realized she hadn't moved. I loaded the box into the bed of the truck and climbed back on to the porch, then stopped before her. It seemed she needed to say something. I waited a few seconds before deciding to head back in and let her work out whatever grief she had alone on the porch without creating another awkward scene.

But before I entered the house, she asked softly: "Dear, did you say you experienced these things while you were at *Bruton?*" A strange, unrecognizable quality had gripped her voice. I was not sure if it was anger or confusion or desperation.

My patience was wearing thin, though. A part of me thought she was going to make some sort of smart-ass condescending remark about hanging out at the most bourgeois of attractions, but there was something in her tone of voice that suggested this might not be the case. Regardless, I had work to do and wanted to stay on task. As much as I didn't want to indulge her emotion, I decided it was best to acknowledge her comment and walk her through it. After all, I was going to need her help loading my rocking chair onto the truck.

"At Bruton," I answered. "In the graveyard. The part closest to Nassau. Just the movement of tree branches, the hum of traffic, stuff like that—probably when an eighteen wheeler was passing through the tunnel underneath. On the Colonial Parkway. Or maybe the voices of construction workers from the airshaft in the next lot." I headed back in to get another load.

When I reappeared at the threshold with another box full of books, she had a look on her face that stopped me dead in my tracks. I initially thought she was looking at me but then realized she was looking slightly over my left shoulder. It freaked me out, and I instinctively turned to see if someone had sneaked up behind me, an axe murderer or something, which I confess has always been a secret fear of mine. But I saw nothing, and when I turned back to ask her what the hell was the matter, I realized she wasn't looking over my shoulder. She was looking *through* me. I suddenly felt like she was at my bedside in the hospital, watching me breathe my last breath. I dropped the box of books. A cold sweat beaded up on my forehead and above my upper lip. My stomach fell to my feet. I felt like I had just been diagnosed with cancer or something.

"*Bruton?*" she asked again. This time, I definitely discerned the emotion in her voice: the impossible mix of dread and hopeful curiosity.

I nodded my head. She slowly bit her upper lip, as if reviewing some sort of calculus in her mind.

"Dear, don't you know the tunnel isn't anywhere *near* Bruton," she finally said, apparently satisfied with her mental computations. "It's a quarter mile east of Bruton. Underneath the Courthouse. The airshaft is hidden in the woodpile outside the east windows, the ones next to the witness stand."

My mouth became impossibly dry. I was suddenly dying of thirst. I had just wanted to load the truck and get the hell out of town. I hadn't wanted to hit DC traffic. Especially not on a hot August day.

"What do you mean?" I finally asked, eventually realizing the scene in which I'd found myself inextricably involved for the past three years was moving toward some sort of end—one much different than any I could have imagined only a minute before.

She sprang to life and moved quickly down to her Subaru, opening the passenger side door and rifling through the glove box. She found what she was looking for and moved quickly back up to the porch without closing the car door. She unfolded a well-worn *This Week in Colonial Williamsburg Map*, the kind I'd handed out a thousand times to tourists and that I used regularly myself.

"Look, dear," she said frantically. "Look—here it is." A trembling forefinger pointed to the cartoon map and its depiction of the Colonial Parkway as it disappeared from the map, entering a tunnel behind Peyton Randolph's House just east of North England Street. The tiny finger moved across the smudged, creased page of the map, crossing over the courthouse, moving west of England Street, and picked the highway back up as it reemerged on the map, just south of Francis Street, close to a half mile away.

It was true—unless the Parkway took a few abrupt turns like the Warren Commission's magic bullet, then the tunnel ran beneath the Courthouse some 600 feet east of Bruton's graveyard. It took a good minute for the full significance of this to register. The strangeness of it. Countless times I had sat in the quiet of Bruton on an afternoon and felt the breeze fan my cheek, heard a distant soft sound like that of children at play, seen the rustle of leaves and heard the faint rumble like distant thunder, only—as Stanbeck had taught me—emanating from the ground. But he had been wrong. Or perhaps he'd just been drunk. As for Carla, the revelation required her to face the most awesome challenge I have ever before seen a human have to face: the recognition that she'd finally found what she most desperately sought in the very thing she most passionately dreaded. I must say, she bravely met this contradiction.

As for me, I was a believer at last. Converted by an atheist. So much for the wisdom of the wise. So it was that what these various things could now mean—what they meant—slowly and silently assembled about me, like the Beaufort clan at a graveside service, quietly welcoming home a returned prodigal, solemnly determined to lay something much beloved to rest.

I sensed then that there was no need to return to the graveyard for verification. To measure the motion of the trees. To record the stirring of the earth or the low hum from a buried beyond. Such efforts seemed vulgar. Offensive. In fact, I vowed then that I'd never return. That would be sacrilegious, I thought—profane. Then a familiar sensation welled up inside of me, the emptiness I'd first felt when I'd learned of my grandparents' death. And I knew at that moment that I wouldn't be heading to DC after all. That I'd be heading home to Texas. To Huntsville. Then just as quickly the emptiness dissolved into something else, exactly what I cannot say. I still can't.

What I do know is this: something had happened at last. My shoulder had been tapped—and on my way out of town. Or rather, I finally realized that it had been happening all along. That I'd been visited after all, and daily. The only proof I needed—the best proof—was this, and I believe it to be irrefutable: that I hadn't even known I'd been visited. That's how it works. That's the mystery. The inexplicable mystery of the ineffably ordinary. I'm convinced of it now. Or, at least, that's how I'd like to think it works. That's how I pray it works. And I don't ever want to pray another lie again. Honest.

Degüello

The truth of the matter was Cassie was a little disappointed at the lack of fight the cattle had been putting up. She figured if there was one thing worth squalling about it was the prospect of losing your balls. If you didn't show any fight, you probably didn't deserve a pair.

As far as Cassie was concerned, there'd been little struggle, less blood, and a totally insufficient display of distress. It seemed the herd had become pretty sedate after getting fed. Though a few were breathing heavily, the only other sound she'd heard had been the wet thump into the bucket and the tinny clang of its handle as it shook with each new deposit. In a rare moment of charity, she thought she might attribute the beasts' silence to a stoic resolve, a grim determination to endure and preserve dignity in the face of such humiliation. She went so far as to imagine that one particular calf was taunting her, resisted screaming so as to hoard knowledge of an event so terrible that it defied expression in sound: an experience Cassie could never know and yet one of which she'd become suddenly, and strangely, envious. When she'd knelt down before the beast and gazed into its black eyes, she remembered thinking to herself that the animal had crossed over—now had knowledge Cassie could never acquire. And for a moment, the very silence itself seemed evidence of the beast's contempt for her.

But that moment passed. There was no scream, and she thought it best not to waste her charity on a farm animal. The beast was no hero. Was too dumb either to realize the future now severed from it or to appreciate the past that should be dear to it. Its time horizons were relegated to the moment. To its belly. And at the moment, its belly was full.

In the distance, lightning tore across the gray sky, but Cassie didn't even blink. Only when another flash forked through the clouds overhead did she finally become aware of the tugging on her sleeve. She looked at her side and saw her twelve-year-old cousin. Then at last all the sounds from that afternoon came bursting in upon her: the thunder's roll and crack, the wind through the grasses, the screaming of a dozen calves, the horn from her aunt's truck, and now the voice of Becky shouting at her side. "It's finished, Cassie. Let go! It's fixin' to pour! Hurry so we can beat the rain." The calf snorted and ran off as Cassie released her grip. She stood up, grabbed the bucket, and followed the darting form of her cousin across the field.

Heading back to the house in the truck, Cassie looked down at her bloodied hands and then rubbed the bruise on her shin. She rolled up her jeans to take a look. Her skin was already a dark purple, but she could not recall how it happened. Judging from the conversation in the truck, she determined that at some point within the past hour, Becky had caught a hoof in the gut and Aunt Judy had been head-butted onto her ass. They were both laughing and carrying on, just as they had been earlier in the afternoon.

"Cassie, you all right?" her aunt finally asked as the truck bumped its way along the narrow road.

"Hmm?"

"You all right, hon?"

"Yeah, I think so."

"You were mighty quiet out there."

Cassie said nothing. The sky was darkening and the rain began to pound the truck. Becky shifted awkwardly between her mother and her older cousin.

"At least until you kicked that frisky one in the ribs and called him a 'little bitch.' Now that's a new one."

Becky smiled up at her mom and then looked up at her cousin, who was still staring distractedly out the window.

"Never heard that one before, Cassie. 'Course I never heard a calf scream like that before, either. Thought you'd like to have killed him."

Cassie remained silent. Her aunt glanced into the rear view to try to catch sight of her niece's reaction without drawing too much attention to her concern.

"Still got that magic touch, hon. Old 'No Quarter Cassie.'"

Cassie remembered none of this and only sat quietly with her face against the cold window. Her breath had fogged up a small patch of glass. Though she was hurtling down a West Texas road with her aunt and cousin, her mind was elsewhere.

She'd had several spells like this since the death of her father earlier that week. She was too afraid to mention them to anyone, though her aunt had grown suspicious. Becky's fidgeting eventually brought her back around as she fiddled with the radio and started jabbering about middle school boys and the State Fair. But Cassie said nothing, only watched the rain as it angled down from the leaden clouds. She didn't know if she were getting hard of hearing or incapable of listening. This uncertainty seemed more of an annoyance than a revelation, though, and it was this thought more than any other that brought her back to the conundrum involving her family and the entire community of Stockbridge, an ordeal that had escalated during the events of the preceding week.

In the past seven days the town's most respected tradition had been declared a nuisance. Most all were agreed by now. But this hadn't always been the case. For the past one hundred and twenty years, a lone bugler had ascended to the top of the courthouse clock tower and begun to play the first eight bars of Reveille at 4:47 each Monday morning, stopping abruptly mid-song. The tradition sought to commemorate what many believed to have been the final Comanche raid in the state of Texas, honoring those frontier pioneers of Stockbridge who had repelled the assault as well as immortalizing the nineteen-year-old soldier who had begun to play Reveille on that morning so many years ago, warning his comrades of the attack and saving many lives even as his was tragically cut short.

Cassie had always imagined her great-grandfather to be a dashing Custer of the plains, swashbuckling his way across the vast Texas waste before an arrow had treacherously stolen his life. Ended his bugling. Bitten into his throat and yanked him away to another place. The fact that a Garfield relative of hers had played Reveille each Monday morning for the past one hundred and twenty years since that tragic day had solidified this image in her mind. And the fact that each Monday morning the playing ceased at the exact note last played by her great-grandfather, who in truth had been a pimply-faced and awkward boy at the time of his death, added a poignancy to the rite, reminding the locals of the fragility of life, the unexpected nature of death, and the impossibility of real closure.

But people grow weary of such reminders, and even of heroes, and when Cassie's father died, and it became clear to all in town that the tradition would be passed on to her—the only child of her parents' stormy marriage—folks in Stockbridge began to mumble that maybe it was time to reconsider how those bold pioneers were honored. Perhaps a plaque or a statue of a bugler on the courthouse lawn was sufficient. So after burying her dad during lunch time on Wednesday and mourning his death throughout the afternoon, she decided to spend the dinner hour confronting the figure she'd pegged as the ringleader of the town coup.

"Bullshit!" Cassie had yelled at Hank Finley, looking him square in the eyes, flecks of spit flying into his face. She was determined to call him out and rip him a new one if need be. She was insistent that the tradition would not die—not on her watch. And so there, early Wednesday evening on the front steps of the Stockbridge Church of Christ—as families were leaving the Bible Study service—she'd lit into him.

"Absolute, total, fucking bullshit! You know it, Hank. And I'm gonna call you on it."

Hank was silent. Stunned. His wife had turned pale and looked away and then down at the sidewalk.

"You think 'cause daddy's dead and mama's sick you can abandon your watch? Hell, he's not even been laid to rest twenty-four hours, and here you want to go and forget all that he stood for. Wipe it all away. Make it like it's never been. Good Lord, Hank, I am glad he passed so he don't have to see you stoop to such treachery. It's shameful, Hank. Shameful. But I guess that's something you know all about, ain't it Hank?"

Hank winced, and Maggie, his wife, bit her lip. But both remained silent. He had no response to Cassie's dig. He knew there was no excuse for the pass he'd made at her when she'd been in high school, but he still thought it was a cheap shot for her to try to work that into the mix—make it seem like a motive for his present actions. With Maggie's support, he'd gotten help for his drinking. He'd beaten that demon. But there were nights when he still lay awake long after Maggie had gone to sleep, and thought of the seventeen-year-old Cassie in that red halter top. He breathed deeply. Then—aware that a small crowd had gathered to hear his case—he mounted his defense.

"Cass, hon, now I understand you been through a lot lately." He reached out his hand to touch her shoulder in a gesture that he hoped conveyed genuine concern. "We all understand." He looked around him, as if in an effort to gather the small crowd to his side and defuse any thoughts that his gesture had been inspired by anything other than concern. "And you know we all thought highly of your daddy. A fine and honorable man, God rest his soul." He paused for a moment, recalling the man who had given him his first job thirty years before. Hank knew that, regardless of all that had happened between him and Cassie, he owed her dad. "And it was a beautiful service you put together for him," he added hurriedly. "It really was, hon. But this here's a different matter. A different matter altogether. But it's no rush, either. And we can talk about it later." He made as if to leave, certain that he'd won her and the crowd over by his calm tone of voice and reasonableness.

But Cassie's arm shot out and jolted him, stopping him dead in his tracks.

"We'll talk now, Hank Finley."

Mrs. Finley turned her head away again, pulling her son close to her side and trying to cover his ears while pretending to be smoothing down his hair. Hank gulped. Left with no alternative, he spoke hesitatingly.

"Things change, hon. Times change. And some of us, well… some of us have come to think that this tradition is one of those things might need changing."

"Over my dead body, Hank."

By now more churchgoers had filtered out of the narthex and gathered at the edge of the strange disturbance. Cassie was un-fazed.

"But maybe that's what you want next, Hank," she continued. "Maybe that's what you all want next," she uttered with contempt, now sizing up the entire gathering. "To get rid of all of the Gar-fields." She shook her head with scorn. "Well a Garfield's played Reveille for the past hundred and thirty years, and a Garfield's gonna be playing it for the next hundred and thirty if I have any-thing to say about it."

"A hundred and twenty, hon," Hank said, unconsciously cor-recting her before catching himself. "But…well, that's—you're missing my point," he said in a tone that was pleading with her to take into account the presence of the onlookers. But she was staring only at him now—and she was staring hard and cold. "Let's talk about this later. Can't we talk about this later, Cass?" he asked. Though he didn't know if he could defend himself any better then, he knew he didn't want his defeat witnessed by so many. "The point is…I know you've got a lot on your mind," he offered sympathetically.

"Oh, I got your point—what there is of it," she said, glancing down at his crotch, he thought. He looked quickly at Maggie to make sure she hadn't seen this, but she was staring at the ground and holding her breath.

"You want to forget the folks that settled this town. I ain't talking 'bout the folks who moved here later, Hank—I'm talking 'bout the folks who made Stockbridge what it is. Who made all this possible," she snapped out, again stepping back from her assault posture and sweeping her hand across the horizon in a gesture that seemed to take in the church, the bank, and the courthouse square.

"You want to forget all this, Hank Finley. But you better never forget. Never! 'Cause while your great grand-daddy was living the high life in Philadelphia, mine was taming the frontier. Fighting back the Comanchero. Laying railroad. Making it possible that an ingrate like you might ever come squirting out of your daddy's little tallywhacker and into your pathetic, miserable existence."

He shook his head at this comment—felt sure everyone would take it as a cheap shot, for most families in town had arrived since the oil boom. But when he quickly scanned the crowd, he wasn't sure they had taken it that way. They all looked scared. Despite all the emails he'd sent out the last week about his research into Stockbridge's past. He'd found a half a dozen articles and historical accounts that seemed to take issue with the town's tradition and Cassie's depiction of her relative. But for the first time that week, he was uncertain about what he'd read.

Nor was Hank sure if a nineteen-year-old bugler could have done everything Cassie seemed to suggest he'd done, yet he knew if he brought that up he'd lose the fight for sure. About the only thing he knew for certain was that this matter of the town's past wasn't about getting at the truth; it was about something else. It was about arguing, perhaps. And he knew if he tried to split hairs now he'd definitely lose the argument. But he also knew he had to make a point, for nearly the whole congregation was now watching.

"Cass," he finally said, summoning the courage to look her square in the eye. "Hon, I hadn't wanted to say this, but you're livin' in the past. A past without a past. A past that's gone."

She was back in his face before he'd gotten out this last word.

"Don't tell me the past is gone, you ungrateful sack of shit! It ain't gone! Hell, it ain't even begun! I'll show you how past the past is," she spat out, half wondering what she meant by these words that seemed to shoot out of her mouth without stopping for con-sultation from her brain.

"I tell you what," she said, looking around her and trying to stare down as many people in the congregation as dared to meet her eyes. "I tell you all what. I'm gonna be playin' that trumpet from here on out," realizing mid-thought that a trumpet wasn't a bugle and that she hadn't played any brass instrument since high school, and she'd only taken up music then because the school board had refused to let her play football. "Every Monday morn-ing. Bright and early. I'll be waking your sorry asses up. Playing Reveille from up there, atop the courthouse my great granddaddy built," she said, now pointing up at the finely restored clock tower atop the noble looking structure. "At 4:47 sharp. Each Monday morning. And then we'll see how past the past really is."

Hank bit his lip as she walked right back up in his face—her nose not two inches from his, her mouth grinning from ear to ear, a half-crazed look on her face. He suddenly grew conscious of her breath; it stank of cigarettes and coffee, and only that terrible smell was able to beat back the thought of the red halter top from his mind. He tilted his head and spoke nervously, avoiding eye contact, looking around her face and over her shoulder. Looking every-where but in her eyes.

"Cass, now don't you even kid about that. You don't want to get these fine folks any more upset with you than they might already be. Upsetting the peace and all. Starting trouble like that."

"Start!" She screamed in absolute disbelief. "Start? Where the hell have you been? It's too late for that. It's on, Hank Finley.

It's on! Hell, daddy was battling you the last three years of his life. Don't think I didn't know that. The whole town knew it, you two-faced son-of-a-bitch. But tell me this, Hank, which face is it you'll be wearing tomorrow when you don't have your church to go to? What's it gonna be then, Hank Finley? What's it gonna be?"

The logjam at the church door had now spilt out onto the portico, and Jimmy Moss, the young preacher, had left his post shaking hands in the narthex to see what the problem was. He soon found out, and it was worse than he ever could have suspected.

"Cass, come on now," Hank protested meekly, his confidence waning in the face of her screeching assault. Even now he was willing to doubt the truth of the recent historical accounts he'd read as he found himself faced with the boldness of a Garfield in action.

"He knew about your plan to put a puny-ass plaque next to the gazebo," she whispered in mock secrecy. The crowd stirred.

Hank looked down at the ground as if he'd been found out in public. This final revelation, coming as it did before so many members of the community, seemed to guarantee that this scene would be remembered by the town for years to come. And though people felt for Hank—there were many co-conspirators in the crowd that day—no one was daring enough to intervene or even try to restrain Cassie. As frequently happens to those in the midst of a spectacle way beyond their control, Hank sensed a need for propriety, believing foolishly that he might offer his own account before the conversation turned into a scene. But it was way too late for such concern. As Hank was desperately planning his next course of action, Brother Moss had apparently sized up the situation and decided it prudent to sit this one out. The cavalry would not be riding in to save the day. The cavalry knew better.

"Cass, that's not fair of you and you know it. We were going to do more than that. We were gonna have an exhibit in the library. Polish up the bugle and retire it in grand fashion. With a big glass case in the lobby. Out in front of the checkout line, so when you get a book you see it. Have some old pictures of the courthouse blown up. Put on easels there in the lobby. Frame a few maps from that era, showing where the first settlers lived. Me and Bernice even started working on a diorama. We'd even talked about going before the City Hall with a plan for a day of remembrance in October."

He looked around the crowd for a show of moral support. A few were tempted to offer it, but the presence of Cassie kept them from it. Young Moss finally made a step in Hank's direction but drew up short when he caught sight of the savage look on Cassie's face.

"A diorama? Are you kidding me? Is he kidding me?" she said, stepping toward Moss. He was too stunned to react but shrank back a step. The rest of the crowd wisely averted eye contact. She rolled on. "And a yearly holiday!" she hollered in scornful disbelief, directing her wrath back upon Hank. "A yearly fucking holiday! Well I'm glad you can carve a day out of your busy schedule to honor the men who founded this town and made your life possible. That's mighty generous of you. A yearly fucking holiday!"

Hank had lived in Stockbridge his whole life. He'd been a successful attorney, a member of Rotary, a deacon, and an officer of the Chamber of Commerce for the past fifteen years, but he was helpless before the assault of this woman half his age, and the entire crowd knew it. Mrs. Finley was in tears—silent tears, for she didn't want Cassie lighting into her, either—and she'd pulled her young son closely to her side, still shielding his face from the wrath of this buxom fury of the prairies. Moss had decided to cut his losses and was now quietly motioning his shaken congregation back into the narthex.

"Oh, I see Hank Finley, I've upset you. Well, I am sorry. Please accept my apologies. After you've stomped all over daddy's grave. Spat on a hundred and forty years of family history. Of Stockbridge history. But tell me, Hank Finley, what are you going to do bout the past? What are you going to do about tradition?"

Hank breathed deeply for a good ten seconds. He couldn't believe it—he was hyperventilating. Like he'd done when he'd had his first heart attack. He was trying to fight through it and muster some response, but he couldn't. Cassie grinned, sensing the dramatic fullness of the moment.

"Oh, I know Hank Finley. I know how I can solve your little

problem. Do what everybody else is doing these days. Do what your high and mighty Chamber of Commerce recommended for us all to do," she said, stepping back from him now, smiling bitterly, and eyeing what remained of the congregation with contempt. "Outsource for it!"

The crowd gasped. A woman fainted. Somewhere in the distance, a child began to cry.

For the past year, Stockbridge had learned all about outsourcing. When local wells had started to run dry three years ago, folks started getting nervous, and as if things couldn't get worse, the fears over mad cow disease further dampened the prospects of the town's other leading industry. But then a peculiar series of events unfolded and changed Stockbridge's place in the pecking order of the universe. A year and a half ago, an executive from Warwick Petroleum had read about Stockbridge's peculiar plight in a Dallas Morning News feature while on an extended layover at DFW International. A plan hatched in his brain, and an unlikely arrangement was shortly thereafter worked out. In a posh London boardroom, half a dozen WP suits had decided that they were going to outsource certain of their company's services. Stockbridge, Texas was never going to be the same.

WP had been making unconventional moves for quite some time as it maneuvered to reclaim the lost glory of what had once been its global reach. It was getting hammered in the stock market and hammered in the press, as its chief competitor had launched a series of snappy commercials that managed to communicate little of substance while winning lots of public attention. WP felt the heat and had even anticipated some of it when the first Gulf War broke out. In the early 1990s, WP had struck a deal with the UN to provide reasonably priced support services and investment capital to English-speaking third-world countries with oil-based economies, some of which had once been a proud part of Victoria's Empire.

In the mid-1990s, WP pioneered the ranching of their oil

properties, ingeniously managing to wring profits from both above and below the ground. Thus, a happy union with its oil partners was expanded. Rather than retrain its staff, the company decided in August of 2000 to outsource a small portion of its service department to a tiny town in West Texas.

Because the company was in dire need of an affordable, English-speaking work force with knowledge of the oil and ranching industries, some thirty residents of Stockbridge now worked, on a trial basis, as service representatives, and support staff of WP, fielding inquiries about rig safety, fluid imaging, reservoir modeling and management, and drilling procedure, while at the same time recommending early detection practices for foot rot and lumpy jaw and advising on seasonal grazing schedules and livestock vaccinations. And so the stock portfolios of a fair number of the English gentry had become strangely dependent on a group of complete strangers who wore Stetsons, listened to Merle Haggard, and celebrated—each July 4th—their rebellion against George III. For even treason, it seems, can be forgiven in the name of commerce.

In truth it was a happy fit for Stockbridge, which had been founded as a stop on the cattle trail to Kansas and was later invigorated by oil found in the region, bordering, as the town did, on the Permian Basin. Nor was Stockbridge without its own legitimate area of expertise, either: before the oil bust, locals had won grants from the Department of Energy to conduct experimental work in converting petrol and related waste water into an affordable and irrigable product. And it was ultimately this experience that WP hoped would be most beneficial to its investment. Such an innovation could reap dividends, and if the benefit could be financed on Uncle Sam's coin, all the better thought the London office. So in one of the company's stranger strategic moves, a deal had been struck in a meeting room of the Dallas Adolphus; the end result brought ranchers and roughnecks who were working lands in New Zealand and the Cook Islands into a first name basis with the citizens of a tiny Texas town who were remarkably well suited to meet their distant coworkers' needs. But only because Stockbridge's citizens had agreed to suffer through weeks of elocution and annunciation classes. Little by little, as "schedule" became "shed-yule" and "garage" became "*gare*-rahj," people forgot the benefits of the traditional work day in favor of what had become a sort of perpetual graveyard shift.

Cassie was incensed at the changes and at how few people seemed to take notice of them. But of all the transformations taking place in her hometown, nothing angered her more than these new accents or work hours. The fake accents made her want to puke, and the new work day was more than cramping her style. Because of the difference in time zones between Stockbridge and New Zealand, many of the local employees were working seven days a week—2:00 pm to well after midnight—with most settling into their second stage of REM at about the time a Garfield began playing Reveille on Monday morning. And this was when the problems with tradition first became apparent to City Hall. The 4:47 Reveille, once a point of community pride—rallying the industrious, hard-working citizenry to a day of toil while reminding them of their ties to a heroic past—had now become an obstacle to that same mission.

For most of the locals liked their new jobs well enough and felt a little in debt to this new practice of outsourcing, especially considering the tough times that the worldwide ranching economy had endured in the wake of Mad Cow Disease and Oprah's untimely remarks. And after a few months at their posts, many thought their new jobs differed little from their old ones, except that instead of capping wells or punching doggies in 100 degree heat they were now emailing solutions to hoof and mouth or describing—in the King's English—the finer details for how to cap a well, all while sitting in an air-conditioned office with reruns of SportsCenter turned down on a Sony flatscreen, sipping designer blend coffee from Amsterdam, their Lucchessis crossed atop their desks. But the truth was that more than one of WP's new employees had grown self-conscious after asking his son about his football "*shed*-yule" or his hunting buddy about when he would be getting the Jeep out of the "*gare*-rahj."

Cassie was sensitive to all of these circumstances and more, for her dad had also ranched, and she frequently helped out on her widowed aunt's property while she worked on finishing her degree at the community college in Abilene. Though she'd shown little interest in bugling during high school, the matter had become of great importance to her lately. She had raised cane at the previous two town meetings when the topic of WP had come up.

"You've let complete strangers turn your world upside down. Turn your day into night. Profane your Sabbath. Make you ashamed of your voice and the way you speak. What won't you do for a buck?"

The mayor just shook his head. He'd heard her rant before on the subject, and he brought out his gavel to stamp an end to it. The call to order failed.

"You gonna moo for them next? Crawl around like a beast if the price is right? Mark my word, it's a-coming. I guaran-damn-tee it!"

The mayor nodded over at the bailiff who made his way over to Cassie and gently touched her elbow to escort her out. She wanted to say more; she was pretty confident that she could drop the bailiff with a sucker punch and then squeeze out another twenty seconds before she was corralled out of the meeting, but she didn't think the time was right for that move. Not yet. She would draw a line in the sand later.

The truth of the matter was folks might not have minded the tradition continuing had it not been that Cassie was the one left to carry it on. Cassie herself knew this but was unsure how to respond to this knowledge. She had rubbed locals the wrong way since she'd been a high school cheerleader, and her ways hadn't changed dramatically in the ten years since. She still broke the local taboos: she swore like a roughneck, avoided bras like the plague, and sat in seats too soon after they'd been vacated by men, thereby not allowing enough time for the manly warmth from the seat to have dissipated. She'd broken this last taboo while only a freshman in high school. The results had been scandalous.

"She did it last night at the DQ," the local mothers would gossip to their husbands on Saturday mornings after high school football games. "She even wiggled her little tush around in the seat after plopping down in it. Puttin' on a show for the whole store. She's up to no good." The husbands would flip through the newspaper, trying to act uninterested. "Flirting it up with all the boys. *All* the boys, did you hear me? She's trouble. I don't want her around this house. She's a bad influence on all the kids. She'll be the first to get herself pregnant—wait and see. It's the damn halter tops. I swear she wears them everywhere. Next thing you know, she'll start wearing them to church. Homer better learn to keep his eye on her, or she'll ruin the family name."

Seldom would the husbands look up from the Sports Page, but their wives' comments had registered, and though they also didn't want their daughters socializing with such a girl, they made a mental note to eye Cassie's sparrow-breasted form more closely when services let out on Sunday mornings.

For her part, Cassie hadn't repented of her wild ways. Anything but. In the weeks before her dad's death, she'd taken to leafing through the hymnal too soon after the sermon had ended, evidence, some thought, of her not taking the preacher's words to heart or reflecting on the message of the sermon. Most were merely irked by the demonstrative and dramatic way she raked the hymnal out of the pew's rack immediately after the end of the sermon—even before the minister had sat back down—thumbing loudly through the pages while the rest of the congregation examined their consciences, offered silent penance, or meditated on the sermon. It seemed to many that she was doing this just to be contrary, but others thought she was trying to get the attention she'd lost when her metabolism slowed down.

Cassie hadn't seen much reason to reflect on these sermons since she'd decided a few years back that most of her young adult Sunday School classmates were not Presbyterians but agnostics or Unitarians and simply hadn't realized it yet. They didn't know what they believed and were a bit resentful of those who did. Whenever she tried to get the class talking about sin or redemption or the afterlife, folks clammed up. They were more comfortable talking about American Idol or the new Hollister that had opened on FM 592.

"Thirty-seven applications in the first hour they were taking them," Kat Norton related one Sunday morning. "Kids lined up around the corner. I didn't know there were thirty-seven kids that age in Stockbridge." Everyone in the class laughed. Cassie began to thumb through the Bible loudly, marking her displeasure at the turn in conversation. She knew that though her classmates were laughing at the store, they'd be the first in line when the place opened. And when she tried to steer the conversation back to sin and predestination, someone else brought up capris pants and cargo shorts. It was a losing battle. She finally realized that hell couldn't compete with Hollister, and that's when she stopped going to Sunday School.

But she'd been determined that day, and she had kept at it for a good fifteen minutes more until eventually everyone in the class began to look nervously around the room as if Cassie had confessed to contracting genital warts and they were afraid it were an air-born contagion. Finally, the class bell mercifully rang, and everyone awkwardly left the room, a few nodding their heads in courteous goodbye to Cassie, but most leaving quickly with the hopes of having to avoid her altogether.

Cassie knew that what they were really embarrassed about, though, was Claire, Cassie's nine-year-old who she'd had out of wedlock, or because—as she laughingly told her own mom—she'd sat too quickly in a DQ booth seat vacated by one of Stockbridge's most virile young men. But she hadn't done this. She'd just had an awkward prom date with Clyde Mills. The truth was she was a little ashamed of this; if you're gonna get knocked up in high school, it's probably better it be by the stud quarterback and not the lone pimply car geek on campus. But Claire was worth it all. Worth all the self-righteous condemnation and scorn and backstabbing the town could dish out. Claire was worth it. She had it all, too; she was smart, kind, cool. Cassie sometimes wondered if Claire could be Clyde's or if maybe there was something to that wive's tale about sitting in a seat too quickly after a man left. She resigned herself to the fact that there were worse fates than being tied for all of time to Clyde. Not many, but probably a few.

Lately she'd thought a lot about her past with Clyde, so much that it had distracted her from writing her most recent paper for her women's history class. She'd come up with some interesting ideas about history and the past and had included a few of them in the paper. But the paper had come back without a grade: only a "Please see me" written in red ink at the top of the title page. This comment quickly became a source of pride for Cassie, and she delayed meeting with the teacher about it for fear the encounter would ruin what she wanted to read into the cryptic remark.

What she wanted was to think her thesis had been too sophisticated for him to understand, and indeed it had been bold. In a scant three pages she had proposed that it was the fate of all true Americans to found either their own internet start up companies or their own religions: each man his own prophet or profit, whichever the case may be. As she saw it, too many Americans didn't like being told what to believe or when to show up for work. Few respected authority anymore, and even fewer respected tradition. The irony that she was the one making this argument was not lost on her. What bothered her the most was the faintly articulated assumption that the majority of folks seemed to have that everyone was doing the best they could and that everything was gonna be fine and dandy in the end. Tomorrow would take care of itself. That was the attitude Cassie herself had had on prom night, she remembered. She could even recall her parents' advice early that evening when they all three started from their seats after Clyde had rung the doorbell.

And that smug satisfaction was the real scandal, she often thought to herself. At least she was willing to admit her mistakes; she should have said "no" when she'd said "yes." She knew that, knew it with a certainty that made most uncomfortable. She also knew that though she might not be the best qualified to deliver the message, that didn't mean it didn't need hearing. "Athens fell, y'all, and so did Rome," she told her Sunday School class one day. "And we're not far behind." It needed to be said, she reasoned, even if the discussion she'd interrupted had been about the new wing of the children's nursery. Hell, she reasoned, if no one else was going say it, it may as well be her. If you're waiting for a messenger whose hands are clean, she thought, you're going to be waiting a long time. To the end of time.

But she also knew that, as a general rule of thumb, neither West Texans nor anyone else likes getting preached to by young single mothers suspected of whoring it up on weekends. The best response to that argument, she thought—while driving back to her house with her aunt and niece that rainy day after castrating the cattle—was "tough shit." So when her daddy had breathed his last on Monday afternoon, she decided that this matter involving the bugle would be where she'd make some sort of stand. "So help me God," she thought, as they lowered him into the ground. "I can do no other." What she didn't fully realize was that this vow would require her to seek out the strangest of bedfellows. Again.

So the first Saturday morning after the funeral, Cassie found Clyde exactly where she figured she'd find him, the place where he always went for a late breakfast after he'd finished his propane deliveries: the Chalk Hill Diner, finishing off a Number Two and nursing a mug of coffee in a booth he always shared with Will Owen and Chuck Finley. It could have been high school all over again. Clyde was just as pimply, Will still didn't have his diploma, and Chuck still had braces on. She'd sized the scene up after entering the diner, deciding to approach the booth in as quiet a manner as possible. It could have been Travis High of ten years ago, when the three were sophomores and ate lunch together in the corner of the cafeteria, and Cassie stopped by to harass them while making repeated trips to the salad bar in an effort to get the attention of as many boys as possible. But their common histories shared even more than these lunchroom squabbles.

At one time or another in the past, Cassie had beaten them all up: Will and Clyde in high school and Chuck back in seventh grade after he'd made some smart remark about her wearing a bra. She'd knocked a front tooth out and given him a scar above his right eye that he still wore his hair long to conceal. He couldn't look in the mirror without being reminded of her wrath or her left cross. She'd vowed two things on that day: never to take shit from anyone and never to wear a bra again. And she'd kept them both.

"Don't you ever forget I whooped your bony little ass," she hollered as the principal peeled her off of him while dispersing the lunchroom crowd. Chuck had never forgotten the incident, and when she asked him to go steady with her two weeks later, he was too frightened to say no. He was still afraid of her, too, though she'd stopped beating up boys up over Christmas break of seventh grade because, as she said, "There's not enough time to beat up all the one's needs beating up."

Cassie's decision had been greeted with a collective sigh of relief from the boys in her class and all of their fathers; no twelve-year-old boy wanted to suffer the indignity of being on—or even near—the receiving end of one of her thrashings. The boys only received a two-week reprieve, though, because Cassie's interest soon shifted from wanting to beat boys up to wanting to make out with them. This horrified the boys' mothers as much as her fists had horrified the boys' fathers.

This history united Cassie and her three classmates, and it loomed silently in the background of whatever conversation any of them might have. Cassie knew this, and as she approached the booth that morning, she sensed it would kill whatever discussion the three were having—not that she figured it would have been a worthwhile conversation to begin with. As it turned out, her suspicions proved correct.

"It's bullshit, man," Clyde remarked, unaware of Cassie's entrance at the far side of the diner. In the minute preceding her descent upon the booth, the conversation had skittered around a variety of topics before settling upon the most crude and shallow topic a bunch of grown men can discuss: high school tits.

"Let me tell my version of events, and then you can tell

yours," Clyde insisted to his eager listeners. The others nodded and smirked and drank from their coffee mugs.

"All right, here's the deal. So long as you've got some sort of living quarters on a semi chassis any sonofabitch can drive it. That's the law."

"Well that's a shitty law," Chuck piped in.

"I think it's a shitty law, too, but I didn't invent it. So just shut the hell up and let me finish my story."

Chuck nodded his head again, nudging Will under the table because they both loved to get Clyde worked up over things.

"So we're stuck behind this bluehair driving sixty-five feet of semi with a Class C license for, I don't know, for how long do you think, Will?"

"Maybe an hour."

"Hell, no. Longer than that."

Will did some primitive math in his mind. "Well, Windthorst to Decatur…"

"Really?" Clyde asked—a bit thrown by his friend's calculations and willing to mull it over for a second. "Ok, well, let's say an hour. Hour and a half."

Chuck nudged Will again as their friend rolled on.

"And I'm honking and flashing my brights and the road construction won't let me pass and Will's cussing up a storm."

"Tell him about the Firebird."

"If you shut the hell up, I will. So about fifteen minutes outside Decatur this little red Pontiac—"

"Firebird. Looked like a '99."

"I was thinking a '98, but it don't matter. Bright red. Little hottie inside, and she starts flirting with her insurance. Weaving in and out of lanes, trying to pass. She's seventeen, tops. Bodies like that don't last past seventeen."

"Tell him what she's wearing."

"If you shut the hell up, you jackass, I'm fixin' to. Will you shut up, huh?"

Clyde's friends did their best not to laugh out loud. Clyde rewarded their effort by looking around the diner real discreetly and then leaning forward as if to share a secret.

"And all she's got on are some Daisy Dukes and a tiny red halter. Tiny! And it's almost November! Unbelievable! And when the construction ends the gate's been opened, and she's loosed and flies by the line of cars, flipping every one of them off as she scoots by. But especially that Winnebago. She slows down, honks her horn to make eye contact, and lets Granny have it."

Will nodded his head, approving of this part of the retelling.

"Yeah, I think me and little Daisy could have really hit it off. She kind of winked at me, too, as she drove by, didn't she Will?"

Will was drinking his coffee and suddenly lurched forward with a laugh, forcing coffee out of his nose. Chuck didn't laugh though, for he was seated opposite his friends and had seen Cassie's approach to the booth. He fell deadly silent. Will picked up on his signal, but Clyde was so thoroughly engrossed in the thought of high school hard bodies that he failed to pick up on their cues.

Cassie had heard the last bit of his tale, and it was more than she could bear. She wondered if these were her options in life: propane or Warwick Petroleum. Reconciling herself to grown men who either chase high school tail or who bend over for the British. She cringed and decided to interrupt the father of her daughter before he could make a bigger fool of himself.

"Hi Clyde…guys," she said curtly, nodding out of courtesy at the other two without so much as looking at them. Chuck slumped down in his seat and stopped gnawing on a piece of greasy bacon. Will dropped his eyes to the table. Clyde burned his tongue on his coffee at the sound of her voice.

"Hey Cassie," he managed, turning his head, dreading having to make eye contact with her. "When'd you get here?"

She dismissed his question and issued an order. "Let's talk," she said in a very businesslike manner, nodding her head over to a corner of the diner. Clyde dabbed his mouth with his napkin, and quietly got up to follow her, as a small town man who has gotten his high school prom date pregnant without asking for her hand in marriage is inclined to do.

When they'd gotten out of earshot of the others, she turned

and looked him square in the eyes.

"You heard what they're trying to do, didn't you?"

He knew it would do no good to try to play dumb. She always broke him down when he attempted such tactics. She'd done it last month when she'd heard he'd gotten a new truck. She wanted to make sure the payments didn't interfere with the support he was giving Claire.

"Uhm, yeah. I'd heard something about it. Not much, though."

He was silent, staring at her right shoulder, unsure if she expected him to say more. But then he caught himself, worried that she'd think he'd been staring at her cleavage again, and so he looked out the windows of the diner. It had been one of life's cruel ironies, he'd always thought, how at the precise moment her bust line had begun to sprout she'd cut him off. He looked back toward her, still avoiding eye contact.

"I don't know, I mean. What can you do?"

"You can not let them get away with it, for starters. Help me out. You know what bugling meant to daddy. Your daddy, too."

This was true. Clyde knew better than anyone else that his dad had always been a supporter of the town and its traditions before he had passed away a few years back. Clyde himself had always been fond of Cassie's dad. He'd even worked summers for Mr. Garfield at the newspaper office. For all the awkward history he and Cassie had, there were undeniable ties between them, and he knew that this was what she was trying to appeal to, though she'd never admit it outright.

"Cassie, I don't know. I mean, you're right, but…"

"But what?"

He was silent.

"Cassie—"

"Don't tell me you're in on it, too."

"No, I ain't in on it. There's nothing to be in on. It's just that…"

"Just that what, Clyde?"

She folded her arms in front of her, shifting her weight onto one hip. He could think of nothing except that every time she assumed this pose, her "war stance," as he called it, he ended up getting humiliated. He was terrified but knew it would ruin his day if he didn't say something. The last time he wussed out in an argument with her it had bothered him for weeks. At the same time, he didn't want to be foolhardy. Cassie played for keeps. He knew that in a fair fight, he was no match for her. His best chance was to offer feints and remain elusive.

"Well, folks do need peace and quiet for their sleep and all. You gotta get rest some time."

"Need their peace and quiet? Daddy's the one needs his peace and quiet."

"Well, they do, too" he managed, eager to misinterpret her repetition of his words as an endorsement of his explanation.

"There wouldn't be any peace and quiet if it weren't for daddy and his type. There wouldn't be a Stockbridge if it weren't for his bugling. There wouldn't be a Chalk Hill Diner, a Jackson's Propane, either. And there sure as hell wouldn't be a Clyde Mills if not for the bugling. Don't you know that? Or have you forgotten now, too?"

Sensing that discretion was the better part of valor, he remained silent. He hoped he'd spoken up enough to get sleep that night, but he wasn't sure.

She wasn't gonna carve him up this time, though. She wasn't even going to punch him, either. She was too disappointed. And tired. Clyde was both shocked and relieved. And a little saddened, too, for it struck him at that moment that her spirit had finally been broken, at the least shaken, by these recent developments. He'd never known this to have happened. Not even when she learned she'd gotten pregnant a week shy of graduation. She'd always had the time or energy to carve someone up in public. Especially him. But she pulled back. This confused him. And it made him wary.

"Well, I'm sorry to have taken you away from your breakfast. I'll let you get back to the boys so you can talk about your new truck and Will's job answering phones for some Englishman ten thousand miles away. All that important stuff." Even these words lacked their sting for they were uttered halfheartedly. He was thrown by it.

"Take care, Clyde," she said. And she was gone. She had schoolwork to finish and errands to run, including getting back over to Aunt Becky's to check on another calf. Clyde returned to his booth, his burnt tongue already beginning to blister. The boys were silent. Clyde was nervous. It struck him that this strange behavior of hers was some sort of portent. But he didn't dwell long on what she'd said or hadn't said. There was food to finish and a belly to fill.

Aunt Judy had called Cassie early that Saturday morning to see if she could come out and help in the afternoon. She needed Cassie to help castrate a few more calves and then check up on a cow she thought might have lumpy jaw. It wasn't a valuable animal, but she wanted Cassie to look at it before she called the vet. Cassie had said she'd be over after running a few errands, so when she left Clyde and his cohorts at the diner, she headed over to her aunt's. After tending to the bloody business with the calves, she and her aunt walked out to the barn to check on the sick cow. The beast looked pitiful. Cassie thought it was too late for antibiotics to do much good—slaughter was the only practical solution. She hated the thought. But she knew they couldn't let the herd get infected.

On the drive home, she recalled the look the last calf had shot her before entering steerhood. It was not angry. Just tired. And very disappointed. Change is tough, and not even a dumb beast can pull it off well. Cassie felt for the animal. She was convinced that if there was one thing you could excuse getting sentimental over it was a pair of balls. That could be forgiven. She almost wondered if she shouldn't have just killed the animal. Kill them all, she thought, smiling to herself. The sick one, too. Lumpy jaw or not. Balls or no balls. "Killin' to save," her dad used to say when a cow got infected. She found herself mumbling this solution to herself while she drove home, and she was still thinking about the look on the calf's face when she entered her living room.

Claire was sitting in the reading chair, absorbed in Harry

Potter. The bologna sandwich she'd made her daughter hours before sat untouched on the end table next to the chair. Cassie's mom was asleep on the sofa. She had been sleeping most of the time since Cassie's dad had died. Her breath was raspy and labored, the result of years of smoking. The emphysema she suffered had made her vigil at her husband's side even more difficult, but she'd been there every day. She drove him to the courthouse each Monday morning to play Reveille, even on the last day—this past Monday, just hours before he died—when the bugle had made practically no sound, emitting only the hoarse, wheezing exhalations of a dying man. No lights came on around the courthouse square. Most of the town just slept through it. Cassie could never forgive them of this final insult.

"Haven't you read that one already?" she finally asked her only child, bending down to kiss her gently on the forehead. Claire was too engrossed in her book to muster a response.

"Just be sure you finish your homework. And eat your supper, for goodness' sake," she added, disappearing into the back. Too tired to bathe, she just splashed water across her face, changed out of her splattered overalls, and threw on some sweatpants and a tee shirt. She returned to the living room a minute later, took the half empty tumbler that sat on the coffee table by her mother's head into the kitchen, downed what was left of its contents, and then washed it out. She dabbed her hands dry on a cup towel and then went to the fridge to get a swig of orange juice to wash the taste of scotch out of her mouth.

She froze at the door, where a magnetic bugle holding up a youth soccer league schedule caught her eye. The house was full of such knick-knacks, and she wondered how tacky they must seem to an outsider: porcelain bugles, paperweight bugles, even lamp stands shaped like bugles. She shook her head in disbelief—bugles presided silently over her every moment. It struck her as pathetic, and she actually forgot what she'd gone to the fridge for. She rubbed her eyes and walked back through the living room.

"Hon, don't stay up too late," she said out of habit, "you're going to church and Sunday school tomorrow, ok?"

Claire was silent, and Cassie slowed her passage down and offered another "Ok?" Without lowering her book, Claire offered a very soft "Yes, mam."

She detected a bit of sadness in her daughter's voice and went over to check on her. She touched the back of her hand against her daughter's cheek and smiled at Claire. Cassie was not real good at being gentle, but with Claire she always tried.

"I love you, hon," she said, patting Claire's head again and brushing a few strands of hair out of her daughter's line of vision. Claire smiled up at her mom then continued to read. "And be sure to eat your sandwich and brush your teeth," she said, continuing back toward her bedroom. "Let grandma get her rest there. She needs it." Cassie figured that her mother had gotten so little quality sleep over the past week that it would be counterproductive to wake her and help her into the guest room. Better let her get some good shuteye whenever and wherever she could.

As for Cassie herself, she couldn't get to sleep. She lay awake a good hour thinking about her father and worrying about her mother and Claire. She wanted her mom to stop smoking, but every time she pointed this out, her mother reminded her of the bargain they'd struck. "I'll quit smoking when you quit swearing." Cassie didn't think these were fair terms because she couldn't stop swearing. She'd tried, but it seemed impossible. She said a quick prayer and rolled over to the cool side of the bed. Still, she couldn't drift off. She finally decided she wanted to renegotiate the terms of their deal and was trying to work out what she'd say to her mom when she suddenly got out of bed and went to her closet. She pulled aside a few dozen hangers full of work shirts and jeans until she got to the back of the rack and found what she knew she'd find—what had been there for years: her old red halter top. She hadn't worn it since high school. She took it off of the hanger and looked at it. She stood there for ten minutes looking through the halter and into the past, then hung it back up.

She got back into bed but couldn't stop thinking about the girl in the Firebird. She wondered if men had once talked about her that way. If they would ever again talk about her that way. And this was the last thought she had before falling asleep.

Not three hours later, Claire's screams shattered the silence in the house. Cassie arose in a flash and was at her daughter's side so quickly it was hard for her to tell if it was a dream or real. Claire was crying and panting.

"What's the matter, hon? Did you have a bad dream? Mommy's here now and it's all right," she said softly, holding her daughter in her arms. "Everything's gonna be all right." She tried to figure out what the problem could be because Claire never woke up in the middle of the night. Scouring the room for some clue, she saw the Harry Potter book on the bed-stand and became immediately angry at Clyde for having given it to Claire at Christmas. She'd suspected all along it was not the right thing for a nine-year-old to be reading. She was angry at herself for not taking the book away from Claire last night and even more angry for not tearing into Clyde at the diner. Her mind was racing with thoughts she half knew were self-serving when her mother came into the room and turned on the overhead.

"They took the horn."

Cassie was completely clueless about the meaning of her mother's words and immediately thought she was still drunk.

"Mama, I'm here with Claire, and everything's all right. You just go back to sleep, and I'll make us a big breakfast tomorrow."

But her mother just stood there in the doorway, a cigarette in one hand—silent and ancient and shrouded in smoke like some sibyl of old.

"The horn is gone," she repeated.

It took Cassie a few seconds to realize that her mother was not drunk and that her words were not sleepy, drunken ramblings but sober truths.

"What the hell are you talking about? Who took the horn?" she said, laying Claire's head down gently on some pillows, tucking her in, and then standing up.

But her mother only motioned her into the living room, where she pointed to the empty mantle—a mantle that was only empty for one hour a week on Monday mornings. She looked back over at her mother, who now stood by the window, holding the curtain back with one bony hand while taking a drag with the other. At that moment, Cassie saw shadows moving across the darkened lawn and heard a familiar voice cussing. She ran out onto the porch.

"Clyde Mills. Don't you dare take another step!"

Two shadows—one limping from apparently having tripped on Claire's bicycle which always lay in the front yard and the other helping its co-conspirator along—stopped dead in their tracks. They turned around slowly. A black F250 was at the curb, and someone in its enormous cab gunned the engine, signaling its accomplices to hurry. But Cassie's voice stopped the thieves, even though she was thirty yards off.

She stepped down off of the porch and into the moonlight. She'd never heard of anyone ever breaking into a home in Stockbridge. It was unprecedented. No one ever locked their doors because the fear didn't exist. It had not been within the realm of possibility. But it was now.

Clyde knew this, too. And even though he was drunk, he dropped his head in shame. Will was anxious. He didn't know if his friend was gonna turn himself in or what, but he didn't want to stick around and let Cassie get a hold of him. He stepped away from his wounded accomplice and backed away slowly toward the truck. The passenger door clicked open. Cassie had begun walking down the long driveway toward Clyde when he suddenly raised the bugle up above his head. She stopped. Though he was staring at the ground still, he knew she was looking at him with the look he hated most. The look that said, "You don't have the balls, so don't even pretend." Raising his head until their eyes at last met, he found his suspicion confirmed. Frustrated and afraid, he threw the bugle down onto the pavement and started stomping on it, twisting his other ankle in the process and falling to the ground in a heap of profanities. Cassie was initially too stunned by his actions to begin her charge, but when she realized what was happening she tore out across the yard. Clyde made it to the cab before she could reach him, and the truck screeched away into the night. Cassie knelt down beside the bugle, cradled it in her arms, and took it into her home. And for the first time in her life, she locked the front door.

Cassie worked five hours straight trying to fix and clean the bugle. Banging it back into shape and doing her best to polish it up into some presentable condition. It had taken her awhile to figure out what she would do, but after she'd gotten Claire back to bed and her mother had disappeared into the guest room, she went out to the garage and found some pliers and a hammer and began to bend and twist the bugle until it regained most of its previous, noble appearance. When she was exhausted and her hands were cramping, she set it down on the coffee table to look at it. Over the years, she had developed a strange devotion to it. Most in the town had. It had become a sort of fetish. An idol. A household god.

And yet it was only a standard infantry bugle. High grade spun brass. Key of C with a B-flat crook. Nickle plated and tempered in a Philadelphia workshop for the best possible sound. In the early hours of the November morning, a shimmer of light moved across the horn's graceful curves as it stood upright on the breakfast table. Cassie looked out the window to see the sun rising. She smiled. In its beautiful simplicity, the bugle was worthy of such devotion. Once again, the noble shape caught the early morning light and seemed to wink at her, eager to flash in use. Cassie knew then what the others did not—that the horn was alive and that she'd be damned if she'd let Hank Finley embalm it and seal it in a glass sarcophagus for tourists in the library to gawk at. And so there in the early hours of Sunday morning, she finally realized what it was she would have to do.

The first thing was to keep the usual Sunday morning routine, and so she woke Claire at 8:15 and helped her and her mother get dressed for church. She dropped them off at nine and picked them up at noon. They spent the afternoon as they did on every other Sunday of the fall—watching football and working on homework. She made an unusually big dinner that evening, and this had been the only departure from the norm. Still, neither her mom nor Claire had any idea about her plan, and both were somewhat surprised—though quietly pleased—at Cassie's composure in regards to the events of the preceding night. Her mother thought the less said the better, and Claire needed no prodding to dive back into her book after dinner. They'd all turned in at the usual hour, and her mom hadn't even sneaked back out at midnight to have one last smoke.

Cassie woke them at 4:00 in the morning, dragging them both out of bed and toward the clothes she had already laid out for them. She disappeared into the living room to gaze through the front curtains, and then returned with winter coats for each. Claire was still groggy, but something in her mother's demeanor told her she should do as told. Besides, Claire wasn't certain of the time—she was too busy to check—and for a while she actually thought it might be the routine of her regular school day. At 4:15, Cassie opened the front door and led her mother and daughter out into the cold November air. By 4:30, they had reached the court-house. But her daddy's key no longer opened the front door. The locks had been changed. Cassie figured Hank Finley must have had something to do with it. But she would not be deterred. So by 4:36 Cassie had entered the building through the men's restroom win-dow—kept permanently ajar due to Judge Canon's gastrointestinal disorder—let the others in through the lobby door, and begun the ascent of the clock tower.

Five minutes after entering the courthouse, Cassie surveyed the town while her mother and daughter huddled on the floor of the tower. Though her mother knew that it all was finally coming to a head, Claire seemed more interested in the contents of the book she'd managed to smuggle into her jacket before being hustled out of the house. She held it up at an awkward angle to catch what little moonlight was available. Cassie's mother had lit another cigarette and was taking slow drags, looking at her daughter with a mixture of pride and fear. From the tiny clock tower platform, the first hornblasts rang out, Cassie's desperate attempt to reproduce a song her wisecracking band director had taught his charges to play during fourth quarter blowouts of high school games from a decade before. Cassie's immediate audience was momentarily confused by her exertions.

But she was oblivious to them both. She brought the bugle down from her lips and pivoted it about in her hands, then returned it to its case, failing to notice the faint smears of blood still on her hands from her weekend chores. She studied the town below. She'd hatched her plan at dawn on Sunday, and now it was beautifully unfolding before her eyes.

Already, lights were coming on around the courthouse square and the blocks beyond. She thought she could even see some folks stare up toward the tower from their living room windows and porches, groggy and confused. For the song that had been played this Monday morning at exactly 4:47 had indeed taken them by surprise. Was unexpected. Haunted them, Cassie imagined, just as it must have haunted the one hundred and thirty-two men who'd hunkered down in a Texas mission to fight equally fearful odds over a hundred and seventy years earlier.

Within five minutes, a dozen flashlights were ablaze in the streets below, shimmering like torches in the damp autumn air. A crowd was gathering on the northeast corner of the courthouse lawn, and shadowy figures were soon motioning up toward the tower, heads nodding in agreement, intent on silencing the bugler. And then the crowd began to move purposefully toward the courthouse doors and the three shivering souls, seventy-five feet above. Only then did Cassie fully appreciate how the Starbucks and its new parking lot had nibbled away at the east and north ends of the courthouse's great lawn, an expanse that had once hosted picnics and touch football games. Four acres had become three, lopped off unceremoniously for commercial interests. She was trying to imagine where it all would end when she was interrupted.

"Cassandra," a voice whispered weakly, as if sharing its final secret. She smiled down at her mother and touched her cheek. She put her finger to her own lips, gesturing for her mother to be silent and conserve her strength. Then she bent down and kissed her daughter, still preoccupied with her book, on the forehead.

And then finally she reached back down for the bugle. It felt good in her hands. Solid. Like a cudgel. It would do. She looked back down to the courthouse lawn, but by then the crowd had passed out of her field of vision and was perhaps already in the lobby of the noble structure itself. So she turned her attention to the trapdoor that served as the one entrance to the tower's top. She was ready. They had the numbers, she thought, but she had the high ground. A chill breeze fanned her cheek. She smiled darkly. And once more a hornblast rang out, lonesome as the bellow of a dying steer, across the windswept plains.